Dandelion summer

Mary ellen Bramwell

Black Rose Writing | Texas

The author grants the final approval for this literary material.

First printing

This is a work of fiction. Names, characters, businesses, places, events, and incidents are either the products of the author's imagination or used in a fictitious manner. Any resemblance to actual persons, living or dead, or actual events is purely coincidental.

ISBN: 978-1-68433-279-3
PUBLISHED BY BLACK ROSE WRITING
www.blackrosewriting.com

Printed in the United States of America
Suggested Retail Price (SRP) $19.95

Dandelion Summer is printed in Calluna

To Erin Horn,

because life isn't always easy, in fact sometimes it's downright hard—

and that's when we truly need an ally and a friend.

DANDELION SUMMER

Part 1

Madelyn had heard whispered tales of butterfly summers—the ones that float gently and beautifully in and out of our lives, and cat summers—narcissistic passages filled with visits to the pool and lazy backyard barbecues, even rainbow summers—the calm after the storm of the school year. But she'd never thought for an instant there could be a dandelion summer. Dandelions are, after all, a weed, and a resilient one at that. But when life is choked by unwanted disruptions, you have to make a choice—do you dig up the dandelions or ignore them? Or is it a little of each?

Summer 1975

Her mother was hiding something, that much Madelyn knew. It was in the subtle things she might not normally notice—Mom was twirling her fingers in her hair more and she seemed almost hesitant to answer any questions, even, "What's for dinner?" It's not as if she couldn't answer something so simple, it was more like she was distracted. Her mind was somewhere else, and Madelyn had no idea where it was.

It had been building gradually for the last month, ever since the day her parents had announced that her dad would be working out of town for the entire summer. He was doing training or some such thing that Madelyn couldn't have cared less about. What she did care about was the absence of the one parent she connected with. It felt like a betrayal, one they hadn't even thought to consult her about.

"He'll be back at the end of the summer. It will be over before you know it," Mom had said. And then Dad said something about his job or a promotion, but by then Madelyn had stopped listening because she recognized what had gone unsaid. They were talking to each other, comforting each other, explaining the value of their decision to each other—she wasn't even part of the equation. Her initial reaction was shock, even anger, but in that split second when she discovered her feelings didn't matter, even as they tried to appeal to them, her mind was made up. If they didn't care how she felt, then she wouldn't care either.

"Okay. Whatever," she said, getting up to leave.

"Wait, don't you want to talk about it?" Dad said. Madelyn shrugged her shoulders, trying to convince herself that it was really nothing. It was nothing that Dad was her confidante. It was nothing that he was always there for her—or at least had been. It appeared that wasn't the case anymore. And it was certainly meaningless when she cried on his shoulder, like when she recently learned her best friend Lori was moving. No, this time, with this loss, crying was not in Madelyn's plans.

She simply replied, "No thanks," registering the almost imperceptible sound of her mom's jaw dropping—and then something else. It was the first she had noticed the nervousness, her mom's furtive glance around the room. Mom would certainly miss him—they were a team, doing everything together from grocery shopping to cooking to running errands. But she was bothered by something else. Madelyn could feel it in the air like a summer storm that was brewing yet still too far off to be seen.

At the time, she shrugged it off, too angry or too busy pretending not to care to give it a second thought. She walked out on the two of them, moving swiftly down the hall to her room.

Jillian found her there a few minutes later, asking Madelyn with her eyes what was wrong. Madelyn gathered her little sister in a big hug and held her tight, grateful that at least she wasn't going anywhere.

It was to be the summer of her discontent, and not all of it was of her own making.

•　　•　　•

Madelyn was 14 that year, and even with the attitudes that often gift themselves at birthdays that end with "teen," she had, up until that point, enjoyed spending time with her dad. When the weather was cold or the evening's darkness advanced, Madelyn and her dad would each grab a book to read. They'd invite the others to join them, but Mom's answer was to toss a Mona Lisa smile in Dad's direction, kiss him on the cheek, and leave them to their reading.

Occasionally, Daniel or Jillian would take them up on their offer, and they would end up sprawled around the living room. But often as not, it would just be the two of them, so they'd move to Dad's study. It's not that they wouldn't be disturbed there—because they usually were—Mom would have a question, or Daniel would be stuck on a homework problem. Rather, for Madelyn, it was like they owned some large manor house, and this was their great library, even if the room wasn't large at all. It held Dad's desk, his office chair, and two overstuffed easy chairs. Dad, tall and lanky, liked sitting upright in one chair while Madelyn would lie sideways in the other, resting her head on one arm of the chair while looping her legs over the other, kicking them up and down as she read. Her long hair would flow over the arm, falling like a blond, tangled mess down the side of the chair. Typically, Madelyn pulled her hair back in a ponytail—except when reading with Dad, choosing instead to let it flow freely, without restraint.

Often as not, Dad would pull out a piece of Black Jack gum to pop in his mouth. Madelyn didn't like the licorice taste of it like he did, but the sound of him softly chewing while he read was familiar and comforting. It created a subtle rhythm that added to the turning of pages and exclamations of surprise when their stories took unexpected turns.

Dad would look up periodically and smile in her direction then take a hand and brush his hair back from his forehead, push up his glasses, and start reading again. He repeated this motion often since looking down at a book made his thinning brown hair fall forward into his eyes and his glasses wiggle their way down his nose. Madelyn didn't have the same problem since she hadn't needed glasses—at least not yet. But she couldn't resist glancing up every so often just to see him there.

Dad liked to read everything—histories and mysteries, tender love stories (as long as they weren't too mushy), and swashbuckling adventures. He often gave her suggestions such as *Pride and Prejudice, Fahrenheit 451, To Kill a Mockingbird,* and anything by Agatha Christie. They even read a few Shakespeare plays together, altering their voices for the various characters until they could no longer keep straight who sounded like what.

But it was other voices she heard now after they told her he was leaving, whispers in the night with an edge to them, anxious, worried. She only caught a phrase here and there, "It'll be fine ... trust me ... you can," and then, "Madelyn will take care of it."

The words felt like a knife in her back. The specific meaning was lost on her—who knew what she was going to "take care of," but the whole idea hit her hard. Wasn't that just nice. Dad was leaving and she got to shoulder the burden, whatever that burden happened to be.

Acting unphased by it all became harder and harder as frustration built inside her. She had questions she wanted answered, but that would mean sitting down and talking with one or both of her parents. Doing that smelled of admitting defeat, and she wasn't about to do that—at least not yet.

She caught herself a few times almost being kind, almost confiding in Dad, almost acting the way she knew she should. It didn't help having Lori gone. If she'd been around, at least Madelyn would have had someone to complain to instead of bottling it up.

But thinking of all the "ifs" didn't improve her situation any. Lori was gone, and now her teddy bear of a daddy was leaving too, all without telling her the whole story of what was going on. What did it matter anyway? She knew enough. She was barely an afterthought. Her feelings hadn't been their concern. So why should she care about theirs?

The only thing was, she cared more than she was willing to admit.

1942

They were called the Screaming Eagles, but to Hazel they were no more than soldiers going off to fight a war halfway around the world. Specifically, they were the division taking her husband away to World War II, to an uncertain future. The thought that he might not return was something she tried hard not to contemplate.

William reached across the kitchen table to grasp her hand. For several nights the two of them had huddled over this very table discussing the available opportunities, as they called them. Their conversation had been intimate and intense, yet quiet for the sake of their sleeping children.

But after so many nights with so many words, there were none left to express what their final decision had wrought. Brushing up against their clasped hands lay the official paper—William Knight was to report in October, just a few short weeks away, for training at Fort Benning, Georgia. Given the past horrors of The War to End All Wars, now downgraded to simply World War I, they had made the decision that William should volunteer, knowing he would eventually be called up anyway. Volunteering seemed the only way to maintain a bit of control in a chaotic and frightening world.

He had signed up to be a paratrooper, part of the 101st Airborne Division. The children sleeping peacefully in the next room had been the deciding factor—paratroopers were paid more. That extra amount would come in handy with Rachel, almost three, and Thomas, still an infant.

Hearing over the radio about the attack on Pearl Harbor less than a year ago now seemed like a world away to Hazel. That night after the Japanese attack, lying in bed, she and William had talked about what war might mean. And at that same moment, she had felt the baby that would be Thomas move for the first time. The joy that overwhelmed her for the small life yet to be born also brought with it a strange sense of guilt—guilt that she could be happy after such a tragic day. It was bittersweet—an affirmation of life at a time when so many lives had been lost, with so many more inevitably being extinguished before it was over.

And now here they were. Without a word, William let go of her hand to push away the paper that separated them and reached up to gently wipe away the tears trickling down her cheeks. Then standing, he opened his arms for his wife, beautiful even now in her sorrow. She gave him a small smile, the best she could muster, then rose into his embrace.

The baby woke not soon after, hungry. While Hazel nursed him, William sat beside her—sometimes reaching up to stroke her hair, sometimes simply looking into her eyes, trying to convey all that he didn't have the words to say. After the baby was settled back down, William and Hazel, overcome by sheer exhaustion, fell asleep clasped in each other's arms.

JUNE 6, 1975

June 6th was her dad's departure day. On the surface, Madelyn had managed to maintain her indifference, but on the inside, she felt as if her legs might give out from under her. The day itself was beautiful. Besides being a Friday, it was the first day of summer vacation. The Colorado weather was a perfect 75 degrees, with just a light breeze blowing wisps of hair occasionally across her face. The Rocky Mountains, at their lower elevations, were alive with green, and even though the peaks were still snow-covered, they were warm and inviting to the eye. Madelyn usually loved those mountains. They reminded her to stand tall and strong—like her dad. But that June day, reminding her of Dad wasn't a positive thing.

She knew it was the thirty-something anniversary of D-Day when the allied forces invaded Normandy in World War II. Supposedly, that day long ago was important because it was the turning point of the war—an indication that the allies might actually win it after all. But every time Madelyn heard about it, the only thing that stayed with her was the chaos and all those dead and injured soldiers. Maybe she should have taken heart from the significance of that day—that something so costly and horrible could lead to something good, like the end of a world war. She should have, but she didn't.

As Madelyn tried to covertly watch Dad gather his bags together, she contemplated a summer without him. He was her rock, her sounding board—helping her with homework, listening to her problems, even making cookies for her. Mom did most of those things too if he wasn't around, but Madelyn didn't give her a chance if he was. What exactly does a Daddy's girl do when her daddy isn't around?

Her little brother Daniel, at eleven, had an independent streak no one could tame. Madelyn believed the prospect of having only one parent to supervise the three of them had his creative and highly mischievous mind working overtime. While he might miss Dad, she was sure he was viewing it as an unparalleled opportunity.

Jillian, being the youngest, cried at the thought of Daddy leaving. But Madelyn knew she'd weather the storm all right since she usually spent most of her time trailing in Mom's shadow. When Madelyn saw her tears, her stomach lurched with uncomfortable emotions. She hadn't cried since they'd told her he was leaving, refusing to give in to the emotions even while something in her told her it was the wrong approach to take.

It's just that Dad had always been there, and now that he wasn't, Madelyn didn't know how to conduct her life. Even the thought of picking up a book brought with it reminders that she should be reading it while he was also reading close by.

But it was more than that. Everything made sense with Dad. Life was predictable and orderly. It made sense in the way he kept a hanky in his pocket for cleaning his glasses or in the knowledge that spring meant planting the garden and cleaning out the gutters. Every year about that time, they would survey their property for animals—good and bad—and perform maintenance on any mechanical device they owned. Madelyn loved sitting on a fence post watching him work on their car or the lawnmower, helping him where she could while peppering him with questions. He never seemed to mind, answering each one the best he could. At lunchtime, Mom would bring them sandwiches with freshly squeezed lemonade, kissing Dad's forehead while laughing lightly at his greasy fingers.

In early May of that year, he was the one who started asking the questions. "Do you think you can take care of the garden by yourself this year? And I know I usually take care of the yard, but could you handle mowing the grass?"

"Sure!" Madelyn answered, on cloud nine, thinking her dad trusted her, not realizing the relevance of such a question was yet to come.

He simply nodded his head and said, "Good," but he said it quietly, more to himself than to Madelyn.

On rainy weekends, when it was too difficult to do yard work, they would settle down in Dad's study. Not many of her friends knew anything about their family's money, or lack thereof, but her dad viewed finances as an opportunity to teach her. Each month they would gather the various bills together. He would write out the checks and let Madelyn record them in the ledger, adding deposits and subtracting payments. At first, he checked her work, but since Madelyn rarely made a mistake, he soon stopped. She even enjoyed helping him when the bank statement came in the mail. He showed her how to ensure that his balance and the bank's balance matched. It felt like a puzzle they were solving together.

Mom wasn't fond of numbers the way Dad and Madelyn were. She liked painting and sewing. Often Madelyn would come home from school to find her experimenting with some new craft like laminated placemats that looked like cute little animals or macramé plant holders. Her materials would be strewn all across the kitchen table, and she would be singing some happy tune to herself. Mom was beautiful by anyone's standards, even when messy. Her face was shaped like a china doll with misty blue eyes that lost the blue aspect when she was angry. Her wavy blond hair was usually held back with a headband, and her fingernails were often accidentally painted with the detritus from her various projects.

Her finished works were amazing. Mom often invited Madelyn to join her along the way. She tried a few times, but Madelyn wasn't good at it like Mom was. Daniel sometimes helped, but only if the project "wasn't too girly," in his words. Even when he did, he did his best to create outlandish things, like making placemats that resembled monsters or sharks instead of cute, harmless bunnies. Jillian always participated—in whatever ways she was able. Since she was seven that summer, Mom tried to do things that she could understand.

Madelyn would watch them, jealous that she didn't fit in the crook of Mom's world like Jillian did, even being reluctant to join Daniel in playfully mocking her projects. Madelyn was the outsider looking in until Dad came in the door from work. After that, Madelyn didn't notice the others.

•   •   •

If she'd actually paid attention, it would have occurred to her sooner that her life was about to change, or at least her perception of it. About the same time as Dad put her in charge of the garden, he asked if Madelyn wanted to balance the checkbook by herself. He watched over her shoulder but never said a word. It was hard to tell whose smile was wider, his or Madelyn's, when she managed it without any trouble.

"Madelyn, you're brilliant. Why don't you take a look at this?" he said as he opened a drawer in his desk and pulled out a file. Inside were several monthly bill charts he had made. They were drawn up on green graph paper with neat columns for amount, date paid, and check number. He showed her the one labeled June. "Here's the list of what bills come due in June, and this is the amount I expect them to be. Does that make sense?" Madelyn nodded. Then he proceeded to teach her the basics of family finance and budgeting.

When they finished, he smiled but appeared more relieved than happy. "Madelyn, this summer –"

Before he had a chance to finish, Daniel burst in on them. "I think Mom might need your help." Then he dashed out as quickly as he'd come, the mysterious grin on his face lingering in the air.

Dad leaped up. "Daniel! What have you done?" He turned to Madelyn. "Will you please go check on your mother? I need to find your brother."

For once, Daniel hadn't actually meant to play a trick on Mom. It was just a happy accident on his part. It seems that after it rained a few days before, Daniel was curious about all the worms that materialized on the sidewalk. He started gathering them up and putting them in the pocket of his jeans, meaning to do something with them later—he hadn't decided what yet. Only, he got distracted climbing a tree and never removed them. It turns out dead worms float in the washing machine!

It was another week before Mom and Dad cornered her and told her of the plans that had already been made. And even though she would have liked to have known sooner, in the end, it made no difference. The decision had been made, and her world was turning upside down.

• • •

Madelyn didn't want to go to the airport with them a few weeks later on that June 6th, but staying home by herself and being reminded of how empty the house would feel without Dad seemed a worse option. So, she went anyway.

Dad and Mom spent much of the time waiting for his flight in hushed conversation as if the rest of them didn't exist. Dad kept reassuring Mom with words like, "Don't worry," although to Madelyn his need to say them meant that's exactly what they should do.

Then he said, "What about your dad?" It seemed a strange question to be asking at this point. Did he think Grandpa was going to step in and help? Madelyn wondered. Grandpa hadn't been around at all lately, so how could he possibly help?

Mom had explained it to her—not to her satisfaction, but that didn't seem to be Mom's concern. Madelyn's grandma had died in a car accident not long ago. Before the accident, her grandparents visited often, but after the accident, Grandpa had been around almost constantly—until the spring. Mom told her simply that his work had changed and he didn't have time to spend with them anymore. It didn't make sense then, and it certainly didn't make sense now.

But, regardless, the fact remained—Grandpa wouldn't be slipping into Dad's shoes while he was away. Apparently, Dad had all kinds of illusions about how their summer was going to go. The knot in her stomach grew tighter, the bitter pill getting harder and harder to swallow.

When the announcement came across the loudspeaker that it was time to board, Dad gave hugs and kisses all around, gathered his things, and walked away, waving to them as he went. "Take care of your Mom," were the final words he called back to Madelyn as he disappeared down the gaping tunnel.

The words almost undid her. Despite her attitude, his leaving threatened to break her heart. Without Lori, she'd counted on him being there. It seemed the safest of assumptions, but she'd been mistaken. It may only be for the summer, but Madelyn needed him—and his final words weren't even for her, they were about Mom.

Madelyn turned to watch for him through the plate glass window. She hated to admit it, but she was upset with herself. She'd wasted the last few precious weeks he was home by turning an indifferent shoulder to him. They had even planted the garden together, side-by-side, but Madelyn had said little to him, grabbing seed packets from the basket while merely raising her eyebrows to ask if she'd picked the right one. Regret and anger mixed like bile in the back of her throat as she leaned her forehead against the cold glass.

Her heart skipped a beat when she saw him emerge onto the tarmac then walk across it and up the stairs into the belly of the beast, painfully aware that a part of her was going with him. Mom was talking to Jillian and Daniel behind her, but Madelyn wasn't listening to what they were saying. She didn't know if she could handle watching the plane take off like they usually did, but she couldn't peel her eyes away either, being drawn to it like a compelling yet disturbing accident scene.

Dad's flight was headed to Atlanta, and later he would travel from there to Jackson, Mississippi, where his training would take place, arriving late at night. As Madelyn watched his plane lift off, self-pity engulfed her despite her resolve not to care.

Driving home from the airport was the longest ride of her life. The day had turned hot with an angry sun beating down. Daniel and Jillian in the back seat were alternately hitting, tickling, and pinching each other. "Mom, he –" and "But she –" continuously played behind her like a radio station with a record that was stuck. Mom kept responding, but Madelyn didn't catch her words even though Mom was right beside her. She just couldn't bring herself to engage, to be part of their lives.

Madelyn rolled down her window and let her hand dance up and down on the air rushing past. The window frame was hot, and when she rested her arm on it, she felt it burn into her flesh. She yanked up quickly and turned to see if Mom had noticed, but her eyes were trained on the road, her hands tightly gripping the wheel. Sighing, Madelyn pulled her arm back in and rested her head on the back of the seat, staring up at the vacant ceiling above her.

Looking back later, Madelyn had sensed something was off. It called to her in the pinched strain in Mom's voice, the way she picked at her fingernails or chewed on her lower lip, and a general nervous unease of her movements—unusual behaviors that the lonely summer ahead couldn't account for on its own. But caught up in her own thoughts as she was, the truth of it didn't hit her at the time. It was like a whispered warning on the breeze, but if you're not listening for a whisper, you can't possibly catch its meaning.

JUNE 6, 1944

"Hey, Knight, move it. You're almost up." The thought of what lay ahead made William shiver, but the presence of the jumpmaster rendered hesitation impossible. Time had just ticked past midnight, starting the soon to be legendary D-Day, and in a matter of seconds, William would find himself leaving the relative safety of the airplane, heading to the ground below. If he was lucky, and lucky was an interesting term, he wouldn't end up dead or captured, just merely behind enemy lines. The plan involved paratroopers from one side of the line making it possible for soldiers landing on Utah beach to successfully attack from the other side. The man in front of William chuckled and said, "I always wanted to visit the French countryside, but somehow I envisioned doing it differently," and then he was out the door.

They had trained for a long time for this very moment—first in the United States and then in England once they had arrived, anxiously waiting for Operation Overlord to begin. All were nervous and excited at the same time. Survival, returning home to loved ones, was never far from their minds, but that, if it happened, was a long way off. Getting ready to jump out of an airplane, however unnatural that seemed, was the here and now.

Already things weren't going quite as planned for the 101st Airborne. Enemy fire had forced their pilot to take evasive action, and even the primed and ready paratroopers could see the heavy fog below.

William jumped just when and where he thought he should, followed by his buddy Frank Stafford, and a trail of others behind him.

As he was finding his feet after landing, he heard, "Hey, Knight, you okay?" The whisper was coming from the other side of the hedge but was the unmistakable gravelly voice of Frank.

"Yeah, I'm okay. Keep it down, will ya, Stank?" While his fellow soldiers were called by their last names, "Stafford" had proved to be too much of a mouthful. However, the combination of his first and last name had gained instant acceptance.

As silently as possible, William pulled out his switchblade to cut himself free from his parachute lines and harness. Before he was finished, Frank was standing beside him. "What's taking you so long?" he said, causing William to jump.

"Man, Stank, stop it. You see anyone else?"

"Nah."

"Okay, help me gather up this parachute and get your clicker handy. I don't want to find out someone's the enemy the hard way."

•   •   •

By the time the first rays of sun became visible on the horizon, the pair had grown to a small, ad hoc unit of twelve. Between the dark night and the fog, navigating by sight had been difficult, but they had at least found each other by clicking their cricket noisemakers and waiting for the answering click of friendly soldiers—always a relief that the rifles they had at the ready were still just a precaution.

Palmer, as the only sergeant in the group, had become their de facto leader. Since he was as hungry as they were, he knew which objective to focus on when a house and a church each came into view. "Hey, Knight, Stank, go check out the church for any holed-up Krauts. Johnson and I will go check out the farmhouse down the road. Maybe we can rustle up a nice breakfast. The rest of you, stay hidden the best you can."

The possibility of fresh eggs in their future added a briskness to their step as they ascended the small hill to the chapel. William tried not to look at the headstones in the adjacent graveyard they came across first. "At least we're not among them, Will," Frank said, coming up behind him.

"Yeah, you said it, Frank." It was a small thing, this use of their given *names, but it expressed what they found hard to articulate in any other way.*

The church was lovely, nothing like the wooden churches in the States. This one was built of stone and would stand for hundreds of years, in fact, probably already had. Although anxious to return to their buddies, the two couldn't help but glance up in the dawning light at the steeple rising in the air above them. A small belfry stood below it, thankfully silent at the moment. Gracing the side of the church was a row of large peaked windows illuminated by the sun, and just past them, they spied an arched entryway.

"C'mon, let's get this over with," Frank said, heading to the heavy, ornate door, gun at the ready.

"Yeah, the sooner, the better."

The door was unlocked and creaked open at their gentle urging. Neither was prepared for what they found inside.

The scent hit them first—a combination of dust and age as if they were stepping back in time a hundred years, but it wasn't unpleasant. The morning light, which had merely exposed the windows on the outside, now transformed them along with the interior of the small chapel. Streaming through stained glass, it draped the wooden pews in blues, greens, and reds and painted the stone floor with brightly colored images of saints.

They immediately found it impossible to walk silently across the interlocking, rectangular stones under their feet. So, they opted instead for swinging their M1 rifles in all directions in case of an enemy presence. How they missed seeing the small man near the altar at the front, they couldn't say.

"Hallo," echoed through the chapel, startling both soldiers.

"Did you see him?" Frank turned to ask William.

William shook his head, "And if anyone asks ... "

"Yeah, right, I spotted him as soon as we came in."

"Like any good soldier," added William.

"Hallo," the man repeated. Thankfully, it was English—heavily accented English, but English all the same.

William and Frank walked toward the older man who they could now see wore priest's vestments, but just as they drew close, he disappeared. They hadn't even had the chance to inquire about the state of the church or the presence or absence of German soldiers.

Exchanging puzzled glances, the two walked to where they had last seen the priest. He had been up against the back wall, and they could now see a full-length curtain still swaying slightly. Frank was just leaning forward to sweep it aside with his hand when the priest reemerged, almost running right into him. He was carrying something in each hand, and his eyes were warily darting back and forth.

"Are you okay?" William said. The priest furrowed his brow, possibly confused by the English or maybe giving his answer. "Krauts?" William tried again, this time swinging his arms wide to hopefully convey the idea of anywhere in the church.

"Non, non," the priest said, shaking his head. Then with wide eyes he added, "Krauts," while indicating with an outstretched arm the darkened windows to the west.

"Krauts? That way?" Frank said, mimicking the priest's motion.

"Oui, oui!"

"Hey, Stank, if that's the case, we've got to go tell Palmer," William said as he turned to leave.

"Non, non!" the priest said, quickly stepping in front of the two men. He held a hand out in front of Frank. In it, in the visible strips of light, lay a brass crucifix. The priest thrust it at Frank. "S'il vous plaît. Take. Make safe." Then he nodded his head in the direction of the Germans.

"Keep it safe? You don't want the Germans to have it?"

"Oui, oui. Take," the priest said, leaving the crucifix in Frank's hand. Then he turned to William. "You take," he said, handing him a fabric-wrapped parcel that he'd been holding in his other hand. "Make safe."

William was hesitant, but the eyes of the priest were pleading, glancing nervously to the west toward the location of their common enemy. William tentatively closed his fingers around the object. It felt like a large, rolled up scroll, but it was hard to tell anything more than that, having been carefully wrapped for protection.

As eager as the priest had been for them to stay, he was now equally eager for them to leave. "Go, go," he said while pointing toward the door they had come in, and when they didn't move fast enough, he started pushing them from behind. It reminded William of the firm push of the jumpmaster only a few hours earlier.

17

"Okay, okay, we're going. Are you all right? Do you want to come with us?" William pointed to the priest and then to himself then indicated the door. "Go with?" he tried again.

"Non, non. You go."

• • •

The rest of the day happened in a flash—eating a hurried breakfast of eggs from a grateful French farmer followed by a skirmish with a thankfully small band of Germans, reuniting with a larger unit, and searching for more enemy troops—equally hopeful of finding them and not. By the time it was over, William hadn't spent a single moment considering the significance of the fabric-wrapped bundle buried deep in his knapsack.

week one – summer 1975

Sunday

By the time Sunday rolled around, Madelyn had decided on one thing—ten was a number she could wrap her mind around. That's how many weeks Dad would be gone. So, if she could break her summer into ten weeks, maybe she could get through it.

Madelyn carefully wrote the numbers one through ten on a pad of paper, circling the one as her starting point. As she did so, Mom walked by her room. There was a melancholy about her; her head was down, and her step was slow. She depended on Dad even more than Madelyn had thought, and a bit of her heart ached for her. Madelyn wanted to reach out to her, she really did. But the hole in her own heart was so big she didn't know how to climb out of it.

Madelyn didn't hear the sermon at church that day, certain it would condemn her. But true to her teenage self, by the time it concluded, she had replaced her guilt with a healthy dose of bitterness instead. Surely the best solution when change is required is to decide it's someone else who needs to do it.

After church, Dad called to let the family know he'd arrived safely, but he was busy "getting the lay of the land," according to Mom, so he didn't talk long. He only spoke to Mom and didn't even ask to speak to anyone else.

Madelyn knew he'd be calling. It was part of the plan, that he'd call every Sunday, but she'd decided she wasn't going to talk to him. She simply wasn't going to care. And then he had the gall to not even ask for her. It felt like a sneeze that's ready to burst only instead it fizzles and fails to materialize— the result more annoying than just sneezing and getting it over with.

MONDAY – FRIDAY

If it wasn't for Jillian, the week would have been a complete loss. She nestled up to Madelyn whenever she found her reading, even asking a couple of nights if she could sleep in Madelyn's room. After they made a little bed for her on the floor, Madelyn sang Jillian her favorite lullaby, "Hush, Little Baby," even though she was much too old for it.

"Good night, Madelyn. I love you."

"I love you too, Jilly." After a minute, hearing no obvious sounds of sleeping, Madelyn whispered, "You really miss Dad, don't you?"

"Well, sure I do."

"It's okay." When Jillian didn't respond, Madelyn added, "That is why you've been staying so close to me, isn't it? Because you're missing Dad?"

"No, silly. It's because *you* do." And with that, Jillian turned over and fell asleep.

Saturday

Mom was up early on Saturday. The kids awoke to, "Come and get it." She'd made a big breakfast of pancakes and sausages for everyone. Even though Daniel was a few years younger than Madelyn, he was almost as tall as she was, and he was always ready for food, especially if he didn't have to make it himself. He came out of his room and shot past her at the sound of Mom's voice. When he entered the kitchen and saw the spread on the kitchen table, complete with toast and jam, he said, "Whoa," with a hushed reverence.

Mom ruffled his curly hair—blond like hers—and laughed in response. "I figured you'd like it, Daniel. You seem to have more energy than the rest of us combined." He took that as a compliment, and smiling, he slid into his seat.

Neither one of them saw Madelyn's eyes brighten at the breakfast Mom had laid out. She'd been nibbling at her food all week, and hunger was starting to get the best of her. Madelyn looked away and pretended to be busy putting her hair into a ponytail. Then, as casually as possible, she moved into her seat at the table, trying hard not to notice Dad's empty chair at the end. "Thanks, Mom," she said softly.

Daniel reached for a piece of sausage with his bare hands, but Mom stopped his motion in midair. "Uh-uh. You will use silverware, and you will wait for your little sister to get here." She gave him a stare that meant business.

Reluctantly he pulled back but rested his elbows on the table, putting his chin in his hands. "Well, then she better hurry up," he grumbled under his breath. Madelyn wasn't going to say it, but she was as impatient as he was.

Jillian appeared a few minutes later, rubbing the sleep out of her eyes and yawning. Her long hair was tangled in brownish wisps pointing every direction. "Why'd you wake us up so early, Mom? I'm still tired." Madelyn hadn't thought about that. Mom didn't usually wake them on the weekends. In fact, she never did. Why now, Madelyn wondered.

Mom didn't answer, just got up, put her arm around Jillian, and guided her to a chair. "Okay, Daniel, since you're so anxious, why don't you offer a blessing on our food." Daniel often expressed gratitude for things in his prayer that made it hard to add an amen—things such as snakes and "the mouse in Madelyn's closet." But today he was on his best behavior—probably because he was so eager to eat what Mom had laid out.

Part way through the meal, Mom stopped eating, laying her fork and knife down on her plate in a purposeful manner. The clank of metal on stoneware made them look up. She cleared her throat. "Things are going to be different this summer. We've had our week of laziness. I hope you enjoyed it."

Daniel's brown eyes grew big, and Jillian started to twist a strand of hair around her finger, her go-to nervous habit. They stared at Mom, wondering what she was going to say next. "There's a lot to do around here that's not going to get done on its own. So, we're going to divvy up the chores and stay on top of everything. I want Dad to be proud of us when he returns. When the work's done, then you can play."

They glanced at each other then quickly nodded. This wasn't like Mom. She seemed to appreciate a slightly messy and chaotic home. Dishes were put away in the kitchen but not always in the same place. Newspapers were stacked haphazardly in the corner by the back door while magazines were found strewn about the living room, opened to various projects or with pictures ripped out, lying nearby.

"Madelyn, I know you miss your dad," Mom said. "We all miss him. It's time to do something about it. You can miss him, or you can get busy making him proud." Madelyn was thinking those weren't mutually exclusive, but she wasn't about to argue the point.

"Okay," Madelyn meekly replied. "What do you want me to do?"

"Mostly I just want you to do what Dad has already asked you to do." That was a relief—until she added one more thing. "But I don't know if Dad talked to you about the dandelions." Her face fell.

Dandelions—dandelions were the second thing about that summer that she hated.

.   .   .

Madelyn's family lived at the end of the street. You wouldn't call it a cul-de-sac because it didn't end in a nice, neat circle. Basically, if you drove down the street and didn't stop, you'd end up in their driveway. That, in and of itself, was fine. The problem was that their property took up the entire end of the block, extending for about a hundred feet on either side of the house and then back farther than Madelyn cared to think. Only part of it was grassed in—a patch in front that stretched around one side of the house and then, behind a fence that stretched to the edges of their yard, a nice backyard section. The vegetable garden was out back, and the rest was made up of weeds mixed with wildflowers.

As far as the lawn went, other than mowing and setting a sprinkler on it occasionally, Madelyn knew nothing about caring for it. If Dad had done something to deal with the dandelions, she had no idea what it was. "Dad didn't mention the dandelions," Madelyn said, her voice timid. "He always took care of that. I don't know anything about it."

"Well, you know how to dig them out of the garden, don't you?"

Her mouth dropped open. "Are you serious? You want me to dig them all out, one by one? That will take forever! The dandelions in the weed patches will just keep blowing their seeds onto the lawn. I'll never be able to keep up." She was certain now more than ever that Mom knew nothing about taking care of a yard, but Madelyn couldn't think of a single way to convince her of that fact.

Mom stopped for a minute, seemingly processing what Madelyn was saying. "Well, your Dad always kept the yard in great shape. We need to keep it looking just the same. We can do it. I'll help you." She smiled as if to reassure her daughter, but it didn't even begin to do so.

When Madelyn mowed the lawn a short while later, she kept thinking about all those dandelions, and she noticed every single one she was cutting down, hundreds and hundreds of them. Surely Dad hadn't meant for her to worry about them, but she couldn't think of any way out of it. If she wrote Dad asking about the dandelions, she'd have to admit to what Mom said, and he'd never go against her. If Madelyn tried to be sneaky and not mention what Mom said, he'd still find out. Then she'd be in even worse trouble. This was shaping up to be a horrible summer.

Thankfully, the day wasn't too hot for June, and the lawn looked nice when Madelyn was finished, as long as someone was looking from a distance. From there, the broad-leafed dandelions weren't as apparent since their tops were momentarily missing.

"Mom, I finished mowing. If I dig up twenty dandelions, may I call my friends?" Madelyn hollered to her through the kitchen window. The plan she'd finally concocted while mowing was to dig up a certain number of dandelions every few days. It seemed like something she could manage. She was also hoping Mom wouldn't realize how woefully inadequate it would be.

Mom's face appeared at the window. Her brow was furrowed as she surveyed the backyard, thinking. Since she couldn't see the tell-tale yellow blooms Madelyn had cut down, she was contemplating just how many dandelions there were. Madelyn smiled inwardly, relishing for once her mom's lack of numerical sense. Mom finally nodded. "That would be fine." She turned to go then stopped herself. "But before you go, there are some bills that came in the mail this week. I left them in Dad's study. We should take care of those before you take off anywhere."

"Okay, Mom." It was the deal Dad and Madelyn had worked out before he left. Madelyn was in charge of the household budget, at least to an extent. Dad had left Mom cash for groceries, gas, and other essentials by putting a certain amount in separate envelopes for all the weeks he would be gone. He'd had to take money out of savings to be able to have all the cash, but it seemed like the easiest way to handle things. Madelyn was responsible for paying all the bills. Dad was having his checks deposited in the bank directly from his company while they were funneling money to cover his expenses straight to him. Once Madelyn called the bank to verify the deposit had been made, she could pay all the bills on his list.

"Your Mom hates dealing with the money," he told her before he left. "It stresses her out to think she might make a mistake, and since you're so good at it ... well, it seemed like a perfect solution." He grinned at her. Madelyn would have relished the compliment if she hadn't been so busy feeling used and abandoned.

Thinking about it now, Madelyn almost let a smile escape her lips, but her first jab into the ground after a dandelion root helped quell the temptation. Digging up her designated twenty dandelions was at least, as she had hoped, quick work.

June's paycheck was already in the bank, so after washing grass and dirt off her hands, Madelyn went straight to Dad's study and sat down at his desk to write out the checks. She felt small sitting in his big office chair, but she smiled when she caught the lingering scent of his licorice gum. Just then Daniel poked his head in, his eyes dancing mischievously as he emitted a loud burp in her general direction. Madelyn looked away, refusing to give him the satisfaction that he'd made her grimace, or worse, smile.

When Madelyn could tell he had gone, she tried to recapture Dad's licorice smell, but she'd already adjusted to the aroma of the room, and it was lost to her senses. She considered stepping out of the room and back in just so she could smell the difference, allowing herself to walk in from the hallway-home-aroma to the familiar and comforting scent of Dad's study. But she feared looking foolish if anyone saw her. Instead, she pulled her legs up onto the office chair and hugged them to her. If only she could cocoon herself in his chair, maybe reality would fade for just a moment. She could imagine she was just waiting for him to join her for their nightly reading— just Dad and her together, the way they were supposed to be. Madelyn reached up to release her hair from its ponytail then hesitated, unable to bring herself to do it. So she hugged her legs tighter instead.

After a few minutes, she let go, telling herself it was because her legs were starting to cramp up in that position while, in reality, the loneliness she felt without Dad was threatening to drown her. Madelyn was surprised by the liquid forming at the edges of her eyes and quickly reached up to wipe it away.

"Okay, Dad, let's do this." She was talking to the air, but pretending she wasn't alone in his study took away some of the pain of its hollow interior. Only a couple bills were waiting for her. Madelyn wrote out the checks and neatly entered them into the ledger, double checking her subtraction to make sure the balance was correct. She found two more unexpected envelopes. The first was a subscription renewal for an outdoors magazine Dad liked to read. "You forgot to add this in, Dad, but I guess I should go ahead and pay it. I hope you didn't forget anything else," Madelyn said aloud.

Just then Mom passed by, then stopped and returned to peer in. "Are you talking to someone?"

Madelyn shrugged her shoulders. "Dad?"

Mom nodded. "I understand." She twisted her face up, and Madelyn could tell she was trying to fend off the tears. Then she shrugged her shoulders too. "I do the same thing." They stared at each other then burst into giggles at the absurdity of it.

"Mom," Madelyn said when she finally stopped snickering, "since you're here, I have a couple checks for you to sign."

"Which ones are these?"

"It's just the electric bill and the car insurance."

"Okay." She slowly moved to Madelyn's side, having lost all hint of her previous mirth. She picked up a pen, reaching for the first check. Madelyn was surprised to see her hand shaking slightly. She carefully and meticulously signed each check then set the pen down with a sigh of relief. "Anything else?"

"No," Madelyn said, but as she did so, she noticed the last envelope. The handwritten address read Rachel Osborne, but there was no return address. "Oh, wait, Mom. This must have gotten mixed in with the bills. It's a letter for you."

Mom hesitantly reached out to take it with a furrowed brow. "I wonder what it is?" But instead of opening it, she clasped the envelope tightly to her and hurriedly left the room.

As Madelyn wondered at her reaction, she glanced at the bills before her. She'd thought once the checks were written out and signed that Mom would address the envelopes and mail them. "I guess I have to do everything around here," she muttered to herself.

As she sealed and addressed the two bills, she spied the magazine subscription. She'd been ready to pay it when Mom came by. Quickly Madelyn wrote one more check, got the envelope ready with a stamp and return address, and grabbing a pen, went to find Mom.

She wasn't in the kitchen or the laundry room like Madelyn expected. She went upstairs and almost ran into Mom as she came out of her bedroom, closing the door behind her. "Madelyn, you startled me!" Her eyes were open wide in surprise.

"Are you all right, Mom?"

"Yes, of course I am," she said while smoothing her dress and straightening her hair as if she were trying to pull herself together. "Did you need something?"

She didn't seem to be fine, but Madelyn didn't know what to do about it. "Yeah, I forgot a check. It's for one of Dad's magazines. Is that okay?"

"Sure. Sure." She took the pen and check Madelyn offered and using the hall table, bent over to sign the check. Madelyn wanted to see if she was still shaky, but Mom turned her back to Madelyn until she was done. "There you go. Thanks for taking care of this, sweetie. I appreciate it." She reached up and gently patted Madelyn's cheek before rushing past her and down the stairs. Madelyn was left standing there, staring at the closed bedroom door, wondering what had her mom so much on edge.

•   •   •

Attempting to shrug off her confusion, Madelyn made her way to the kitchen for a quick lunch. Whatever was going on, she figured it was time to make her escape. "Bye, Mom. I'm ...," when it dawned on her that she didn't have anywhere to go. Madelyn hadn't adjusted to her new reality yet, that Lori had moved. Madelyn stood frozen in the middle of the kitchen, unsure what to do.

Jillian was next to her, doing dishes at the kitchen sink. Madelyn glanced behind her to see Daniel vacuuming the hallway with an impish grin lighting his face. She knew what that meant—as soon as he finished his chores, he'd find a devious way to run off some of his energy. It wasn't reason enough by itself to get out of the house, but coupled with Mom's newfound cleaning frenzy, Madelyn figured she should take off as soon as possible.

Running back to Dad's study, she grabbed the bills. "Mom, I'm putting the bills out in the mail then I'm heading over to the park on my bike. See you later," she said, in a hurry to leave before Mom thought of something else for her to do.

As Madelyn shut the mailbox, she heard Mrs. Burnham, their next-door neighbor, behind her. "Don't forget to put the flag up, dear." Madelyn rolled her eyes. Didn't she think Madelyn knew that?

Madelyn moved the flag up with a deliberate motion. "Of course. We wouldn't want to confuse the mailman, would we?" she said, giving her an exaggerated smile. Maybe it wasn't the nicest response, but Madelyn rationalized that it was much nicer than it could have been. Then she grabbed her bike and set her foot on the pedal, but Dorothy Burnham wasn't done with her yet.

"I heard your father left for the summer. That must be hard on your mother."

Her foot froze in motion, "My mother? We *all* miss my father, thank you."

"Oh, I'm sure you do. I just didn't know if your mother would be up to the challenge of running the place by herself."

Her words left Madelyn speechless. Unfortunately, Mrs. Burnham didn't suffer from the same affliction. "I can't imagine what the inside must look like," she said, "but I don't give a never mind about that. I do, however, worry that your yard might become an eyesore. It's already messy enough with all those wildflowers, but I'd hate to see the dandelions take over your lawn."

Madelyn was stunned. The problem was she agreed with her about the dandelions, at least she had an hour earlier. "My mom ...," she trailed off, not certain how to defend her, or even if she wanted to. Instead, images formed in her mind—the typically messy house, the bills she was paying along with balancing the checkbook, the yard work that was suddenly hers. Even though Madelyn didn't like Mrs. Burnham, her assessment didn't seem far from the truth. Taking her side, however, wasn't something Madelyn was ready to do.

Mrs. Burnham had never been known to be warm and friendly. It was a wonder that Dad made a point to talk to her from time to time. From Madelyn's perspective, she was a pathetic character. She liked to wear wigs of varying styles and colors—often just throwing them on, or so it would seem, as they tended to sit at an angle, giving you the urge to reach up and adjust them, if only you could do so without actually touching her. It's like her attempt at having perfect hair was half-hearted at best, sort of like her attempt at wearing clothes that matched. But her eyes, well, there was nothing half-hearted about her eyes. They could burn holes right through you. Madelyn and her friends had nicknamed them Burnham's burners.

Wanting to extricate herself from the whole situation, Madelyn sat up on her bicycle seat as straight as she could and said, "Don't worry about it."

"Oh, but I am. I don't want your yard making mine look bad—you know guilt by association. Your father, if he were here, wouldn't let that happen."

That hit a nerve. "Well, my dad trusted me to take care of the things he usually does. So, like I said, don't worry about it. I'm sure it will turn out just fine. And if not, all your friends will just be able to see how much better you are than all the rest of us." Madelyn turned away with a smirk, riding quickly down the street.

It wasn't until Madelyn was nearly to the park that she felt a twinge of guilt about her words, and it was only because she thought of Dad. He never would've said what Madelyn had. Here she thought she'd finally found a great comeback, only to have it ruined by the thought of disappointing Dad. It was a cruel comment, made worse by the fact that everyone knew Mrs. Burnham had no friends. No one would be coming to visit her. No one would see her lawn. No one cared about Dorothy Burnham.

There had long been speculation, at least among the neighborhood kids, about the whereabouts of the Mr. who went along with her Mrs. title. Had he ever existed? If so, what had she done with him? Madelyn's favorite idea was that he lived in Siberia, having escaped to the one place on earth she wouldn't go searching for him.

It was a nice day for the park, but instead of riding around on the path that circled it, Madelyn stopped her bike on a small crest from where she could see but not so easily be seen. Below, in the center of the park, was a small pond that the city called a lake. She and her friends often waded there, but her heart wasn't in it today.

Self-consciously, Madelyn twirled her ponytail in her fingers, wondering what to do now that she was here. She could see a group of people below. She thought she recognized a few of them, but Madelyn wasn't sure she wanted to be around anyone right now. Climbing off her bike, she laid it and herself onto the cool grass and started watching the clouds go by, imagining they were strange and mysterious creatures. Soon, she closed her eyes, stopped thinking, and let the warmth of the sun attempt to comfort her.

"Are you okay?" Madelyn opened her eyes to see Zane standing above her, the sun putting his wavy hair in silhouette.

Delia, Zane's older sister, had been Madelyn's babysitter when she was younger, and she often brought Zane, who was Madelyn's age, along with her. At the time, it felt like he was just another member of the family, but during junior high, they hadn't seen each other as often. They were now friends when they were together but nothing to each other when they weren't.

Madelyn pulled herself up to sitting then squinted in the sun as she peered into his face. For a split-second, she wanted to tell him about her dad, but as she opened her mouth to speak, she saw Delia walk up behind him. Changing her mind, Madelyn turned her gaze away. "It's nothing ... just dandelions." Madelyn hadn't meant to say anything, but the words just came out.

Zane looked puzzled by her response. "Dandelions?" he said.

Madelyn stood up and brushed the grass from her shorts. "Well, there's always something to deal with, isn't there? But it'll all blow away soon enough, you know, like dandelions do." It wasn't what she'd meant, but he didn't need to know that, Madelyn thought as she climbed on her bike and pedaled her way home.

As Madelyn drew near their house, she noticed the flag was down on the mailbox, so she walked over to it, glancing around for any sign of Mrs. Burnham. Thankfully, she was nowhere in sight. With a sigh of relief, Madelyn opened the box. Stuffed inside were a couple letters and one tattered-looking package. She couldn't remember the last time anyone in their house had received a package. Curious, she turned it over. Madelyn

Osborne was written clearly on the front. It was for *her*?

With her heart racing, Madelyn dumped her bike in the garage then ran into the house. "Mom, I'm home, and I got the mail," she said, holding out the package.

Without looking up, Mom said, "Thanks, Madelyn. Would you mind taking care of it? I'm busy getting dinner ready."

"Sure, but look, Mom, there's something for me! Do you know what it is?"

Mom's head came up. "No, open it!" she said, clearly now as excited as Madelyn.

Ripping open the package, a book fell out, *The Hobbit* by J.R.R. Tolkien. No note accompanied it, but since it was a book there was only one possible explanation—it was from Dad. Madelyn dropped the wrappings and started dancing, hugging the book to her then pulling Mom into her embrace as well. "He didn't forget about me, Mom. He didn't forget."

"Of course he didn't," Mom replied.

Madelyn paused, wondering how Mom could be so sure. A mixture of happy and sad played with her heart. It was hard to reconcile the loss she felt from Dad being gone with this lifeline he'd sent.

"Well, go ahead and go read. I don't need your help right now," Mom said, misinterpreting Madelyn's change in demeanor. "Just take all the other mail with you," she added while smiling and waving her off.

"Sure. No problem," Madelyn said, picking up the mail and walking out of the kitchen without even noticing the remnants of the package scattered about the floor. The book was warm in her hands, and she held it up to examine it closer. It did look interesting, and Dad would want her to enjoy it. In spite of herself, a smile began to spread on her face.

"What's up with you?" Daniel said, "You seem happy."

She laughed. "Oh, it's nothing," she said as she ducked into Dad's study. She forced herself to sort through the rest of the mail before allowing herself to open her new book. Most of it was junk mail and went right into the garbage. The one bill in the mix Madelyn decided could wait for later, so she set it on the desk before once again picking up and embracing her new book.

Snuggling down into one of Dad's easy chairs, Madelyn mentally distanced herself from the rest of the world. She took her ponytail out of its elastic and shook her hair free while thinking of all the times she read in this room with Dad. A dose of fiction would be a good addition to her real life right about now. The feeling of Dad being gone was still there—and it still hurt—but this was a nice band-aid. It may not heal that wound, but it could at least cover it for the moment, and Madelyn was willing to take what she could get.

Reverently, she opened the front cover. Madelyn was wrong about there being no note. Under the inside title, *The Hobbit, Or, There and Back Again*, Dad had written in his flowing script, "I may be away—or 'there,' but I will be back again. Love, Dad." Madelyn hugged the book hard to her chest again before delving into the world of Bilbo Baggins.

1944

The first sense of stability for the allied forces after D-Day—which stability was, in and of itself, an oxymoron in wartime—showed itself not in the battles won, but in the simple act of mail call. Word from home, the smell of home, the promise of home all came as bittersweet. For William, it was something more. Other than the "Dear John" letters soldiers were receiving, bad news was expected to flow west across the ocean—news of dead, injured, or captured soldiers—not the other way around.

It was, of course, wonderful to hear from Hazel. He missed her something terrible. She was his lighthouse, his source of comfort and guidance. But the end of her letter wasn't the same as the beginning. Thomas, his baby boy—who was no longer a baby, although that's the only way William knew how to picture him—had been slow to develop. But with the concerns of war, they kept telling each other that, surely, he would grow out of it, catch up, be fine. They were lies that got harder to believe and harder still to tell the more time passed. The truth was he wasn't fine. Hazel had waited until the end of the letter to tell him, working hard to soften the blow. Their son had just been diagnosed with cerebral palsy. William didn't even know what that meant or entailed, but it didn't sound good.

Hazel explained it to him in the letter, but what the disease was and what it meant for their son were two different things. While one was known, the other wasn't. Walking and talking were things that William, up until this moment, had taken for granted. But now he had to confront the idea that his son might never do either one. Apparently, Thomas' prognosis was good. Because of the sounds and movements he was already making, his case was "more on the mild side," Hazel had said. Mild or not, however, his son had cerebral palsy.

The mail call had reminded him about the bundle he had faithfully carried with him since landing in France. It was time he mailed it home, and as he grabbed it, he hastily penned a letter to his wife, knowing as he did so that his quickly scrawled sentiments would be completely inadequate to ease the burden she now carried. For half a second, he wondered if he could get a hardship discharge, but Hazel had assured him in her letter that she was managing fine. The letter, potential proof of hardship, was also the very thing that would negate it.

He stuffed his brief note into the package before heading off to regimental headquarters to mail both item and letter home.

*   *   *

Hazel couldn't believe it when a couple months later the mailman knocked on her door with a package from William. "I know how much letters mean these days, so I figured a package might mean even more, Mrs. Knight. It's certainly better than a telegram," the mailman said, wishing he could take back the words as soon as they left his mouth. "I'm sorry. I didn't mean …," he said, knowing telegrams usually came from the war department, and they never brought good news.

She smiled at him and reached out to pat his arm. "It's okay. I know you didn't mean anything by it." Taking the package from his extended arms, Hazel retreated inside, leaning against the door once it was shut. Despite what she'd said, her breath caught in her throat. Why did everything have to be so hard? But, yes, thankfully William was safe, and it wasn't a telegram.

Opening the package on the kitchen table revealed a strange trussed-up parcel and a single sheet of paper.

My Dearest Hazel,

I'm so sorry that you're there dealing with our precious son all on your own. I thought that here I was serving the greater good, fighting for our country and the freedom of the world. But now, all that seems unimportant. I wish I could be there with you. Know that I love you and that all my prayers will be with you.

As always, give hugs and kisses to my two little munchkins, but save some for yourself!

Love,

William

P. S. Don't worry about the package. An old priest gave it to me for safekeeping. I didn't even dare open it since it was wrapped up so securely. Just set it aside, and I'll deal with it when I come home—and I assure you, it's when and not if.

She picked up the parcel, deciding whether or not to be disappointed it wasn't something special for her or the children. But as she thought of William, she realized the only thing she really wanted coming to her from across the ocean would be William himself. Hazel set it down and instead held the letter to her nose, trying in vain to catch the scent of her husband. She had an inner feeling that he would indeed return to her, but how soon she didn't know. People dealt with hard things all the time, but she felt that while God had given her and her sweet child some difficult challenges, He wasn't going to take her husband too. She knew that wasn't always the case, but for some reason, she was being given this gift. After a silent prayer of gratitude, she pulled down the ladder to the attic and climbed it, slipping the parcel up inside. Then she went to tell her children there was a letter from Daddy.

week Two – summer 1975

sunday

Hidden in the drawer of her nightstand was the small pad of paper Madelyn had written numbers on. If anyone saw it, they wouldn't understand what it was about, and she preferred it that way. Early Sunday morning, she took out a pen and colored in the circle that surrounded the number one. One week down. Madelyn carefully circled the two. She could do this. Before she knew it, the summer would fly right by. She was likely fooling herself, but it was worth a try, she reasoned.

It felt odd going to church without Dad, just like the previous week, but Madelyn didn't mind as much this time since as soon as it was over, they planned on calling him. The long-distance bill was going to go way up with these weekly phone calls, but Mom and Dad decided before he left that it would be worth it. It was an extravagance they didn't usually take. As inadequate as she thought phone calls could be when they'd told her about it, she was incredibly grateful now.

Madelyn could hardly sit still, waiting for each minute to pass. Even Jillian put her to shame, sitting politely and quietly through the entire service. Daniel, too, was stiller than Madelyn was, but he kept making faces in her direction in an effort to make her laugh. Mom only noticed the faces Madelyn made back at him, while Daniel returned to innocently sitting bolt upright complete with a pious look on his face. The look should have been his giveaway since he was rarely innocent and certainly not pious, but Mom merely smiled at him.

With the promise of the approaching phone call, she'd forgotten it was Father's Day—until the sermon began—as if Madelyn needed one more reason to miss him. She went from feeling excited and happy to feeling remorseful. She hadn't really been doing much to honor her father lately.

As they were leaving church, the pastor came over to talk to Mom. "How are things going, Mrs. Osborne? Do you need any help while Roger is away?"

"Oh no, Reverend, we're just fine, thanks."

The pastor continued to offer help to Mom, while she continued to decline it. Madelyn didn't care either way. She just wanted them to stop talking so they could go home and call Dad. As their pleasantries continued, Madelyn finally said, "Mom, I'm not feeling well. Could we go now?"

Madelyn could tell Mom knew it was a lie by the frown she gave her, but Mom gathered them up and headed out the door all the same. "If you're not feeling well, maybe you should go lie down while we talk to your father," Mom said on their way to the car. Surprised, Madelyn swung around to see if she was serious. Only then did she see the twinkle in Mom's eye. "Regardless of your good intentions, it's not nice to lie, young lady. Don't do it again." Mom's twinkle had been replaced by a stern glare, and Madelyn knew she meant business, but she was still relieved.

"Okay," Madelyn said while under her breath adding, "but he was never going to stop talking."

"I heard that, and yes, he's long-winded, but I'm sure you could have handled it better, don't you think?"

Madelyn looked down at her feet, shuffling them on the ground. "I suppose so."

"All right then. Let's get in the car and go home so you can call your dad." She was smiling again as they drove the short distance home.

•   •   •

When it was finally her turn to talk to Dad, Madelyn chose to speak to him on the phone extension in his study. There she could listen to the sound of his voice in a room that was alive with her thoughts of him.

"Happy Father's Day, Dad."

"Thanks, Madelyn. So, how are you doing?"

"Okay," Madelyn said without realizing she'd released her hair from its elastic, idly running her fingers through it.

"Really? Somehow I think you can elaborate a little bit more than an 'okay'."

Madelyn smiled even though he couldn't see it. "You're right." He may not have known what he was unleashing, but the floodgates opened as Madelyn proceeded to tell him about her run-in with Mrs. Burnham, going to the park, talking briefly to Zane, finishing with finding *The Hobbit.* She didn't know if he could follow her stream of consciousness, but she didn't care.

He chuckled lightly. "That's quite a lot for a week, although it sounds like all of that happened yesterday. What about earlier in the week?"

"Uh. Well, Jilly and I kind of ..." Madelyn didn't know how to finish the thought knowing none of the time they'd spent together had been her idea. Her hand dropped, letting go of the hair she hadn't realized she'd been playing with. "Jilly's a great little sister," she finally said, almost in a whisper.

"Yes, she is. And, Madelyn, I'm glad you're back. You really couldn't pretend *not* to care forever." She tried to sputter a denial but choked on the truth of his words. "So, have you forgiven me for leaving?"

Chagrined, Madelyn said, "Yeah, I guess so," then quickly added, "but it doesn't mean I don't still miss you."

"Of course you do. I miss you too. You're my bright spot—you always have been. Have you started reading *The Hobbit* yet?"

"Yes, and I love it! But I want to spread it out over the summer. So, I only let myself read a few pages then I read one of my library books instead. I want to finish *The Hobbit* the day before you come home."

"All right. I'll do the same."

"What do you mean?"

"Well, I saw it in the airport bookstore in Atlanta. When I was younger, I loved it. So, I bought you a copy and then one for me. I figured we could read it together."

Madelyn squealed with delight. "I love that, Dad! What page are you on?"

"I haven't started yet. I wanted to make sure you got it in the mail first before I began."

"Well, I'm at the start of the second chapter, but I won't tell you what's happening until you read it, just in case you've forgotten."

"Sounds good. How about I catch up to you and then read two more chapters by next Sunday? Then we can talk about it. Okay?"

"Sure." Madelyn was having a hard time relaxing the smile on her face, until he spoke one last time.

"How's your mom? Are you taking care of her?"

Why did he have to go and ruin it by asking about Mom? "Sure. She's fine, Dad. She's taking charge of things. She's just fine." Madelyn realized that for some reason, with all she'd told him, she hadn't mentioned the dandelions. Even as it dawned on her, she held back, not certain why.

"Okay. Just keep watching out for her, will you? You might find ... well, she just might surprise you."

"Surprise me? How is Mom going to surprise me?"

"Oh ... never mind." He was flustered, something he rarely was.

Madelyn brushed it off. "Okay. Do you want to talk to her now?"

"Yes. Thanks, Madelyn. I love you."

"I love you too."

When Mom picked up the extension in the kitchen, Madelyn settled down right where she was to read chapter two of *The Hobbit*. She couldn't wait to find out what would happen next to Bilbo with a handful of dwarves and a wizard thrown in. As Madelyn twirled her hair in her fingers, she thought about just how hard it was going to be to save the third chapter for later in the week.

MONDaY

Madelyn woke early Monday morning to a quiet house. It was actually too early to be up, even earlier than for a school day. But hard as she tried, she couldn't fall back asleep. So, she threw on some clothes and made her way downstairs to grab a bowl of cereal for breakfast. She didn't usually read the newspaper—that had been more Dad's thing than anyone else's—but she decided to give it a try. It was then that she remembered Dad had canceled the subscription for the summer.

When Mom entered the kitchen soon after, she was surprised to see Madelyn going out the back door. "Where are you heading?"

Madelyn shrugged her shoulders. "I thought I'd check on the garden, and you know ...," leaving the rest unsaid, instead nodding to the whole outside. Mom smiled and nodded in return, silently acknowledging that Madelyn was doing something she'd rather not.

Mrs. Burnham discovered her a short while later in the front yard. "Hello, Madelyn. What are you doing?" Maybe she meant it to be a friendly question, but it came off sounding like an accusation, especially when combined with the piercing stare that accompanied it.

Without a word, Madelyn held out a recently plucked dandelion in her grasp. Why Mrs. Burnham felt the need to ask a question with such an obvious answer was beyond her. "Just digging up dandelions," she said, wishing she had a snappier comeback. But then she whispered, conspiratorially, "You know, the ones you were worried about."

While Madelyn was debating whether to feel bad about her retort, Mrs.

Burnham decided to walk onto their lawn and survey the work ahead of her. "You'll never finish, you know—at least not with your half-hearted attitude."

Madelyn sat up from where she was bent over the lawn. "Mrs. Burnham, you don't know anything about my heart—half, full, or otherwise." With that, Madelyn turned back to her task and attacked with a vigor previously unknown to her. Mrs. Burnham may be right that Madelyn didn't much care about this particular task, but if she was that observant, surely she'd noticed Madelyn helping her dad with other projects and knew she was quite capable. She smiled a little as she worked, thinking about her new friend, Mr. Bilbo Baggins. The dwarves didn't think much of him to start with either, but he was determined to show them. Madelyn could do the same.

The problem with that thought was that Mrs. Burnham didn't go away, and Madelyn was having to actually continue to dig up those nasty dandelions. Mrs. Burnham said nothing more, just stood over Madelyn blocking the sun. She'd lost count, but by now Madelyn was sure she'd reached her twenty weed count for the day. The problem was she didn't know how to quit without giving Mrs. Burnham the upper hand.

Fortunately, or unfortunately, Daniel picked that moment to turn the hose on Madelyn—full blast. She was dripping mad from head to toe. "Daniel!" she yelled, running after him, Mrs. Burnham momentarily forgotten. It was then that Madelyn came across a laughing Jillian at the spigot.

She reached out to grab Jillian when, out of the corner of her eye, she saw Mrs. Burnham walking away in a huff. Jillian squealed as Madelyn picked her up, certain Madelyn was going to do something to get even, but was surprised by a hug instead. Jillian looked at her in confusion then burst out in giggles.

Daniel soon returned to see what was happening. The shocked expression on his face at their laughter was the best revenge Madelyn could have wanted.

•   •   •

After the warm day, the cool breeze felt pleasant flowing through Madelyn's bedroom window that evening. She picked up a library book, but it failed to capture her interest. So, she opted instead to comb the kitchen cupboards for a snack. Crackers in hand, she wandered toward the living room where she discovered Mom and Jillian curled up on the couch reading a book. She recognized the words Mom was reading. They were from one of her old children's books. Madelyn had three favorites— *Where the Wild Things Are; Go, Dog. Go!;* and *Are You My Mother?* It seems like when she was little Mom read those same three books to her over and over and over, so much so that Madelyn could recite the words from memory. Even after she could sound the words out for herself, Madelyn still preferred to listen to her mom read them, resting in her arms, feeling like all was right with the world.

Madelyn leaned up against the wall just around the corner from where they were reading, not wanting to be seen but letting the warm comfort of the familiar words envelop her. As she relaxed, her body slid down until she was sitting in the empty hallway up against the wall, soaking it all in.

She smiled as they moved from one book to the next—her three books—everything the same and nothing so. Madelyn listened to each word and the turn of each page as if it were a graceful two-step being danced before her. She closed her eyes to shut out all distractions so she could participate in the dance, seeing the pages of the books before her, each detail of the illustrations twirling in front of her—one page following the next, turn after turn.

Suddenly everything stopped, and her eyes flew open. The sound of her mother's voice continued, but something was wrong. The dance was all wrong!

Madelyn jumped to her feet and rounded the corner into the living room to where they sat. She choked in surprise at the scene in front of her— not because things were out of place, but rather because they weren't. Mom and Jillian were curled up just as Madelyn had discovered them earlier. The two books already read were to one side, and Mom was finishing *Where the Wild Things Are* with Max coming home to find his soup still warm. But Madelyn was cold, and she had no idea why.

TUESDAY

Madelyn tossed and turned that night, racking her brain to understand what was wrong, but she could think of nothing that should have left her so upset. Nothing had been unusual or different that she could put her finger on. The only logical conclusion was that she was losing her mind—not any more of a comforting thought. As the first hint of daylight trickled into her room, Madelyn finally fell into an exhausted sleep.

It was fully light when she pulled herself out of bed, still tired but no longer able to sleep, hearing the giggles and conversation of her family seeping in under her door. After getting dressed and eating breakfast, she went in search of her younger brother and sister. For reasons she couldn't explain, she wanted to spend as little time as possible with Mom.

She spent much of the day with the two of them—playing tag outside, Monopoly inside, even taking them on a bike ride to the library. Although Madelyn hadn't planned on it, she found that being a good big sister made the rest of life more bearable, and even her strange unease around Mom began to dissipate. She even considered reading *The Hobbit* out loud to Jillian and Daniel, before realizing she couldn't bring herself to share that one thing that was just hers and Dad's. As Madelyn curled up in Dad's study to read another chapter, she decided maybe next summer she could read it again and share it with them. But for now, she was content to be slightly selfish.

THURSDAY

Every other Thursday marked the day they visited Uncle Tommy. He was Mom's younger brother, although Madelyn wasn't sure how much younger—just a few years she thought, since he was a baby when his dad, her grandpa, went off to fight in World War II.

Uncle Tommy lived in a group home because of his cerebral palsy. They often visited him there or at the sheltered workshop where he spent most of his days. After the half hour car ride, Madelyn loved being able to get out and stretch her legs, but mostly she liked the walk that took her straight into the workroom a few feet inside the front door. There a small group of adults with various disabilities was employed working on items for businesses.

Every eye turned her way when they heard the sound of her shoes on the tile floor. As Uncle Tommy's head came up from where he was bent over his work, his eyes lit up, and a crooked grin spread across his face. "Madly!" It was his name for her—much easier for him to say than the entire Madelyn. If anyone else called her that, she'd have been upset, but on his lips, it was perfect. He swung out of his chair and stood up to make his labored way to her. Madelyn used to rush to him to save him the trouble of moving across the floor, but one day he told her, "I can make it, Madly. You just be more patient." Since then, she stopped as soon as he noticed her then patiently waited for him.

Of course, that meant that someone else would usually reach her first. It was often Eliza or Annie, or both. "Madelyn, I see you," Eliza said.

"I see you, Eliza." It's what they always said to each other even though Eliza was legally blind. Her thick glasses merely kept her from running into things when she wasn't using her white cane, which she hated. "It makes me look blind," she'd say, not aware that her visual impairment was obvious with or without it. But she liked to pretend her sight was perfect, so whenever Madelyn was looking for someone or something, she always asked Eliza first. "Hey, do you know where Annie is?"

"She right there," Eliza said, pointing behind her without looking and not even close to where Madelyn could see Annie. "She comin'. She just slow today."

Slow or not, she still beat Uncle Tommy. When she reached Madelyn's side, they wrapped each other in a big hug. Annie pulled back to reward her with a great, big grin. While Eliza was just over five feet tall—short by any standard—Annie was tiny, likely four and a half feet, but that would only be if you could straighten her up enough to take full measure of her height. Madelyn didn't know if she was bent over from the ravages of time or if she was just born that way, probably a combination of the two.

Annie had never said a word to Madelyn. She honestly didn't know if Annie could speak at all. "How are you today?" Madelyn said. Annie half-closed her eyes. "Tired, huh?" She nodded. It had taken her a bit to figure out Annie, but once Madelyn did, she had no trouble communicating, words or no words. Apparently, Annie really was tired because she shuffled away, but rather than return to her workstation, she moved to the hallway. Madelyn watched as she made her way toward the breakroom where there was a couch she was particularly fond of napping on.

By now, Mom, Jillian, and Daniel had joined Madelyn, and Uncle Tommy had at last arrived. His sandy colored hair was always slightly messy, a few stubborn cowlicks made certain of that, but he always tried to wet them down all the same. "Jilly, Danny, Sissy," he said in turn as he doled out hugs. Madelyn didn't know if he'd ever called Mom by her name Rachel. As long as she'd been around, Mom had just been "Sissy." Finally, it was her turn. He bent down to give her a big hug. The contradiction of it always struck her—he was mentally stuck in childhood, yet he was taller than her dad. "How you, Madly?"

Daniel started to snicker. "She's mad, you know, crazy, just like her name."

Madelyn glared at him. Then to Uncle Tommy she said, "I'm just fine. How are you?"

"I'm good. Want to see what I'm making?"

"Of course I do." It took them a while to make it back to his spot. He had several large bins around him. In one were small foam pillows, in another were blue covers, and in another still were his finished product—the foam pillows inside their blue covers.

"These is for airplanes. You know, in case airplanes get tired." He burst out laughing.

"Uncle Tommy, you made a joke," Madelyn said, laughing along with him. For some reason, Uncle Tommy had a tremendous ability to surprise her. He couldn't add two and two, but he could make jokes or understand when Madelyn was sad better than most people she knew. "Are you ready for lunch?" He nodded vigorously.

During the summertime, they tried to time their visits during lunchtime. Much as Uncle Tommy loved their visits, he hated leaving his work. He was very conscientious about his job, and since he was paid piecemeal for whatever he did, stepping away from it was always hard for him to do. He may not have been able to add, but he understood the growing numbers in his bankbook and what they meant—a small measure of freedom in the form of going on shopping trips or visiting the commissary at his group home for extra snacks or treats. Often, he bought things for his nieces and nephew, saving them for the next time they came to visit.

When the picnic lunch they brought was finished, Uncle Tommy said, "Thank you for lunch, Sissy. Can you stay?" He was usually reluctant to have them leave once they arrived, forgetting about all else but what was in front of him.

"No, Tommy. It's time for us to go. Don't you want to get back to work?" Mom said.

He brightened at the thought, but then his face clouded over again. "Where's Pop Pop? I want to see Pop Pop." He was talking about his own father, Madelyn's grandfather.

"I know you do, but Pop Pop can't come. Remember, he lives too far away now."

"He does?" Madelyn said, confused.

Mom brusquely cut her off with, "Yes, he does," adding, "Right, Tommy? You remember, don't you?"

He hung his head. "Oh, yeah."

Mom ruffled his hair. "Don't worry. We're here, and we'll keep coming to visit you—always."

"Okay." However, he wasn't cheered up any.

"Uncle Tommy, can you show me how many airplane pillows you've made today?" Madelyn said.

"You bet!" he said as he hustled her, in his snail-like way, back to the workroom. Madelyn knew it would save the moment, but she glared at her mother as she followed her uncle to his workstation.

· · ·

As soon as they were in the car, Madelyn said, "Did Grandpa move and you never bothered to tell us?"

"No," was all Mom said without any explanation.

"Then why did you tell Uncle Tommy that Pop Pop lived too far away to visit?"

"There's more than one way to be far away."

"What's that supposed to mean?"

Mom turned toward her before answering. "There's a lot more that goes on in this world than meets your eye. Besides, it's what Pop wanted me to tell him. Tommy wouldn't understand the truth—Pop and I both know that. Trust me, it's best this way."

"But I thought Grandpa was just busy with work, and that's why we haven't seen him lately."

"Yes, and don't you think Tommy would have a hard time understanding that?"

Mom seemed to have an answer for everything. Even worse, it made sense, but Madelyn didn't want to be placated. "Of course he would. *I* don't understand it." Her words came out angry, but she wasn't mad, not really. She should have stopped right there, but she pushed onward, giving in to her frustrations. "First Grandma dies, then Grandpa basically disappears. What grandfather goes from being there all the time to suddenly being 'too busy'? Who does that?"

Mom glanced at her sideways. "We talked about this before. I thought you were okay with it."

"I was, but ..." She was feeling abandoned on every side, but putting it into words and opening up to Mom was not what she had in mind.

"It happens. It just does. All right?"

"But ..."

"No, Madelyn. No more buts. Leave it alone."

Madelyn folded her arms with a loud "humph" for emphasis and stayed that way for the rest of the drive home. Her summer just kept getting better by the minute.

1945

Life—whether a war is being waged on the other side of the globe or not—goes on. For Rachel that meant going to kindergarten. And when her daddy still wasn't home at its end, it meant moving on to first grade as if nothing else mattered or existed in her world.

Rachel liked school, at least all the art projects. The rest of it was a lot for a six-year-old to take in, especially with so much happening—or actually, not happening—at home. Her baby brother was now three, only he wasn't doing the typical toddler things. For one, he wasn't "toddling," but at least he'd recently taken his first step. As her mom said, "That's a HUGE step for him." For another, he wasn't talking, although Rachel could get him to make more sounds than anyone else. Even at six, Rachel knew she was needed, and being where she was needed was where she felt most comfortable.

It might have been different if her daddy hadn't gone to war, but then again, she'd never know for sure. It was hard for Rachel to remember him— only snippets like particles of dreams floated in her head to remind her she had a Daddy. He read her bedtime stories, or at least she had a memory of him doing it once, that much she knew for sure. And he would rub noses with her, giving her Eskimo kisses. There had been other memories, but before she knew she needed to hold onto them, they were gone, and even the hint of having memories had all but faded away.

•   •   •

Hazel tried to keep Daddy alive in her daughter's thoughts, but fighting for their country by being in a different one on the opposite side of the world was hard to explain to someone so young. The effort seemed futile. Besides, most of Rachel's friends were in the same situation. What should have been unusual was the norm. And, of course, there was so much to worry about with Tommy.

She had taken him from doctor to doctor. What she learned was that she was becoming more of an expert on cerebral palsy than any of them. She often marveled that Tommy was fortunate enough to have even received a diagnosis, although it came with little advice on how to proceed. The best doctors expressed little understanding of what to do, and the worst suggested her only option was to institutionalize him. She was adamant that that was not going to happen.

Hazel had finally come to one conclusion—since he had little to no muscle tone, then she would just have to help him develop some. It was exhausting—physically, mentally, emotionally, and any other way she could think of—but she was not willing to stop trying.

She didn't know whether she should be proud or ashamed at how much she had come to rely on Rachel's help with her little brother. Rachel tirelessly moved Tommy's legs and arms, being the first to get him to sit up and crawl. And now he'd actually taken a step. It seemed when Hazel didn't know what to try next, Rachel instinctively did. It wasn't so much that she thought it out but rather that she didn't need to. She was just a child relating to another child—it wasn't any more complicated than that. Watching them, it was hard to say whether baby Tommy adored his big sister more or the other way around.

.   .   .

As for Rachel, she had no problem helping her brother—it was the highlight of her day. She would hurry home from school to do her own version of "homework"—the work she did at home helping her little brother. And, in her eyes, it was the very best homework of all.

FRIDAY

Madelyn dreamed about her grandpa that night. They were on an outing together, enjoying a picnic in the shadow of a museum. Only, before the dream was over, the shadow turned menacing, transforming into a fierce thunderstorm they couldn't escape.

She woke in a cold sweat. Disagreement or not with her mom, the thought of her comforting presence was reason enough to hop out of bed. "Mom?" she softly called down the empty hallway. When there was no answer, she went searching for her.

Mom was in the kitchen. She was holding a picture she'd ripped from a magazine with one hand while sorting through her box of craft supplies with the other. Periodically, she'd pick up something from the box, compare it to the picture and mumble to herself—so preoccupied that she didn't notice when her daughter walked in.

Madelyn cleared her throat, startling Mom such that she dropped the paper and the spool of ribbon she'd been holding. "Oh, hi. I didn't see you there." She was shaking slightly, and her eyes were darting around the room.

"Are you okay?"

"Yeah, I was ..." She shrugged her shoulders, then with a knit brow said, "Wow, you're up kind of early. Something on your mind?"

"Well, I, uh, just had a weird dream, that's all."

Before her mom could respond, the phone rang. "Osborne's," Mom answered. Her voice was steady, saying only an occasional, "Oh my," or "Really?" but nothing else about her was steady. Mom's eyes were growing bigger by the minute. She was gripping the phone receiver so tightly that her knuckles were turning white, and with her other hand she was twirling the phone cord in her fingers into a tangled mess.

Madelyn waited for her to say something when she hung up the phone, but it took her a few minutes to collect herself. "Someone broke into your grandpa's house last night. I don't know if anything's been taken, but apparently, the house is a mess."

"Is Grandpa okay?"

"What? Oh, yeah. He ... he's fine." She took a deep breath. "Could you go wake up your brother and sister? We need to go check on the house."

After a hurried breakfast, they were all loaded into their car on the way to Grandpa's house. It wasn't until they were almost there that her mom's words struck her as strange. Why were they checking on the house and not on Grandpa?

It had been quite some time since they'd been to his house. Driving up to it brought a smile and a shiver to Madelyn—a smile for the memories like playing card games with Grandpa and enjoying backyard barbecues, but a shiver for the thought of someone breaking into it, violating its safety. As she walked onto the porch, it was impossible not to notice where the front lock had been jimmied. It was too broken to hold now, the door swinging open with a simple turn of the knob—their extra key being completely unnecessary.

If driving up to the house had brought familiar memories, walking inside did just the opposite. It didn't even look like the same house. The furniture was turned over, exposing the dusty undersides of couches and chairs. Paintings had been removed from the walls. Cupboards and drawers hung open. Even the refrigerator had been pulled out of its space. There was, however, the problem about Grandpa—he was nowhere to be seen.

Jillian beat Madelyn to the question. "Where's Grandpa? Is he okay?"

Mom quickly replied, "He's fine. He wasn't here when it happened." She caught Madelyn's angry glare and added, "Don't worry about it. Right now, let's figure out what needs to be done here." Then she turned away with an air of finality and began to right the chairs in the living room. "The police, supposedly, left everything the way they found it," Mom said over her shoulder. "Maybe they thought it would be easier for us to figure out what was missing if we could see where the thieves had been."

"Yeah, I don't see that being a big help," Daniel said. "It's all such a mess, how could anyone tell anything?"

Jillian had gone quiet, but her eyes were big, surveying the turmoil created in a place usually filled with happy memories. "Jilly?" Madelyn said. "Do you want to just go play out back?" Jillian nodded her head but then proceeded to help put things back where they belonged.

They were at it for several hours, and although they couldn't be certain, it didn't appear that anything was missing. But it's always hard to catalog someone else's things—what they care about, what they keep close.

When Mom declared that they'd done as much as they could, they all scampered out to sit on the front porch. Other than the broken lock, the porch still felt the same, like Grandpa's porch. The relief of the mundane yet familiar was like a cooling breeze even though the temperature was in the high 80s.

It was only a moment before Grandpa's neighbors, Nadine and James Chapman, found their way to the small gathering on the porch. James lifted his hand in greeting. "I'm sorry to see you under such circumstances. I thought about going through the house for you, but I knew I'd be terrible at it. So, I asked the police to leave things as they were as much as possible."

"Ahh, so it's you we have to thank for that. It didn't paint a pretty picture, I admit, but it did show us where they had been," Mom said.

"That was pretty much everywhere," Daniel said under his breath.

"How did you know someone broke in? Did you hear them?" Madelyn said.

"No, dear," Nadine Chapman said, "It was because of Lydia. There was a commotion at Lydia's this morning, a break-in as well, with police cars and such. We walked down to see if she was all right. On the way back, we noticed the door to your grandpa's house. It wasn't even shut."

Mom was staring at the house that must be Lydia's without saying a word.

"So, did the police just come from her house over to my grandpa's?" Jillian said.

"They did, dear. We walked them around, and then they called your mom."

"But why wasn't Grandpa home?" Madelyn said, directing it at her mom, but Mom was still studying the house next door. Then without a word, she stood up and walked toward it. Madelyn swung around to see if at least the Chapman's could tell her what was happening, but they had grown quiet as well.

Jillian glanced from one to the other, finally settling on Daniel. They shrugged their shoulders at each other then Daniel grabbed her hand and said, "C'mon." And with that they were off to the stream behind Grandpa's house, leaving Madelyn standing next to the Chapmans.

"Is that the Holliwell's house?" She seemed to remember Mr. and Mrs. Holliwell being good friends of her grandparents, but it had been a long time since she'd talked to them. Nadine Chapman simply nodded, but she wasn't smiling.

Not sure what else to do, Madelyn ran to catch up to Mom as she stepped onto the Holliwell's front porch. Lydia Holliwell answered the door almost as soon as the doorbell rang. When she saw them standing there, her eyebrows arched but then relaxed. "Hello, Rachel. This must be Madelyn. You've grown since I last saw you. Won't you come in?"

Mom took a step inside, but instead of going for the offered chair or couch, she swept Lydia into a huge embrace. "I'm sorry, so sorry." They stood that way for some time, the only sound the soft rumble of crying women.

When they let go, Lydia led them into her living room. "It's okay. Well, it's getting better, anyway. My kids live close by, and they visit all the time. I don't know what I'd do without them." She intentionally trailed off, looking uncomfortable.

"I came over ... I should have ..." Mom heaved a sigh. "I heard your house was broken into. So was my ...," she motioned over her shoulder.

"Your father's house," Lydia finished for her. "I see the house every day. I know whose it is. I also know he's not there anymore. And, Rachel, I'm sorry he's not there." Just then, she caught a glimpse of Madelyn's face. Confusion mixed with anger had spread across it. Turning to Rachel, she said, "I thought ..." When she shook her head, Lydia said, "I'm sorry."

Madelyn looked from one to the other, but neither of them would meet her eyes. They all sat in icy silence for several minutes before Madelyn abruptly stood. "Fine, don't tell me," she said as she left to go find her brother and sister.

. . .

"So, Mom, it's just the two of us. Tell me what's going on with Grandpa," Madelyn said. It was later that evening after Jillian and Daniel had finally gone to bed. Mom had been sitting quietly in a darkened kitchen, sipping some herbal tea when Madelyn came up behind her, surprising her when she spoke.

Mom jumped, spilling tea all over her robe. "Madelyn, don't you know when to leave well enough alone?"

"I'm sorry. Here," Madelyn said, handing her a towel. She watched while Mom dabbed at her robe, hoping she would give some kind of explanation, but Madelyn was met with silence instead. "What's going on, *Mother*? Where is Grandpa?"

Mom looked up to meet Madelyn's gaze, but her eyes held no warmth, turning from blue to gray. "Did I not make myself clear yesterday? It's none of your business, young lady."

The edge to Mom's voice blew Madelyn back a step, leaving her astounded that *she* was mad at *her*! Wanting to know about her grandpa couldn't possibly put her in the wrong. She was the one who had the right to be angry. Madelyn folded her arms for effect. "What are you talking about? How could Grandpa not be my business? We were constantly inviting him over after Grandma died, and now he's nowhere?" Mom tried to interject, but Madelyn wasn't done. "You were right, I was trying to be understanding before, but today changed everything. He wasn't in his house. I poked around. There wasn't anything in the fridge, not even much in the cupboards. Even Mrs. Holliwell said something about it. He's not living there right now, is he?"

Mom's gray eyes were now black, but Madelyn's words had shaken her. "There is much that you don't know or understand. The world isn't as cut and dried as you'd like to believe it is. And it doesn't conform to your way of thinking, just because you wish it so. We decided it was best to leave you out of this."

The words stung, and Madelyn grabbed the table to steady her thoughts. Not only wouldn't Mom tell her, she'd decided to deliberately shut her out, even deceive her. It was a gut punch, and she had no breath left for words.

"This discussion is over." Then Mom's voice softened. "You just need to trust us on this one, Madelyn," she said before turning away. Then, surprisingly, her shoulders started to shudder. She was crying. Madelyn almost felt sorry for her—almost. Instead, she spun on her heels, stomping off to her room, making sure the slam of her door could be heard all the way to the kitchen and beyond.

Sitting upright on her bed, arms folded, fists clenched, she was certain the steam coming out of her ears could be seen seeping under the door. She sat there—waiting. But if she thought Mom would come after her, she was mistaken. And it turns out a good pout isn't nearly as good without an audience. Mom, it appeared, recognized her sulk for what it was and chose to ignore it rather than indulge it. Another word didn't pass between them that night.

SATURDAY

Mom was up early again the next morning making a nice breakfast—waffles with fresh strawberries. For a few minutes, Madelyn forgot or at least pretended to forget, how mad she was at her.

She ate in silence, listening instead to Jillian and Daniel's chatter beside her and ducking to avoid the mini food fights they started every time Mom's back was turned. She finished every last bite of her waffle. Lifting her head, she caught Mom watching her, but the look on Mom's face was hard to read. "Thanks for breakfast, Mom, I ..." She deserved an apology, but Madelyn was having trouble forming the words, in part because she wasn't completely sorry about what she'd said. Finally settling for a quick shrug of her shoulders, she said, "I'm heading out to work in the yard."

The kitchen window was open, and Madelyn could hear the noise of children and dishes and chores being assigned while she tended to the garden. By the time she was ready to move onto the yard and those cursed dandelions, the sounds were fading, coming from more distant places in the house—a vacuum, probably from the upstairs, the clatter of Legos being thrown into a toy bin, the rinsing of water in a tub or sink somewhere. She didn't want to be in there doing those chores, but she didn't like being outside all alone either. At least she'd chosen to focus on the backyard today, hoping to avoid Mrs. Burnham. Despite being lonely, sometimes it was the lesser of two evils.

Lost in those thoughts, Madelyn jumped when Mom said, "What can I do to help?"

"I didn't see you. When did you come outside?"

"Just now. So, what can I do?"

"With what?" Madelyn said, confused.

"The dandelions. I promised to help you."

"Oh." She'd forgotten about the offer. "Even after ... you know ...?"

Mom took a deep breath. "Madelyn, I'm sorry about what I said. I could have handled that better. We made a decision not to involve you—for your sake, but I should have known that would be confusing. I'm sorry I don't have anything more to offer you than 'just trust me'."

Madelyn was about to respond when Mom continued, "And, whether you believe it or not, I was a teenager once, and I didn't always get along with my mother. But, regardless of what I did, she was my mother. She always loved me. I will always love you." Mom took another breath, "Even if at times you make it hard to do so." She was smiling as she said it, and it softened her words and Madelyn's heart even more.

"Thanks, Mom." It came out as a whisper.

"Okay, so how do we do this?" Mom said, motioning to the endless sea of yellow blooms.

For the next hour, they worked side by side digging up dandelions. Madelyn had to show her how at first since she'd probably never done such a thing, but she caught on right away. It wasn't quite the magic moment from the movies, but it was better than being alone.

It was a warm day. When the sweat started to drip down Madelyn's face, and she felt her skin start to ripen and burn, she sat down on the ground, letting her tool slip from her hands so she could wipe her forehead.

Mom followed suit. "Shall we call it good for the day?" she said. It was truly a question and not a statement. They were both pretty tired, but Mom was deferring to Madelyn, asking permission to quit.

Madelyn just nodded. Without wasting any more words, they gathered their tools and weed buckets, slowly heading back to the garage. Taking one last look behind, the spot where they had worked was delightfully green— with no yellow polka dots. Madelyn's smile started to grow until she spied the rest of the yard. It was covered with a blanket of yellow. She quickly turned away—not able to face the thought of the impossible task ahead or the possibility of failing Dad.

WEEK THREE – SUMMER 1975

SUNDAY

The first thing Madelyn did Sunday morning was open the drawer of her nightstand to retrieve her pad of paper. Coloring in the two for the previous week was satisfying, even if those seven days hadn't passed nearly fast enough. She tried not to think about what those days had contained, only anxious for the afternoon when she could talk with Dad.

"How are you doing, Madelyn?" were his first words.

"Okay, I guess."

"How's your summer going without Lori around? I'll bet it's kind of quiet."

"Yeah, it is." She smiled to herself that he remembered. And then, despite what Mom had said, she found herself saying, "Hey, Dad, what's the story with Grandpa?"

"Why are you asking?"

"Because Mom told Uncle Tommy that he lived too far away to visit, but she told me he was simply too busy for us right now."

"Well, that's just two ways of looking at the same coin, isn't it?"

Madelyn didn't think so. And he'd answered so quickly, she didn't even have a chance to point out Grandpa wasn't living in his home.

It was then she realized that she'd squandered a perfect opportunity. If she'd asked more indirectly about Grandpa, like where he was living now

mary ellen bramwell

because Mom had forgotten the name of his new town or something like that—anything other than what she'd said—he might have told her more. And he would have done it without realizing what he was revealing. But it was too late now.

"So, how do you like *The Hobbit* so far?" he said, deftly changing the topic. She was disappointed by his earlier response or actually her missed opportunity, but reluctantly Madelyn warmed to the sound of his voice, whether she wanted to or not. And much to her chagrin, she found herself enjoying their brief conversation. All too soon he was gone—talking to Mom, hanging up—gone.

It was only then that something occurred to her. When her mom had said *we* decided to leave you out of it, she wasn't talking about her and Grandpa, she meant her and Dad.

Mixed emotions flooded her mind—disappointment, confusion, even sadness. She trusted Dad, or at least wanted to. Was Mom right, that it was better left alone? She refused to believe that. It just couldn't be the case. But what if it was? What could that possibly mean? Her head started to hurt from everything she was trying to contemplate. Maybe there really was a different perspective, one other than her own.

Jillian saved her from that uncomfortable thought. Poking her head into Madelyn's room, she said, "Do you want to play a game? Daniel says he'll behave himself and play with us."

"Sure," Madelyn said, brushing her other thoughts aside. "Thanks, Jilly."

Jillian smiled and said, "You're welcome."

•   •   •

Since last week's reading about Bilbo Baggins had been over too quickly, Madelyn determined to wait until Friday or Saturday before picking it up again. That resolve lasted about an hour, as long as it took to finish the game with Jillian and Daniel.

Anxious for a connection with Dad—since she missed him, but also to repair any earlier doubts about how much she trusted him, or maybe, how much he trusted her, Madelyn was determined to right the ship, to find safe ground. *The Hobbit* was safe and also common ground.

61

Snatching it from her nightstand so she could read it in Dad's study, she rushed into the hallway and crashed headlong into Mom. "Oh! I'm sorry."

Mom had fallen back against the wall and was trying to catch her breath. For just a moment, she appeared small and vulnerable. Madelyn reached out a hand to help her.

Mom gave her a weak smile in return. "Sorry, Madelyn. I didn't even know you were in there."

Tipping up *The Hobbit* so she could see it, Madelyn said, "Just getting my book."

They stood there silently facing each other. She'd been such a good sport with the dandelions the day before that Madelyn wondered in that moment if maybe her way *was* best. "Mom, I *am* sorry," she said, only this time they both knew it meant something different. Mom nodded slightly, but her creased forehead was careworn.

"I ... I, uh." Madelyn wasn't sure what to say next, or even if there was anything else she was prepared to admit. Glancing at the book in her hands, she said, "I was just heading to Dad's study to read. Have you ever read this before?"

"No, can't say that I have."

"Well, do you have a favorite book?" Madelyn had never talked books with her mom before. That had always been something she shared with Dad. But standing in the hall, she was trying to fill the void with something akin to a conversation. The book she was holding was the only thing that came to mind.

"Um," Mom wrinkled her forehead, "I don't suppose I do. There's not much time to read when ..." She motioned to the house around her and the toilet plunger in her hand that Madelyn had failed to notice earlier.

"Oh." Madelyn started to giggle. "I guess I should let you go."

The edges of Mom's mouth curled up. "Yes, I think that would be a good idea."

"Not Daniel, was it?"

She laughed, "No, not this time."

Madelyn was still smiling as she pulled out her ponytail and settled into a chair in Dad's study to read.

Tuesday

Over the next couple of days, Madelyn regretted having already finished her allotted chapters in *The Hobbit*. Life instead became a monotony of chores, nibbled meals, sleep, and the reading of random books.

She tried not to think about missing Dad, but as soon as you decide not to think about something, that seems to be exactly what you do. Madelyn saw him in every corner of the house whether it be one of his books or just his office chair. And even though the scent of his licorice gum had faded, the smell of newly mown grass and faint honeysuckle on a passing breeze taunted her with his absence. With him gone, a sadness had settled over her that Madelyn was having a hard time shaking.

Mom silently acknowledged what Madelyn was dealing with in her own way. Dad would have asked her outright about it, and they would have talked it over, but Mom didn't—that wasn't her style. Mom would smile or nod in her direction, and Madelyn was surprisingly grateful, even if she didn't completely understand why.

Mindlessly working on the dandelions, Madelyn started to ponder her family, almost as if she were an outsider, a non-participant in it. It's funny the things you learn when you actually pay attention. They must have always been there, only Madelyn never bothered to notice before—like Mom. Madelyn always knew she was a creative, messy sort, but she hadn't realized just how much. Madelyn had watched her make dinner the night before—soup and cornbread. She gathered ingredients and threw them in the pot with a devil-may-care attitude, tasting and whistling as she went.

Even her cornbread seemed haphazard at best. She didn't follow a recipe, just used a scoop of this and a pinch of that.

She was a good cook, but until Madelyn thought about it, she'd never realized before how much she cooked by feel. Madelyn liked making things the way Dad did, like following the recipe to the letter for chocolate chip cookies. It's doubtful she could ever learn to cook from Mom in such an arbitrary way.

With Jillian, certainly, it would be different. She could likely learn anything from Mom. Thinking about her little sister made Madelyn smile—even as she threw a handful of dandelions into her bucket. Jillian was like Mom in so many ways, but also vastly different. While they both were incredibly creative, Jillian was somehow more organized about it, maybe even the more practical of the two. As soon as that thought entered her mind, Madelyn wondered why. What made her consider Jillian, at only seven, practical?

She was still puzzled by it when she came in to wash her hands, happening upon Jillian and Mom in the kitchen. Madelyn silently watched them while pretending to clean her fingernails. The answer to her question was immediately obvious. Madelyn had seen it yet hadn't recognized it before. Mom was getting ready to go to the store, randomly opening and closing cupboard doors, haphazardly noting what was low. It was Jillian who kept Mom on track with comments like, "Mom, you didn't check the cereal cupboard," or, "You forgot we ran out of cinnamon last week." Madelyn stared in surprise and awe at her little sister who was so aware of what they did and didn't have.

"Oh, that's right. Why don't you remember for me?"

This kind of exchange went on throughout Mom's check of the kitchen, the pantry, and the bathroom cupboards. It seemed that little Jillian was making a mental list of what they needed at the store. Mom finally noticed Madelyn as they were completing their routine. "Oh, hi, Madelyn. Would you mind finding Daniel? We're leaving for the store in a few minutes."

When they all piled out of the car at the grocery store, Madelyn continued to watch in amazement as Mom grabbed a cart then looked expectantly at Jillian. "Vegetables first, Mom," she said.

The rest of the shopping trip was much the same, as if Jillian were the parent and Mom the child following directions. Madelyn didn't know what to make of it. When they came to a display of pudding, she was relieved to see the roles right themselves. "Mom, can we get some butterscotch pudding? Please, please?"

Mom scrutinized the box Jillian had plucked off the shelves while Madelyn wondered at her hesitation. "I don't think so, sweetie."

"But I'll cook it up and everything. I bet I could do it if Madelyn helped me. Would you, Madelyn? Please, please?"

Madelyn was studying Mom's face when she realized she'd read her wrong. Mom didn't seem to mind buying the pudding, but something else was bothering her, only Madelyn couldn't figure out what. "Sure, I'll help. But, Mom, you don't have to buy it. Or we could get a different flavor?" she added, trying to guess at Mom's reluctance.

"No, no, that's fine. I'll take Daniel with me and go get the flour I need. You two can figure out which flavor to get and make sure we have all the ingredients to make it."

Jillian tugged at Madelyn's sleeve. "I like butterscotch. Do you?"

"Yeah," Madelyn said, still unsure what had Mom on edge. Checking the box, it looked like the only other thing they needed was milk, and they always had plenty of that. "That should work, Jilly."

She turned to follow Mom and ran right into Zane. "Hi, Madelyn."

"Oh, I didn't see you. What are you doing here?"

He held up a paper. "Mom sent Delia and me to the store. This is my half of the list of things to find." Then he grinned and added, "But I could use some help."

"Do you really not know where things are?" He shrugged his shoulders, his puppy dog eyes begging so innocently that Madelyn couldn't help herself. "Sure," she said, rolling her eyes. "Hey, Jilly, would you take this pudding to Mom? I'll meet you at the front of the store when I'm done." Jillian grabbed the pudding and skipped down the aisle to where Daniel and Mom were adding baking supplies to the cart.

"So, what's on your list?"

"Bread, eggs, cheese to start with."

"Do you have a cart?"

He gave her a sheepish grin. "Delia does."

Rolling her eyes again, Madelyn said, "Come on. We'll see how much we can carry."

"So, other than grocery shopping, what are you doing for fun this summer?" Zane said.

"Not much—I mean, there's lots of stuff to keep me busy, but the only fun part is reading. What about you?"

"Pretty much the same. Delia has a job this summer. Don't tell her, but I kind of miss when she's not around. I can't wait 'til I can get a job. I mean a real one. I have a paper route—the same one I've had for a while. It keeps me out of trouble."

Madelyn laughed. "Like you need that. You don't seem the sort that goes for trouble."

He winced. "Nice of you to say, but I'm not that much of an angel. Of course, Delia would kill me if I did something really stupid. She wouldn't even give our parents a chance to do it first. But what about you? Aren't you babysitting this summer?"

She shrugged her shoulders. "I was, during school, but this summer's different. I guess I could, but ..." She didn't know how to explain the responsibility she felt with her dad being gone. She hadn't even told Zane her dad *was* gone. "Hey, how did you know I babysit?"

"Um ... I don't know. I've seen you at the Foster's house. That seems like the only reason you'd be there. Anyway, I just assumed ..."

She elbowed him. "That's okay. I'm just giving you a hard time. Do you still like going fishing?"

"Yeah. Delia doesn't, but I go with my dad and grandpa pretty often."

They chatted on about mundane, trivial things, but none of it felt mundane. It was a nice break, talking to a friend. Madelyn was disappointed when they gathered the last of the items on his list.

"Thanks," Zane said. "Hey, Delia and I are going on a bike ride in the foothills. You want to come?"

"That sounds fun. Could Jilly and Daniel come too?"

"Sure. I know Delia misses seeing them. We were planning on Saturday morning."

"Oh shoot! I can't. That's when I mow the lawn and do a million other chores." Madelyn shook her head, disappointment overwhelming her face.

"That's okay. I'll call you next time we go." He smiled as he walked away.

The whole drive home Madelyn kept thinking about Zane, hoping he would call, afraid that he wouldn't—surprised to realize she cared more than she used to. It was a scary thought. The last thing she wanted was to be disappointed by someone else. Shaking off her feelings, she tried to convince herself that she was simply desperate for someone to talk to since Lori was gone. Zane just happened to be in the right place at the right time.

Climbing out of the car at home, Madelyn gathered an armload of groceries. In a rush to retreat to her room to contemplate these thoughts, she made a beeline for the front door. She stood there waiting for Mom to come unlock it, but as she leaned against it, the door fell open. "Mom, I thought you locked the front door when we left."

Mom approached her with a worried brow. "I did. The latch must have stuck. Too bad Roger's not home. If he were here, he'd know how to fix it."

"Yeah," Madelyn said to herself as she made her way into the kitchen. "If he were here, that would fix a lot of things."

1946

Rachel didn't know what to make of William when he returned home. She had only vague recollections of her daddy from before, and most of them were now just memories created by stories her mother had told her. And then there was the other Daddy, the one who wrote letters that started "My Dearest Hazel" but ended with "Kiss the munchkins for me." She loved that Daddy, too, just like the one in the buoyed-up memories.

This new Daddy was someone else. He seemed to have tired eyes—not like Tommy's eyes when he needed a nap, but tired like they had seen things they wished they hadn't. They were sad eyes. Those eyes brightened a little around Tommy, and when Tommy called him, "Pop, Pop," the tired almost went away.

Rachel took to calling this new Daddy "Pop," sort of like Tommy did. It was as if she'd never actually known him before, and so giving him a new name just made sense.

• • •

For William, it was a transition he awkwardly made. The nightmares of war haunted him at night, to only awaken to new concerns in the day. The words "cerebral palsy" were now more than words on a page, and as much as Hazel had explained what they meant for their son, it took time to fully accept them—to embrace the fact that their son had cerebral palsy, but he was still Tommy. As that understanding grew, so did his hopes and dreams for his son. Tommy was amazing. William loved him with all his heart, but it also broke that same heart watching him struggle to do things others took for granted.

Rachel was William and Hazel's breath of fresh air—the relief of, "Thank goodness Rachel can run. Thank goodness Rachel can talk a blue streak. Thank goodness Tommy responds so well to Rachel. Thank goodness we all have Rachel."

They settled into a routine—this new little family. William would come home from work, kiss Hazel, then find Rachel. "Hi, sweetie. How's my sunshine today?" Before she would even have a chance to answer, he would sweep her up into his arms. "You're such a perfect little lady. What have you and Tommy done today?"

Rachel would grin and squirm out of his arms. "I'll show you." Then grabbing his hand, she'd pull him past his newspaper, past her school bag, past the easy chair, and into the family room where Tommy would be surrounded by blocks.

"Sissy!" he would gleefully shout. No name made her prouder. No moment made William happier.

And through it all, the rolled-up parcel lay forgotten and collecting dust in a corner of the attic.

THURSDAY

In her better moments in the following days, Madelyn found herself enjoying spending time with Jillian and Daniel—playing catch with them outside and even appropriately screaming when Daniel put a rubber snake in her bed. True to her word, she made pudding with Jillian. In those times, she caught herself smiling and honestly forgetting about Dad being gone.

In her more self-centered moments, she retreated into books, even rereading her precious *Hobbit* chapters for the week, being especially intrigued by the strange, solitary Gollum creature. At first, he struck her as nasty and mean, but the second time through, even though she still thought that, she also felt sorry for him. How could anyone endure such a lonely existence?

She hurried on, not wanting to dwell on that thought for long, and when Bilbo and his friends were saved by the eagles, Madelyn found her mind wandering to Zane. Even their short visit in the store had been a lifeline. Could it be more than that, or was she just kidding herself?

It was the thought of Zane and then his sister Delia that made her think of Daniel and Jillian one evening. They'd already gone to bed, but she decided to look in on them. Daniel was doing his best snore imitation, so Madelyn pretended to be fooled by it. But as she slipped out the door, she whispered, "I love you, Daniel."

With hardly a break in his "snores," he responded, "I love you too."

Cracking the door to Jillian's room, Madelyn could see her curled up in bed, her arms wrapped around Buster, her bedraggled yet beloved stuffed dog. Her eyes were closed, but her fingers were rubbing Buster's threadbare, floppy ear—a habit since she was a baby.

Madelyn quietly made her way into the room and sat down on Jillian's bed. Reaching up, she gently brushed the hair back from her face. "Hi," Jillian mumbled, almost asleep.

"Hi, Jilly. I love you."

"Love you too. How come you're here?" she said without opening her eyes.

"I don't know. I was just thinking about Delia, I guess. When she used to babysit, she'd come into my room—probably yours too—just like this, although you were pretty young then."

"Oh," she said as she rolled over.

Madelyn sat still, watching the rise and fall of the blanket, the signs that her little sister was falling asleep. When she stood up to leave, Jillian surprised her by saying, "You like him, don't you?"

"What? Who?"

Jillian turned her head, her eyes wide open, with a grin on her face. "You know who," she said then turned back away before adding, "Good night, Madelyn. I love you."

Madelyn still wore the faint wisp of a smile when she wandered into the kitchen where her mom was putting away the last of the supper dishes. She opened her mouth to say good night, when she heard the unmistakable creak of the front door.

"What was that?" she mouthed, afraid to speak out loud. Mom shook her head, but her eyes were as wide as Madelyn's. As they strained their ears to listen, the creaking grew more pronounced until it ended with a muffled thud, surely the sound of the door meeting the wall.

Without realizing they'd done it, they'd reached for each other's hands and were squeezing them tightly. Together they begin to slowly creep toward the living room. Before they reached the arched entry, before the door came into view, a man cleared his throat.

Madelyn froze, her mom's hand in hers turning to ice. Simultaneously screaming, they threw their arms around each other. Other sounds reached their ears, unidentifiable amidst their own clamoring. Clinging together, they started shaking, nearly crying, their chests heaving in heavy, deep breaths. In that one moment, Madelyn wouldn't have traded her mom for anything in the world.

But moments like that pass.

As the silence of a dark night once again settled around them, Mom said, "Come on," motioning *toward* the living room.

"Are you kidding?" Madelyn whispered.

Mom nodded and tiptoed forward, Madelyn following in her shadow. When they rounded the corner into the living room, Madelyn quickly scanned the room to discover ... nothing. No one was there, and not a thing was out of place—at least not any more than normal. The only exception was the front door swaying back and forth at the hand of a strong wind, the storm having invited itself inside.

They stared at each other, not knowing what to think. "Didn't you lock the door?" Madelyn finally said, letting her words be angry to hide her fear.

"Well, I certainly thought so. I usually do when I put the others to bed. But ... maybe ..." She let the thought hang. "I'm sorry."

"Well, that's –" Madelyn stopped. Her mother's fingers were shaking as she reached up to push hair out of her eyes. "I mean, it could have been the wind, or maybe Daniel ..."

"Daniel, now that makes a lot of sense." They laughed nervously, trying to convince each other that must be the answer.

As they both moved to securely close the front door, they couldn't help but notice the weather outside. It was stormy and dark with barely a streetlight visible in the swirling gloom. Without saying another word, they closed the door and leaned against it, tilting their heads so they just touched each other.

When they found their voices again, the words they spoke were, on the surface, ordinary: "Would you like some hot cocoa?" "Let me help you." "This tastes good." While what they were really saying was something else— only they weren't sure what that was just yet.

It turns out you can love someone without ever feeling like you need them, and you can even need someone desperately without even liking them, but loving someone and needing them at the same time is an emotion hard to contain—especially when you've never owned up to it before. The meaning of it was heavy in the air, but neither of them reached out to take hold of it, not knowing what it would mean if they did. Instead, they waited for it to subside then slowly dissipate, more comfortable with things the way they'd always been. Predictable and known can be appealing simply because it's easier.

Saturday

The following two mornings, Madelyn made a stop in the living room on the way to breakfast. She felt the need to check the front door, making sure it was still securely latched from the night before. It was, but she mentioned this fact to no one.

She and Mom both seemed to have decided the same thing—that nothing actually happened, especially between them. Instead, they went about their days as normally and casually as possible.

Saturday, as Madelyn was putting the lawnmower away and gathering her dandelion tools, Mrs. Burnham appeared in the driveway. She just stood there, watching. "Hi, Mrs. Burnham," Madelyn said in a tone that she hoped meant *go away*.

"What are you doing?" It came out as an accusation.

Madelyn put a hand on her hips. "Well, what does it look like I'm doing?"

"Like you're haphazardly doing some yard work, but I –"

Madelyn cut her off before she could complete her thought. "You know, Mrs. Burnham, I was just wondering why you bothered to ask what I was doing since it seems you've already decided. Now, if you'll excuse me, I need to go gather some of the dandelions that have gone to seed—that is unless you want me to let the wind blow them into your yard?"

"Well, I never ..."

"That's what I thought. Have a good day, Mrs. Burnham." Then in spite of what she'd said, Madelyn walked into the backyard to work on the dandelions there. She smiled, knowing they weren't much of a threat to

Mrs. Burnham's yard, not like the ones in the front. And certainly Mrs. Burnham knew that too.

She'd just gotten started on her dandelion count when she heard "Madelyn?" Her face flushed as she recognized Zane's voice. Before she had a chance to find him, he'd found her. "Sorry to bother you, but Jillian said you were out here."

"What are you doing here?" she blurted out before thinking. "I mean ... how are you doing?"

Zane laughed. "Delia and I just finished our bike ride. I thought maybe you could use some help?"

Madelyn had a hard time hiding her smile. "As a matter of fact, I can. That is if you don't mind digging up dandelions."

Zane just shrugged his shoulders and sat down beside her on the grass. "Do you have some more tools?"

"Yes," she said, having a hard time believing he was actually going to help. "I'll go get them."

When she returned, he silently got to work. After a few dandelions, he said, "So, are these the dandelions you were talking about?"

"What?"

"That day at the park. You said dandelions were bothering you."

She laughed. "You're right. I did, didn't I. Yes ... and no."

"What does that mean?"

"It means that I don't like dealing with dandelions, but it really means I miss my dad," she said, surprised that her lips quivered a little at the thought.

"Where's your dad?"

She hadn't meant to when he showed up, but she found herself telling him everything about Dad—how they told her, how she felt about it, even how she'd been acting self-centered because of it. He raised his eyebrows a few times, but always followed it with a nod and something like, "I understand," or "That must be hard." And when she was done telling him, he paused, letting her decide where the conversation should go.

"You know you're nicer than I remembered," she said then gasped when she realized how that sounded. "I didn't mean it that way. I mean ... you were nice and all when we were younger, but ... well, we didn't talk then.

Well, of course we didn't ..."

He laughed. "Madelyn, I'm going to always remember that. Someday, at some party, or to our grandchildren, I'm going to tell them I'm nicer than I used to be."

He hadn't meant anything by that word grandchildren. She could tell in the way he picked up his tool and continued to dig up dandelions all while still chuckling to himself. It was just a funny scenario to him, but past being mortified, Madelyn's heart was pounding so hard she was sure he could hear it.

"What do you want to do when you grow up, Zane? Who do you want to be?"

"Geez. I have no idea what I want to do. I hardly think past next week." She was right after all. He hadn't meant anything by it, and yet, that was okay too. "But what I want to *be*," he continued, "now that's a different story. I want to be like my dad. He's nice to everybody, especially my mom. He calls her his queen. They still fight sometimes, but just over little stuff, never anything big.

"I know people trust him too. If he says he'll do something, he does. Some of my friends want to be famous, playing professional baseball or something, but I don't. I don't care if anyone outside of town even knows who I am. But I want the people who do know me to always feel like I'm worth knowing."

"That's nice," Madelyn said. Then to herself she added, "I want to be like my dad too."

They didn't actually dig up a whole lot of weeds, but they continued to talk about everything and nothing. It turns out it was even better than talking to her dad.

Part 2

When Madelyn was little, she kept a careful watch on the dandelions. When they were yellow, they made a bright bouquet for her to give Mom, but she loved them best when they turned white. Then she would carefully pick them from the yard and blow their seeds as far as her little breath could take them, dancing in delight as they floated away.

At some point, she stopped noticing them—they were simply an unimportant distraction from what mattered in life, and although what mattered might change from day to day, dandelions never crossed her mind. But at times, it's those things we are least aware of that can have the greatest impact—and when they unmistakably enter our sight, it's time to figure out, not just what matters, but what matters most.

Week Four – Summer 1975

Sunday

Madelyn had an agenda when she talked to Dad on Sunday. They'd barely gotten their hellos out when Madelyn said, "Dad, you know the latch on the front door? I think it must be sticking because we locked the door before we went to the store the other day, but when we got home, it just swung open. And then I think it blew open a few days later."

"Really? Are you sure?" He sounded alarmed.

"Well, pretty sure. I think the mechanism just stuck and never actually locked. How do I fix it?"

"Well, it's never done that before, but I suppose it's possible," he said, sounding relieved. "In the garage, on one of the shelves is a can of WD-40. You can spray it anywhere you think the latch is sticking. Then just turn the handle of the door back and forth several times to spread the lubricant around. That should do it."

"Okay. I'll take care of it."

"Madelyn, how are things with –"

Before he could derail her agenda, Madelyn interjected, "And tell me how to fix Mrs. Burnham."

"What?"

"Mrs. Burnham. She always manages to be outside when I am. She wants to know what I'm doing or feels the need to tell me that the way I'm doing something is all wrong. She even walks onto our lawn or comes up the driveway just so she can make some snide remark."

He laughed lightly, which had the effect of making her mad. "This isn't funny, Dad. She's annoying."

"Calm down. Believe it or not, she likes you."

"No, she doesn't!" Madelyn couldn't believe this was Dad she was talking to.

"Madelyn, listen to me for just a minute, will you? Dorothy Burnham is just lonely. She doesn't have a lot of practice talking to teenagers, so she's inventing any excuse she can to have a conversation."

"Somehow I think she could do better than that," Madelyn grumbled under her breath, but loudly enough so he would hear.

He just laughed again. "Then why don't you come up with something better to talk about?" When she didn't respond, he added, "She likes you because if she didn't, she wouldn't be trying to be your friend."

Madelyn used to think Dad was the smartest man on the planet, but right about now, he was sounding like one of the dumbest. "That's a strange way to be a friend," she said.

"Are you still missing me?"

He'd cut right to the heart of everything. "Yes," Madelyn whispered, her brave frontal assault gone. "I do," but even as she said it, her thoughts drifted to Zane, and a smile crept into her lips. Much as she loved her dad, talking to him about a boy felt awkward, so she gave no voice to her thoughts.

After that, they only had a few moments to share thoughts about *The Hobbit* before it was time to hand the phone to Mom. The last thing he said before saying goodbye was, "How's your Mom doing?" She was almost annoyed by the question—but not as much as she used to be.

Madelyn made her way to her bedroom, the happy chatter of her mom's side of the phone conversation dwindling behind her. She'd realized when talking to Dad, that she hadn't marked off the completion of week three.

As she was putting her notepad back in her nightstand, Jillian said, "What's that?"

Madelyn spun around. "I didn't know you were there."

"Well, that's obvious," Jillian said, rolling her eyes.

Madelyn shrugged her shoulders then retrieved the notepad from its place. "I'm marking off the weeks Dad's gone. It helps the time pass."

"That makes sense. But it's not terrible, you know. My friend Sally, her dad left, but he never came back—at least not yet. I don't think she even talks to him on the phone."

"Yeah, I guess you're right," Madelyn said, plopping down on the bed. She gazed over at her little sister who often felt like the older, more mature one of the two of them. "Hey, Jilly?"

"What?"

"You're also right about Zane. We've been friends, but now ... well, now I think I like him. But what do I do about it?"

Jilly climbed up beside her on the bed. "I don't know," she said then burst out in giggles.

Madelyn ruffled Jillian's hair. "Okay, so you don't have a lot of experience in such matters. But isn't he cute? And he's so nice." They both squealed and chatted well into the night.

MONDaY

Early the next morning Madelyn made her way to the garage to find the WD-40. She sprayed it on every locking mechanism she could find on their front door then turned every handle and lock to distribute it, just like Dad had instructed. It was a simple fix—she'd certainly tackled harder projects before with Dad. Surveying her handiwork, Madelyn couldn't help but be pleased. Yet, even though this was more her thing than Mom's, Madelyn was still secretly annoyed that she wasn't taking care of such things, or that Dad wasn't here to make that train of thought unnecessary.

She kept herself busy throughout the day, just wanting time to pass. Madelyn wrote a short note to Lori in Ohio and hoped she would write back. However, since she hadn't heard a peep out of her yet, she wasn't going to hold her breath.

In the afternoon, Madelyn set up a sprinkler in the backyard for Jillian and Daniel to run through. They alternately squealed and giggled as the cold water shocked then refreshed them. Jillian decided to try doing cartwheels into the sprinkler, but mostly she just fell over sideways, soaking herself even more. She giggled every time, and Madelyn found herself laughing as well.

In one of these unguarded moments, Daniel snuck up behind her and doused her with a bucket of cold water. Screaming, Madelyn jumped up to chase after him, but he made a dash for the sprinkler. Madelyn ran right after him, grabbed him, and held him right over the nozzle of the sprinkler, even though in the process she got just as soaked as he did.

If she'd noticed, her own concerns were taking on less and less significance.

· · ·

After dinner that night, Madelyn curled up on the couch in the living room to read her library book. She was determined to have more self-control with *The Hobbit* this week. Soon, the rest of the family trickled in to join her.

Jillian would be starting second grade in the fall and was beginning to read simple chapter books. Tonight, she settled down on the couch between Mom and Madelyn, determined to make it through the book in her hands. Madelyn smiled as she half listened to her stop-and-go reading.

When Madelyn snuck a glance in their direction, she was surprised by what she saw. She assumed Mom would be following along with each word, correcting any errors along the way, but instead, her head was back, her eyes closed, with a blissful expression enveloping her face. Madelyn stopped what she was doing to study her mom.

To Madelyn, Mom was the one in charge, the one who ordered her life. She sometimes forgot there was more to Mom than that, that she could simply be proud of her children, loving them unconditionally. There was never a question about whether Mom loved her, but in the day-to-day ins and outs of life, Madelyn sometimes forgot that was at the core of everything. It's like forgetting trees have roots—you know they do, but it's not what you think about when you're looking at their branches and leaves. Madelyn smiled to herself. It's good to be reminded that you are loved and cared about, even when you're a teenager—probably especially then.

When Jillian finished her book, she picked up the old standards and begged Mom to read them to her again before she headed off to bed. Madelyn gave up reading to listen to her favorite childhood books once more, only keeping up a pretense that she was still reading by holding her open book in front of her. Her eyes, however, were on the well-worn pages of *Where the Wild Things Are.*

Madelyn settled down to listen to the rhythmic cadence of the words while letting her eyes wander over the playful illustrations. She had her favorite beast—the one with people feet, and her favorite words—"wild rumpus." They dripped with potential mischief. A wistful smile played on her lips, and Madelyn closed her eyes to listen, watching the familiar illustrations come to life in her mind—when everything went wrong.

It happened so fast, Madelyn wasn't sure she'd heard correctly. Her eyes flew open in time to watch her mom turn the page. It was the identical spot she'd been listening to before, and it was playing out precisely the same way. Madelyn had known then that something was off—only this time she knew what it was, she just couldn't bring herself to believe it—because if Madelyn was right, it meant her mom couldn't read!

1950

Tommy was the center of everyone's universe. It was mostly out of necessity, but no one in the family minded. He was a happy child, and little by little he was making progress, which made everyone around him happy as well.

Rachel might have resented her portion of attention being given to Tommy if it weren't for her pop. He stumbled upon the very thing she needed without even realizing what he was starting.

The shared ritual could be traced to a single day about a year after Pop's return from the war. One day, when Pop knew he would be at work late, he left a handwritten note for her to find. "What does this say, Mommy?"

Hazel took the note from her daughter. "It says, I love you, little munchkin. Always be good, and remember to save me a hug."

Rachel smiled. Taking the note from her mom, she had an idea. Gathering paper of her own, she painstakingly copied the words. She would give the same note back to him. When she was finished, she found her mother working with Tommy. "Look, Mom!"

"Aren't you a sweetheart. You copied it word for word, didn't you?"

"Yep!"

"You did a great job. Here, let me show you how to fix a couple of these letters. You just have a few of them turned around."

When Rachel went back to fix the note, she had a better idea. She took out a new paper and put it right on top of Pop's note. She could see his dark letters through the thin sheet. When she was finished tracing each letter, she was pleased with the result.

When Pop found the note late that night, he was pleased too.

It didn't happen all the time after that—not so often that it became commonplace. But notes from Pop ended up in her lunch box or her sock drawer or under her pillow. Every time they did, Rachel would put a paper over the top of the note and carefully trace each letter. With each motion of her pencil—each line, each curve—she could feel how much he loved her. Tommy may occupy much of their time, but she knew she occupied a place in Pop's heart.

By the time Rachel was in fifth grade, you'd have thought the notes might have changed, but they didn't. The tradition was about more than the words or the simple handwriting. The pencil strokes were actually heartstrings that bound them together.

It was in fifth grade that the other tradition began. It was the year the school placed all the kids together in one large reading class instead of the smaller, individualized groups Rachel had been used to. It was the year she would discover favorite classics like Anne of Green Gables *and* Nancy Drew.

The first book her teacher handed her that year was Little House in the Big Woods *by Laura Ingalls Wilder. When she got home, Mom was busy with Tommy. So, she waited to ambush Pop when he came in the door. "Pop, will you read this with me?" He was moving slowly. It had been a long day. She followed his eyes as he determined what the situation was with Tommy. A smile gradually spread across his face. "Sure, Rachel. We always do things for Tommy, don't we? Let's just you and I read."*

Two or three days a week, Rachel could convince her pop to take ten or fifteen minutes out of his day to read to her from the books she was bringing home from school. When she heard his footsteps, and if things were going well with Tommy, she'd race to her school bag to find her book. If there were papers from the teacher, or even other homework, it was quickly tossed aside in favor of her time with Pop.

"Hey, this is where we left off a few days ago. Aren't you reading any of it on your own?"

"I don't want you to miss anything. You do want to know what Nancy

Drew discovers don't you?" Rachel would answer.

Pop would laugh. "Well, I was kind of wondering. I guess we better get started before I need to go help make dinner and you need to help with Tommy. Come here, my perfect little Rachel. Let's find out what happens."

There was a lot they did find out—but a few things they didn't.

Tuesday

The next day was consumed with thoughts of what to do with what she'd witnessed. Could Madelyn prove her suspicions? There were certainly ways, but how could she be subtle about it—not letting on what she knew, or thought she knew.

It was the first of July, and Madelyn should have been pleased by the milestone. After all, Dad would be returning in August. But even though Madelyn tried to focus on that, she couldn't. So, despite her resolve not to read *The Hobbit* too quickly that week, she figured it might be a welcome distraction.

Madelyn settled herself into a chair in Dad's study, *The Hobbit* and a library book, for good measure, in her hands. She opened *The Hobbit*, but after the fifth time rereading the opening sentence of the chapter, she closed it and set it aside. All she could think about was her mom and how she couldn't read. No wonder she didn't have a favorite book. No wonder she never joined them when they gathered to read. And no wonder Dad kept asking if she was okay. Was he worried that Mom couldn't get along without being able to read, or was the concern that Madelyn would stumble onto their secret? Much as Madelyn had thought it could have been her escape, it was anything but.

She picked up the library book instead, thinking that something not so directly connected with her family would be better. Only it wasn't—the reminders not hitting her in the face as with *The Hobbit* but whispering to her all the same. It had been right in front of her, and she'd never even seen it. Or at least she'd never taken notice before, and now that she had, she could think of nothing else.

Madelyn gazed around the room. How would she see it differently if she couldn't read? The books were obvious, but there were other things—the mail that came—bills, letters, all of it. A phone book sat on one corner of Dad's desk. That would be useless to her mom.

She got up and began wandering around the house, opening drawers and peeking in cupboards. Cleaning supplies had safety warnings. Children's aspirin had dosage information. Hot cereal provided directions. Even their clothes came with washing instructions. None of it was accessible to Mom. Madelyn didn't know whether to be angry at her mom or feel sorry for her.

wednesday

The next morning, with the beginnings of a plan, Madelyn casually walked into the kitchen where Mom was cleaning up breakfast dishes. Pulling out the one cookbook they owned, Madelyn flipped to the chocolate chip cookie recipe Dad used. "Mom, would it be all right if I made some cookies?"

Mom's head came up, but she looked perplexed. "Um, sure, if you can make them on your own. I don't really have the time right now."

"That's fine, but could you tell me what this part means?" Madelyn held the book in front of Mom's face, pointing to one of the directions.

Mom barely glanced at it before replying, "I'm not much for recipe directions. I just like to throw in a pinch here and a pinch there."

"Yes, I noticed that."

Mom looked at her as if Madelyn might say more. When she didn't, Mom said, "Just make your best guess. I'm sure Jilly and Daniel would love some fresh cookies."

Madelyn hadn't actually planned on making cookies, she just wanted to watch Mom's reaction. But not seeing any way around it, she gathered all the ingredients and even convinced Jillian and Daniel to help. Jillian sat on the counter and measured ingredients, and Madelyn was surprised by how helpful rather than destructive Daniel was. He read the instructions to them as they went along and particularly loved turning the mixer on as high as it could go. They had so much fun, Madelyn momentarily forgot about Mom.

When the cookies came out of the oven, they could smell how good they were going to taste, breathing in the scent before even setting down the hot pan. It reminded her of Dad—and thinking about him made her think about their last conversation. She didn't believe he was right, but why not check it out for herself. "Mom, would it be all right if I took some cookies over to Mrs. Burnham?"

Mom poked her head in from the other room. Her eyebrow was raised, but after a pause she said, "Sure," even though her face told her Madelyn must be crazy.

Jillian decided to tag along, but Daniel was too busy eating a cookie to care, smears of chocolate on his cheeks giving away the fact that it wasn't his first. The two of them made their way past a mass of dandelions that Madelyn tried to ignore, up to Mrs. Burnham's front door. Madelyn couldn't remember the last time she'd stood on this doorstep—probably back when she was young enough to go trick-or-treating.

The doorbell echoed deep and hollow through the house. It sounded strange, almost eerie—enough so, that Madelyn almost turned and ran. But it also sounded lonely. So, she planted her feet, and with the hand not holding the plate of cookies, grabbed Jillian's hand to give her courage.

Mrs. Burnham didn't come to the door right away, and Jillian and Madelyn glanced at each other, shrugging their shoulders. Maybe she wasn't home. Just as Madelyn breathed a sigh of relief, thinking they could simply leave, the door opened a crack.

"Who is it?" It was more like an accusation.

"It's me, Madelyn, and Jillian's with me," she said, trying to sound more cheerful than she felt.

The door creaked open a tad more. Mrs. Burnham appeared disheveled, and Madelyn noticed she wasn't wearing a wig. "What do you want?" It didn't sound as gruff as before, but Madelyn still wouldn't call it friendly.

"We made some chocolate chip cookies and brought you some."

She thought the door would swing wide open at that, but it didn't, and Madelyn was taken aback when they were met with silence. Not sure what to do, they just stood there waiting.

Finally, a very small sounding voice said, "Why? Did you burn them or something?"

Madelyn didn't know how to respond, but before she knew it, words were flying out of her mouth with a mind of their own. "Mrs. Burnham, I don't like you very much, but I wouldn't bring you something that was burnt—out of pride if nothing else. They're good cookies. You can have them if you want. If not, we'll take them back home and eat them ourselves!"

Finally, the door opened all the way, and Madelyn could look the woman she had just insulted in the eye. But those eyes were red and puffy. Had Mrs. Burnham been crying? At first, Madelyn thought her words were the cause, and she felt a twinge of guilt. But then she noticed a damp tissue in her hand—her crying was not new.

Before Madelyn could stop her, Jillian said, "Were you crying?" Mrs. Burnham didn't answer but quickly wiped her eyes and nose with the used tissue. "Why?" Jillian said while Madelyn squeezed her hand to hopefully shut her up.

Mrs. Burnham stopped wiping her nose and stared into their eyes, but for once her stare wasn't full of condemnation. Madelyn sensed she was deciding whether to actually talk to them. In the end, she simply whispered, "No one in this neighborhood has ever brought me cookies before." Then, all in one motion, she took the plate of cookies and shut the door behind her as she disappeared into the darkness inside.

.   .   .

The incident with Mrs. Burnham disturbed Madelyn and stayed with her throughout the afternoon. She found herself wandering outside to work on the dandelions just so she could be alone with her thoughts. Mrs. Burnham hadn't even said "Thank you" for the cookies, but then again, Madelyn hadn't used kind words herself.

But the sadness is what struck her the most. Dad was right after all—Mrs. Burnham was lonely, and it seemed that loneliness had turned her into a bitter woman or a nosy one or something else, she wasn't sure what.

Somehow, she'd always assumed adults had everything figured out, but that didn't seem to be the case with Mrs. Burnham, or her own mom, for that matter. If Mom wasn't a testament to not having it all figured out, Madelyn didn't know who was. With a reignited resolve to find answers,

Madelyn thought through what to do next.

Striking upon an idea, she quickly put away her weeding supplies and went inside to clean up. Finding a piece of paper, Madelyn jotted a note for Mom and handed it to her as she moved toward the front door.

Mom's voice stopped her as she put her hand on the doorknob. "Where are you going?"

"Didn't you read the note?" Madelyn said.

Mom looked bewildered, lifting her eyes from the note she'd had thrust into her hand to meet Madelyn's gaze. "Since when do you write me notes when you can use your voice?"

Madelyn opened her mouth, the accusation on the tip of her tongue, when the phone rang. It was Zane.

• • •

"Hey, Madelyn. How about that bike ride?" The sides of her mouth started to inch upward until she caught sight of her mom crumpling the note in her fist.

"Uh, yeah," Madelyn said. "When?"

"Well, Delia and I were thinking about tomorrow around eleven, maybe just riding around the city park, but we could have a picnic lunch. Would that work?"

"Sure. That sounds great." She turned her body so she couldn't see Mom, not wanting the pleasant sound of his voice to be diluted with her own frustrations.

"Oh, and Jilly and Daniel are welcome to come."

"Okay. I just need to check with my mom. I'll call you right back."

It took some figuring to work things out because the next day was their day to visit Uncle Tommy. Madelyn didn't want to miss seeing him, but the thought of spending time with Zane had her stomach doing delightful summersaults. It also came with the added benefit of avoiding all that time in the car with Mom—but that was clearly only a secondary consideration.

"Well, I suppose it would be all right since I'm bringing Tommy back to spend the Fourth with us," Mom said. Madelyn had totally forgotten that Friday was Independence Day. Usually one of her favorite holidays, she wasn't sure how she'd feel this year without Dad being around.

"Thanks. And Jilly and Daniel?"

"Better not, just you. Tommy looks forward to our Thursdays. He'd be really disappointed if none of you kids showed up, even if we're just bringing him home with us."

Madelyn quickly called Zane to tell him it was okay before Mom changed her mind. It's funny how a moment ago she was ready to yell at her mom, and now she was trying to curry her favor.

THURSDAY

The next day Madelyn watched from the garage, sitting astride her bike, as Mom pulled out of the driveway with her siblings in tow. Madelyn waved and smiled at Jillian and Daniel but dropped her hand when she saw Mom. The image of her face was replaced with other images, and Madelyn started to see them the way that Mom must—the street signs she couldn't decipher or the diner that they never stopped at unless Dad was with them, surely because of the written menus.

Madelyn loved her mother, but the thought of her not being able to do something so simple as reading left a strange distaste in her mouth. How could someone, an adult no less, not know how to read? It was a confusing and troubling thought. Could her mom really be that stupid?

Delia and Zane rode up a short time later, and the three of them took off for the path that circled the city park. Madelyn almost lost control of her bike a couple times because she wasn't paying attention to the path or the obstacles in front of her—her mind still on the mother who was now a stranger to her.

After enjoying a picnic lunch, Delia ran off to throw a Frisbee with some of her friends, leaving Zane and her to talk.

"What's up, Madelyn?"

She hesitated to look at him, more content to mindlessly watch Delia and her friends. Madelyn finally shrugged her shoulders, not sure how to respond.

Zane scooted around until he was facing her. "Madelyn?" She had pulled her knees up to her chin and wrapped her arms around them. So, when he spoke, Madelyn hid her face in her knees, unwilling to meet his gaze. She felt him touch her bare feet where she'd kicked off her sneakers and flinched as he did so. "Madelyn, talk to me. What's up? You seem different."

Madelyn let out a short laugh and lifted her head. "I don't know if I'm different, but everything around me apparently is." He raised his eyebrows, clearly needing more explanation. She took in his earnest look. She wanted to tell him about her mom, but forming the words was hard. So, she said, "I guess I'm just missing my dad," even as she said it knowing it for the half-truth that it was. Yes, it bothered her, but it had become the itchy wool sweater that you learn to live with.

"I'm sorry," Zane said, reaching up to tuck a loose strand of her hair behind her ear.

It was a kind gesture, honest and sincere, making her feel bad that she wasn't being completely honest with him in return. She shrugged her shoulders and started playing with the blades of grass that were tickling her feet. Despite her words, missing Dad had become secondary to everything else—some of it bad, but some of it not, she thought, as she cast a furtive glance in Zane's direction.

Zane was quiet but turned to sit beside her, gently laying his hand on top of hers. It was protective and warm, and before Madelyn knew what she was doing, she said, "I do miss him, but my mom's the real problem. I just found out –" Madelyn stopped herself, fearful of what he would think if he knew. She yanked her hand away and buried her face in her palms.

Zane surprised her by not responding, instead pulling his knees up like hers while gazing off into the distance—waiting, waiting for her to decide what to share. Madelyn tipped her head to the side so she could see him through her fingers. His expression was neither passive nor expectant. "You have to promise not to tell a soul."

He turned to meet her eyes, and with sincerity said, "Okay, I promise." But his brows were furrowed in concern.

"My mom is illiterate." Saying it out loud made it real and Madelyn took in a sharp breath.

"Really? Are you sure?" He sounded surprised, but not repulsed like Madelyn had expected.

"Yes, I am. I wasn't at first, but I am now." Madelyn found she couldn't look at him as she talked.

"Well, how do you know?"

"She was reading one of our favorite children's books, and she messed up the pages. She's read it so much that she has all the words memorized –"

"Wait. How could she have the words memorized if she can't read?"

"I don't know. Maybe my dad taught her or something. She's been reading the same book since I was little. In fact, now that you ask, I think my dad was the one who used to read it to me. I would sit between the two of them. Dad would read, and Mom and I would listen. But somewhere along the line, she took over the 'reading.' I'd forgotten about that." Madelyn could picture that long-ago bedtime routine, and it was all clicking into place. She brushed the memories away and continued. "Anyway, she was reading it to Jilly, and she had all the words right, but they didn't match up to the pages. It was one of the pages near the end—she read words for the next page before she actually turned to that page." He knit his brow in confusion. "Don't you get it? She's just memorized all the words, kind of like I did when I was little, only she doesn't know which words match with which page. She slipped up."

"I know that doesn't seem right, but it doesn't mean she's illiterate. It could just be –"

"Then there was yesterday," Madelyn continued before he could interrupt further. "I asked her about a recipe, and she wouldn't read it to answer my question. And I've been thinking about other things too. My dad stopped the paper for the summer, and I'm paying the bills, but my mom just barely gets through signing her name on the checks, and –"

He put up his hand to stop her mid-sentence. "Maybe you're right, but how could she be illiterate? Didn't she graduate from high school? I mean, it's just hard to believe. You could be right, but that would be incredible ..." He was staring past her as he started to ramble.

Madelyn reached into her pocket and pulled out the note she'd written for her mom the previous day. She'd found its crumpled remains in the kitchen garbage that morning. "I had that same argument with myself yesterday, but then I wrote her this note and pretended to leave the house. I tricked her into thinking it was a note about where I was going. She held it in her hand, even looked directly at it, and it never registered." Madelyn handed him the note.

He smoothed it out then quietly read what was written, "You can't read this, can you?"

"She couldn't, Zane. She had no idea what it said. I can't believe my own mother can't read—not even a children's book. Jilly can read, and she's only seven years old. How could a grown woman not know how to read? Everyone knows how to read!" Madelyn didn't even try to hide the disappointment bordering on disgust in her voice. "You know, I was watching her listen to Jilly read a chapter book. She had me convinced that she was sitting there listening with a big grin on her face because she loved Jilly and was so proud of her. I don't know what to make of it now. Was she pleased with what she was getting away with? Was it jealousy?" She shook her head. "She's fooled us all—but not anymore."

It was too much to contemplate, and Madelyn abruptly snatched her sneakers and stood up. "I'm sorry for dumping on you, Zane. I wanted to talk to someone, but hearing myself say it out loud ... I wish I could take it all back. I'm sorry. I shouldn't have said anything." He started to protest, but she stopped him. "No, it's not you ... I just don't want people to know," she said, not sure if she was more embarrassed for her mom or for herself. "Please don't tell anyone." Then before he could object further, Madelyn grabbed her bike and raced home, leaving a trail of shame following behind her.

FRIDAY

The Fourth of July was typically a fun day for the family. They always caught the city parade in the morning, had a big picnic in the backyard, and then watched the fireworks from their front yard when they were shot off in the city park not far away. Then Dad would supervise them lighting sparklers, and they would dance around with them until way past their bedtime.

But Madelyn was having a hard time warming up to it this year. It would have been bad enough not having Dad around, but now Madelyn was uncomfortable around Mom. To top it off, she had brought Uncle Tommy home with her the previous day as planned. And while Madelyn liked having him around—he always spent holidays with them—Grandpa was usually there too. It didn't feel right not having them here together.

When everyone left for the parade, Madelyn decided to stay behind. Mom raised a questioning eyebrow, and Uncle Tommy tried to convince her to join them, but Madelyn succeeded in fending them off. Wallowing in self-pity was all the hoopla Madelyn had scheduled for her day.

It was a warm day, so she planted herself on the front porch, sitting on the edge with her feet swinging below her. Uncle Tommy was the only adult who wasn't a terrible disappointment in her life right now. The list included Mom—the woman raising her, who had been lying to her her whole life; Grandpa—the man who, for some unknown reason, wasn't around; and even Dad—simply because he wasn't there. If this is what adults were like, she wasn't sure she ever wanted to be one. Just then, Mrs. Burnham walked out her front door—as if Madelyn needed further confirmation.

She waved. "Hi, Madelyn. How come you're not at the parade?" Her typical accusatory tone was still there, but it was tempered with something else, almost a touch of friendliness, but Madelyn didn't trust it.

"I decided to take a pass." The next logical response finally dawned on her. Madelyn stood up and without thinking about what she was doing, walked over to Mrs. Burnham's yard. "Why didn't you go?"

She shrugged her shoulders. "The last parade I went to was during World War II. We watched rows of soldiers march by, looking so sharp in their uniforms." There was a wistful quality to her voice, and she was focusing past Madelyn, as if to a distant memory. She stopped talking, but it was clear the memory was still playing itself out before her eyes. Madelyn stood silently waiting for her to continue.

After several minutes, she shook the past from her head and jumped slightly at seeing Madelyn standing there. She pulled herself together before replying, "At any rate, I haven't been to a parade since." Abruptly, she turned to head back inside. It made Madelyn wonder why she had come out of her house in the first place.

Curious, Madelyn called after her. "Mrs. Burnham, did you need something?" She stopped in her tracks and turned to eye Madelyn with her familiar glare but said nothing. "You must have come out of your house for something. What was it?"

"Well, I saw you sitting there alone. I wanted to make sure your mother hadn't skipped town too."

"Too?"

"Well, yes, like your dad."

"He's just out of town for work. He'll be back. And my mother wouldn't leave town without me." Her desire to be friendly to Mrs. Burnham was quickly evaporating.

Mrs. Burnham just shrugged her shoulders. "Well, you never know."

Madelyn was so surprised by her callous words, and said with such ease, that she hadn't a clue how to respond. With a huff, Madelyn turned and purposely marched back to her house, opened the front door, and slammed it behind her. She couldn't believe what Mrs. Burnham had said—and just when she was about to invite her to join her family for their Fourth of July picnic.

By the time the family returned from the parade—Mom and Tommy with smiles and slight sunburns, Jillian and Daniel with pockets full of candy that had been thrown to them—Madelyn was full of regrets for not having gone with them.

She helped Mom prepare the food for their picnic, but as she did so, all she could think of was the fact that Mom couldn't read a recipe. They were stuck with the things she had already learned how to make—dishes Madelyn assumed she learned how to make from her mother. Dad might be able to make something new, like he'd learned how to make chocolate chip cookies, but not Mom.

Later, when they all gathered around the picnic table out back, eating their same-old, same-old picnic, Uncle Tommy kept glancing at her. "Madly, what's wrong?"

"Nothing, I'm fine."

"But this is your favorite—corn on the cob, baked beans, potato salad, hamburgers –"Madelyn stopped him with a wave of her hand. She didn't want to be reminded of her favorite foods that now churned her stomach. Without saying a word, she ran inside, hiding in her bedroom.

Her window was open, and as Madelyn sat curled up on the floor, voices drifted in from outside. They were going on with their picnic as if nothing had happened. Madelyn couldn't believe that on top of everything, they just didn't care.

Defiantly, she marched back to the picnic outside, sat down at her place, very purposely picked up an ear of corn, and loudly started to gnaw on it. She didn't know how to confront Mom about her illiteracy, so she did the next best thing. With her mouth full of food, Madelyn said, "So, Mom, why isn't Grandpa here?"

Mom got red in the face, but even Tommy was looking at her, waiting for a response. "*Madelyn.*" It was a single word, just her name, but Madelyn knew what it meant. She'd thrown open a door Mom had purposely locked. It was a betrayal of her trust. Mom stared at her, but Madelyn averted her eyes, knowing she'd gone too far.

"Tommy, Pop would be here if he could, but he can't. He just can't, that's all," Mom said.

"Why can't he?" It was Tommy, stepping in where Madelyn could no longer go. She peered up to see how Mom would respond.

Mom was taking in all their expectant faces, deciding on an answer. "He's too far away. He can't get here."

Madelyn wanted to press the issue, but she knew she'd already crossed a line, and Mom's glare confirmed it. Instead, Madelyn returned to her food—silent, but unwilling to look Mom in the eye.

The rest of the day passed, as all things eventually do. Uncle Tommy produced yo-yos he'd bought for them, and Jillian and Daniel had fun trying to master them—with mixed results. Uncle Tommy seemed caught between playing with them and trying to draw Madelyn out. After unsuccessfully trying to talk to her, he shrugged his shoulders and gave in to the fun of the day. Madelyn sat in full mope on the back step watching them without really seeing them, and unsurprisingly, Mom instinctively avoided her.

Madelyn went to bed that night with the nearby nighttime giggles of Jillian, Daniel, and Uncle Tommy infiltrating her dreams until they became monsters from *Where the Wild Things Are*, taunting her and boiling her in a pot of soup that was still warm.

She woke up in a sweat while the world was still dark, but the reality of life hit her, and she felt in the pit of her stomach that it was certainly worse than her nightmare.

SATURDAY

By the time Madelyn went back to sleep and woke up again the next morning, Mom was getting ready to leave with Jillian and Daniel. "Madelyn," Mom called from down the hall, "we're taking Uncle Tommy back. Are you okay staying here?"

She rolled over and rubbed her eyes. Her clock said it was 10:45. The thought of Uncle Tommy brought her fully awake. Guilt washed over her as she recalled her behavior from the previous day. Jumping out of bed, she shot down the hall. "Is Uncle Tommy still here?"

Mom was the only one standing there, but she nodded. "Just barely. He's getting in the car right now."

Without saying a word, Madelyn raced around her, heading directly to the garage. The car doors were open. Jillian and Daniel were climbing in the back seat, and Uncle Tommy was leaning on the door, watching as they got settled.

She ran to his side and wrapped him in a huge embrace. "I'm sorry, Uncle Tommy. I love you. I'm so sorry."

"For what, Madly?"

Looking up at him, Madelyn could see he was asking a serious question. "For wasting the holiday with you by being grumpy," she said, not believing that he had to be told.

He broke into a broad grin and shrugged his shoulders. "You just had a bad day. I sometimes have bad days too." Madelyn couldn't help but grin back and hug him again.

"If you want to get dressed, you can go with us," Mom offered, having followed her into the garage. What Madelyn wanted was for Tommy to stay longer, but she knew that wasn't an option. He liked his routines. Being away from the group home for more than a day was something he wasn't comfortable with.

"No, that's okay. I need to get started on the lawn." Working outside on the garden or the yard was just part of her routine, but today it felt like a self-imposed punishment for bad behavior. She would attack it with vigor.

After they left, Madelyn hurriedly threw on some clothes and downed a bowl of cereal. They would be gone at least an hour—that's how long the drive up and back would be, but Madelyn assumed they would stay and visit a bit until he was settled. How much could she get done in that time?

She started with the mowing. That alone usually took an hour. The day was hot, and Madelyn could feel the sweat drip down her back as she cut swaths back and forth. It went quickly, the grass too languid in this summer heat to put much effort into growth. Dust, kicked up from the parched earth, followed her every movement. By the time she was finished, the sun was directly overhead.

Despite her late breakfast, her stomach kept growling, but Madelyn was determined to get more work done before she allowed herself more than a water break. After setting the hose to water the garden, she began to gather weeding supplies from the garage. The sound of a car drew her attention. Madelyn glanced up to see if Mom and her siblings had returned, but it was only a sedan, apparently lost since it turned around and sped off. She was both sad and relieved it wasn't them.

The patch of dandelions Madelyn decided to attack that day was smack in the middle of the front yard, the ones most visible from the street. Kneeling on the hard, dry ground soon grew uncomfortable as the dandelions stubbornly refused to budge from the cracked soil. A good rain would certainly help, she thought. Maybe in the future she could set the sprinkler on different sections of the lawn before trying to weed.

The more Madelyn worked, the drier the ground seemed, and the wetter her forehead got. Sweat dripped down her face and occasionally into her eyes, making them sting. But she was determined to finish digging up dandelions in her little area. Dig—pull, dig—pull, went on and on, but most of the roots ran deep into the arid ground. One after another snapped off, leaving long roots buried, the ground refusing to give them up.

Dig—pull—snap—sweat, dig—pull—snap—sweat, until Madelyn could bear it no more. "Why? Why?" she cried, stabbing her spade into the ground. "Why won't you come up? I'm trying so hard!" She beat her fists on the ground. Mrs. Burnham was probably watching from her front window, but Madelyn didn't care. She pounded the hard earth again and again with her fists until her knuckles started to bleed.

Hunched over, she planted her hands flat on the ground. A drop of liquid fell into the grime on the back of her hand. Madelyn watched it run across her bloodied knuckles, partway down her finger before sliding off the side, leaving an unmistakable path behind. Another joined it, then another.

She, Madelyn Osborne, was crying. That realization made her cry harder, the tears mixing with sweat to pour down her face in great dirty streaks, falling to the ground to be swallowed without a trace.

She sat back and let them flow, feeling defeated and yet somehow free. Giving herself over to the tears, Madelyn cried about the dandelions then about missing Dad, and her cries turned to sobs. Finally, the tears flowed for a mom who couldn't read a simple children's book—no longer sure if she was angry or sad.

She was still crying—how long she'd been that way she couldn't tell—when Mom came upon her. Madelyn hadn't even noticed the car's return, nor heard the engine, so lost in the sobs that shuddered her body.

"What's wrong?" Mom said, concern spreading across her face. When your child has refused to cry and then is suddenly bawling like a baby, it must be a shock. But Madelyn couldn't answer her. All she could do was sob harder.

Mom tried again, this time touching her shoulder and softly saying, "Madelyn?"

Madelyn twisted away from her touch. "Go away! GO AWAY!" she said without looking in her direction.

When someone touched her again some minutes later, Madelyn jumped, ready to attack anew, but when she whirled around, she saw it was Jillian. "I thought you might like something to eat." Jillian was holding out a paper plate with a peanut butter and jelly sandwich that, by its messy nature, had clearly been made by her own hands. Madelyn smiled, tears still streaming down her cheeks. "You look funny," Jillian said, wrinkling her nose. "Your face is all streaky."

Madelyn laughed and reached up to wipe the tears away. Jillian burst out laughing. "You just made it a lot worse." Madelyn couldn't see her face, but the backs of her hands were a dirt and blood-smeared masterpiece. Jillian set the plate on the ground and sat down beside her, following her gaze to her hands. "What happened to them?" she whispered.

"The dirt, well that's obvious," she said, indicating the earth around her. "But the other—the blood, the tears—I ... it's complicated."

Jillian looked up into her face and with her hands brushed back the hair that had come loose from her ponytail. "It will be okay. I promise."

Madelyn laughed. "That's sweet, Jilly, but you don't even know what's wrong."

"I know, but that's what Mom says to me when I cry, and it always works out."

Madelyn put her arm around her little sister and pulled her tight. "I wish it were that simple, but thank you, Jilly."

"I love you, Madelyn."

"I love you too."

They ended up splitting the sandwich, which tasted amazingly good, even though Madelyn wasn't a big fan of peanut butter and jelly. Then Jillian helped her gather up her things, including the broken off bits of dandelions, and they went inside to wash up.

Madelyn spent the rest of the day avoiding Mom as much as possible. That included, from time to time, ducking into her bedroom and pretending to be asleep. Upon "awakening" after one of these close calls, Madelyn spied *The Hobbit* sitting on her nightstand.

She picked it up and turned it around in her fingers. Earlier in the week, she couldn't bring herself to read it, and after that, she'd honestly been so caught up in thinking about Mom that she'd forgotten to even attempt it.

It was just a cheap paperback, but Madelyn liked the feel of the smooth cover in her hands. She brought it close to her face, capturing the scent of paper—subtle but intoxicating. Opening to chapter seven, Madelyn began to read, attempting to disappear into Middle Earth.

Only it didn't work. With each word, each line, each turn of the page, Madelyn was reminded of what her own mother could not do. This book was supposed to be her connection to Dad—and it was, but it also was a link to *Where the Wild Things Are* and her mother—her illiteracy, even her deceit. Anger welled up. Madelyn was reading about some man-beast creature named Beorn, but Madelyn kept thinking of an illustration in that other book—the beast with human feet, only in her mind it kept transforming into a beast with a human head that looked just like her mother.

When Madelyn finished reading the chapters she and Dad had agreed upon for the week, she realized she could recall very little of what happened. She'd read words only, reciting them in her head, simply because she could. Staring at the page in front of her, she sighed. She didn't know what she could do to change things with her mother, but at least she had Dad—even if he was on the other side of the country.

With a deep breath, she worked hard to let go of thoughts of her mother. Then she flipped back several pages and once again started to read chapter seven.

1957

William, Hazel, and Tommy sat in the seats of the auditorium, proud as they could be. Rachel wasn't receiving any academic awards, but her high school classmates had voted her the friendliest student.

The award came as no surprise; Rachel always had one or more friends over every night of the week—working on homework, talking about life, and always interacting with Tommy. Any friend of Rachel's was a friend of Tommy's—she wouldn't have it any other way.

Rachel, for her part, was nervous walking across the stage to accept her diploma. She couldn't believe it was real, that she was here on this stage with her family watching. She had no plans for any further education—she could get a job and, of course, continue to help out with Tommy.

It was something she had tried to explain to her friends. Many of them were headed off to college, including Roger Osborne, who was starting to become more than a friend. They had a date later that night, and she was planning to explain herself more fully to him then. She wanted to tell him everything. Then, as he left for college, he'd have a ready excuse if he left her behind as well.

Just a few more steps and it would be real—accept the diploma, walk across the stage, breathe a sigh of relief. Now, if she could just make it through talking with Roger.

WEEK FIVE – SUMMER 1975

SUNDAY

Madelyn would love to say that Sunday's phone call with Dad was a wonderful cleansing experience, that she confided in him everything she now knew, that she admitted her complete loss as to what to do about it. After Madelyn passed the phone to Mom, she regretted that it hadn't been.

Madelyn went outside to sit on the front porch to process her conversation instead. Dad had been cheerful, asking about their celebration of the Fourth, even telling her how he had watched fireworks from his hotel room. It was as if everything was right with the world. But, as Madelyn thought of how messed up her side of the world was, it dawned on her that he knew all about Mom, probably always had—and he had done nothing about it. How could she ask him for advice, ask him what to do about Mom, when he had already chosen to do nothing—for years!

Mrs. Burnham came outside and made straight for her. For once, Madelyn didn't care. She seemed benign compared to the people around her. "Hi, how are you doing today?" Madelyn said. Mrs. Burnham stopped mid-stride, caught off guard by the friendly words. Madelyn smiled to herself. She'd found the perfect cure for Mrs. Burnham's usual snide greeting by beating her to the punch with something nice. That hadn't actually been her plan, but she had to pat herself on the back with the pleasant result. "Come on over, Mrs. Burnham, and tell me about your day."

Madelyn was enjoying watching her squirm, all while being as nice as she could be.

It took Mrs. Burnham a few moments to decide how to proceed, but eventually, she came over and even sat down next to Madelyn on the edge of the porch. "Hi, Madelyn." She didn't seem to know what else to say.

"So, you didn't tell me how your day was."

Mrs. Burnham furrowed her brow and took a sideways glance at Madelyn, apparently trying to determine if she was serious. "It was quiet, but quiet is good," she finally responded.

"That's nice. I was just talking to my dad. His day was quiet too."

"I miss him," Mrs. Burnham said quietly. Madelyn turned to look at her. A tear was forming in the corner of her eye.

"Why?" Madelyn said.

"Madelyn, your father is kind. He's one of the few people that wished me a good day as he drove off to work or asked about my flowers during the summertime."

"Oh. I didn't know."

"No, I don't suppose you would have." She smiled and reached over to squeeze Madelyn's hand. They sat that way in silence, watching the clouds overhead waft by, hoping in vain that one of them might drop some moisture down upon them.

"You know, I like your hair—without the wig," Madelyn finally ventured to say. She was going to add that she'd seen it when they brought over cookies, but since that wasn't the friendliest of exchanges, she thought better of it.

Mrs. Burnham turned to face her, neither smiling nor frowning but eventually nodding in quiet acknowledgement.

"What happened to Mr. Burnham?" Madelyn said it softly so Mrs. Burnham could pretend not to have heard if she didn't want to answer.

When she didn't stir, Madelyn figured that was the case—until she began to speak. "I was a wartime bride. We were in love. Under normal circumstances we would have married about a year later, but with the war ... well, Johnny got called up, and that settled it. We had a quick wedding. It was beautiful. We had even pulled together flowers—roses, like in my front yard." She stopped, and Madelyn wondered if that was all she was going to say.

When she started up again, her voice was small and hard to hear. "I was so proud watching him march in uniform before heading out. After some basic training, he was shipped out to Europe. I never saw him again."

Madelyn didn't know what to say. After a lengthy silence, she said, "My grandpa served in World War II, but I guess we were lucky because he came home."

Mrs. Burnham wiped away her silent tears and said, "It's been a long time since I talked to anyone about Johnny. I wished we'd had more time together, that we'd been able to have a family. But you know what they say—if wishes were horses, then beggars would ride." Without another word, she stood up and walked back across the lawn and into her house, the air of loneliness thick in her wake.

MONDAY

The next day brought with it some bills for July along with a bank statement. Madelyn was so caught up in writing checks and balancing the checkbook that she didn't hear Jillian enter the room, not even aware she was standing in front of her until she cleared her throat.

"Hi," Jillian said, smiling.

"Hi, Jilly. You surprised me. What's up?"

"You know, don't you?"

"What are you talking about?"

"About Mom. You're acting funny around her—I mean differently than you usually do. Did you figure it out?"

"You know Mom can't read?" Jillian just nodded and smiled. Madelyn's mouth dropped open. "How do you know, Jilly? Did she tell you?"

"No, I just figured it out. Ever since I learned to read, I could tell Mom didn't know how. She doesn't follow the words. Half the time, she doesn't even look at the book." She giggled a little like this was funny instead of deadly serious.

"Really? Why didn't you tell me?"

She shrugged her shoulders. "Because it wasn't important."

"What do you mean it wasn't important? Do you know how much you can't do when you can't read?"

"Well, I figured out a few things. I help when we go to the store. I can't read everything, but I read the things I can. It must be kind of scary for her." She wasn't upset, and Madelyn couldn't figure out why. "She's not stupid, you know. She just didn't learn to read for some reason."

Jillian made it sound so simple, but it couldn't possibly be that simple. "Does Daniel know?"

"Nope. Mom doesn't even know that I know. I figure she'd be embarrassed."

•   •   •

Later, when Madelyn watched her mom struggle to sign the checks for the bills she'd written out, she kept thinking about what Jillian had said. She didn't know if it changed anything, but maybe it should.

Wednesday

Madelyn was in the garage Wednesday morning when someone said, "What are you doing?" By the question, she half expected Mrs. Burnham to be standing there, but the voice was all wrong. When she located its source, she saw Zane standing there.

"Hi, I didn't see you come in."

"Sorry, I didn't mean to sneak up on you. What are you doing?" he repeated.

Madelyn had the hood raised on the car, and she was a mess. "I'm just checking the oil and other fluids in the car."

"What?" he said, clearly surprised.

"My dad and I do it all the time." She showed him the oil dipstick in her hand for emphasis.

"Oh, you know how to do that?" When she nodded, he said, "I don't."

"It's not hard. Do you know how to change a tire?" He shook his head. "I'll show you sometime then," Madelyn said, closing the hood.

"Okay, that's just … well, I don't even drive yet."

"Neither do I." They both laughed. "So, what's up? You heading out on a bike ride or something?"

He had regained his composure by now, and a sly little grin spread across his face. "No, something better. I have a great idea about your mom." He reached his hand out for hers. "Come with me."

Madelyn pulled her greasy hand back. "Where are we going?"

"Delia's waiting in the car. She's going to drive us over to the high

113

school."

"Delia? You told her?" Madelyn was shocked.

"No, no. She thinks we're just checking out the school. I kept my promise—well, mostly. There's a summer school teacher there who I told about the situation, but I didn't tell her who I was talking about. She said we could come in and talk to her."

.   .   .

That evening as Madelyn sat in the living room holding a book that she wasn't reading, Mrs. Cutler's words from earlier that day came back to her. It was like she already knew her mom even though they'd never met. Initially, all Madelyn had told her was that she knew someone who she thought might be illiterate. Instead of asking about that person's reading ability, or lack thereof, Mrs. Cutler's questions had gone in a different direction. "Does this person have difficulty with numbers?"

Of course she does and always had. Madelyn had almost given Mom away in her response, "Yes, I have to handle, well, I help this person with her banking because she's unsure of herself."

Mrs. Cutler had simply nodded. "Would you say she's an organized person, always on time, keeps a neat house, that kind of thing?"

She'd had to stifle the laughter with that one. "No. I think she thrives on a certain level of chaos. We always seem to make it to church on time, but then that's probably because –" Too late, Madelyn realized her subterfuge was lost. So, she straightened up and owned it. "If it were up to my mother, we'd never be on time, but my sister Jillian has an overdeveloped sense of responsibility. She manages Mom." Until Madelyn said it, she hadn't realized how much of an adult Jillian was, or more likely, had to be. Madelyn didn't know if she was proud of her or embarrassed for her—maybe a little of each.

Mrs. Cutler nodded again, without acknowledging the complete confession or even looking in Madelyn's direction. "Those are behaviors that are consistent with someone who is illiterate. You might be overreacting about your mother's reading ability, but those other signs wouldn't likely be things you would know about. It could, of course, be nothing. I would need to meet with her." Before Madelyn had a chance to decide if she was being insulted or not, Mrs. Cutler said, "Have her come see me tomorrow."

Madelyn kicked a dust bunny at her feet, "Well, she ... she doesn't know ... I mean she ..."

"Oh, I see. Well, here's my number. Call me when she's ready."

The whole meeting took no more than five minutes. Madelyn was grateful Zane was there. He didn't say much, but she knew he was standing behind her. It gave her courage to speak. Or maybe Madelyn sensed her escape route was blocked. Either way, she was taking the first step toward helping her mom rather than being ashamed of her. It was definitely a better feeling.

Mulling over these thoughts behind her open book, Madelyn watched Mom. Jillian and Daniel had gone to bed, and it was just the two of them now. Mom was pouring over the pictures from another craft magazine, the lamp beside her reflecting light off the glossy pages, illuminating parts of her face. Madelyn found her features to be both familiar and foreign.

How could someone be so different from who you thought they were, especially someone you'd known your whole life? Madelyn wasn't sure, but she was finding that the more she learned, the greater her concern and empathy grew while her judgments lessened.

Madelyn followed Mom's movements as she dropped her magazine to the floor and then began to gather materials for a project she and Jillian had planned for the next day—pictures of the finished project, felt, glue, scissors, and so on. She was taking them into the kitchen, but her arms were too full.

"Mom, can I help?" Madelyn said, setting down her book.

"That would be wonderful."

Together it took them only one trip, and they spread out all the materials on the kitchen table so they would be ready for the next day. When they finished, their eyes met. Mom's were questioning, knowing Madelyn had been upset, and now hopeful that she might be ready to talk.

Madelyn wanted to be, she truly did, but being disappointed in a parent is not something one gets over easily. She opened her mouth to ask her mother straight out, to put everything into words, but she couldn't do it. Instead, she simply said, "Sleep well. I'll see you in the morning."

THURSDAY

Early the next morning, Madelyn made her way outside to think, taking her weeding supplies with her. When a weed came up easily, she would be determined to talk to her mother, confront her, challenge her to learn to read. But when the weed was stubborn, she just as easily decided that leaving things alone would be best. Her mom had made it this far in life without reading, surely she could continue on in the same way. If she'd really wanted to learn, she'd have done it by now anyway, right?

She heard the door swing open behind her and Jillian was soon casting a shadow over her patch of ground. "Would you like some breakfast?"

Her stomach rumbled an answer. "Yeah, that would be great. I haven't eaten anything yet this morning."

"Here's a banana," Jillian said, producing the yellow fruit from behind her back.

"Wow. Thanks, Jilly."

As she started to eat, Jillian sat down beside her and began to pluck up blades of grass. Madelyn gave her a sideways glance. Her face was troubled. "Are you okay, Jilly?"

"It doesn't matter to me that she can't read, Madelyn. But you're right. It is important. I guess it probably matters to her." She shrugged her shoulders. "I can't go to the store with her forever, you know."

Madelyn grabbed her in a big hug. "How did you get to be so smart? I'll talk to her, all right?"

"Today?"

"You don't make this easy, do you? All right, today."

. . .

Madelyn waited until Mom and Jillian were almost finished making their decorative pot holders before she ventured into their space. When she entered the kitchen, Jillian's head came up, and she smiled encouragingly in Madelyn's direction.

"Mom, I'll be back to help clean up. I just need to run to the bathroom," Jillian said as she slipped out of the room.

"I haven't seen you much today, Madelyn. Have you been keeping yourself busy?"

"Well, I suppose so." She cleared her throat and braced herself. "Mom, I'm not sure how to say this, but I'd like to help you ... if you know what I mean."

Mom looked up from the materials she'd been gathering together. Her expression was bewildered, oblivious. Madelyn took a deep breath and tried again. "What I'm trying to say is that I'd like to help you learn to read."

Mom's face registered the direct hit. It was a mixture of shock and something else akin to shame or possibly even anger. She looked down at the items in her hands, carefully laid them on the table then silently walked from the room.

Jillian was standing at the doorway and watched her go. "I'll clean that up, Madelyn. I know where it all goes." But before she touched a single thing, Jillian reached out and hugged her sister. It was just the thing Madelyn needed.

SaTurDaY

Mom said little to Madelyn over the course of the next couple of days. She wasn't exactly rude—she'd say things like "Good morning"—but she wasn't eager to engage in conversation either.

When Madelyn finished mowing the lawn on Saturday, she noticed Mrs. Burnham tending to her roses. After putting away her things in the garage, she walked over. "They're beautiful. I hadn't really paid attention to them before, but I love this one," Madelyn said, reaching out to touch the velvety petals of a cream-colored rose edged with pink.

She waited for the snide comment to come, but it didn't. Mrs. Burnham simply nodded in her direction to acknowledge her presence. "It's called a peace rose. It's one of my favorites as well."

Madelyn sat down cross-legged on the grass close to where Mrs. Burnham was working. "What do you do during the day, you know, to keep yourself busy?"

She had been cutting off the dead rose blooms but stopped at the question. "I write books."

"Books? Like published books?"

She nodded. "Would you mind grabbing a lawn chair for me? There's one in the garage. You can grab one for yourself if you want."

Madelyn set up the chairs on the driveway where the shade from one of the trees shielded them from the July sun. "So, tell me about your books."

Mrs. Burnham gave her a genuine smile. "I write children's books—mostly picture books."

"I didn't know that. How many have you written?"

"I've published over twenty different titles."

"Wow. How long have you been writing?"

"You really want to know?" Madelyn nodded vigorously. "Well, when I became a widow, I made a point of finishing my education. I became a school teacher and taught elementary school for several years. You don't make a lot that way, but I didn't have a lot of places to spend it either, so I salted it away. When I felt I had enough, I quit teaching so I could write children's books. I've been doing that ever since. It hasn't made me rich, but it has made me enough." She looked at Madelyn to see if she was still interested before adding, "Would you like to see them?"

The books were charming stories that instantly softened Madelyn's opinion of Mrs. Burnham. She found herself captivated as she flipped through the pages of each one. Jillian would love them, she thought—and maybe Mom would too. Before she could stop herself, Madelyn said, "Could you help someone learn to read?" She hadn't intended to say anything, but now that she had, she wondered where it might lead.

"Certainly. I love opening up a child's mind to the world of books."

"What if it's not a child?" Mrs. Burnham raised her eyebrows. Madelyn continued, "I don't know why, but my mom can't read. Could you help her? I mean, if she's willing to learn?"

The strange expression on Mrs. Burnham's face made Madelyn instantly regret her words. What if she had just set her mother up to be an object of ridicule? What might Mrs. Burnham say to her mom? The only comforting thought was that at least it would go no further. After all, if Mrs. Burnham wanted to, who could she tell anyway?

Madelyn moved away, anxious to leave, but before she could, Mrs. Burnham grabbed her arm. "Please wait." Turning back around Madelyn was surprised to see tears running down her cheeks. "Please?"

She nodded slowly, unsure of what was coming. Mrs. Burnham dropped her arm then started walking toward her kitchen. Madelyn followed her without a word.

Not until they were sipping lemonade at her kitchen table did she speak. "I've been terribly mistaken." She was shaking her head. Madelyn didn't ask what she was talking about—torn between wanting to understand her odd behavior and wanting to escape it. After a few minutes of head shaking, she took to wringing her hands, and Madelyn began to wonder if she should go for help.

Just as she had determined the best way to sneak out, Mrs. Burnham spoke once again. "Madelyn, I have misjudged your mom. All these years I could have helped her. Instead, I resented her, thinking she was unfriendly and cold."

"But she isn't! She –"

"I know that now. That's what I'm trying to tell you. Your dad always greeted me, but I couldn't understand why your mom rarely did. She never made an effort to get to know me. Even if I said hi to her, she wouldn't engage in a conversation. This explains a lot of things."

"What are you talking about? How does her not being able to read have anything to do with it?"

"Madelyn, think for a moment about what your life would be like if you couldn't read—especially if others didn't know and you wanted to keep it that way."

"Well, I've thought about what she couldn't do. She couldn't read books or magazines or even recipes. And, of course, street signs would be hard. Oh, and I already thought about the grocery store—or at least Jillian did."

Mrs. Burnham was nodding, but Madelyn could see she was still missing something. "Madelyn, that's part of it, but quite honestly it's just the tip of the iceberg. You use reading more than you know—reading a map, following written directions, checking your child's homework or even understanding a note sent home by a teacher. The list could go on and on. But what about the other side of things? If you couldn't read, and you didn't want others to know, like your neighbors, what would you do?"

"I don't know. I guess I'd avoid situations where I'd be expected to read—definitely no book groups, I'm thinking." Madelyn laughed at her attempt at humor, but Mrs. Burnham merely smiled.

"Sure, but wouldn't there be other, not-so-obvious moments?"

Madelyn had never thought of it in terms of having friends or being neighborly. "Well, I think other times might be hard to predict—like you wouldn't want to go out to lunch and have to read a menu, or maybe talk about something from the morning newspaper." Madelyn was beginning to see the larger concerns.

"Wouldn't it be easier to avoid conversations and interactions altogether? Then you wouldn't have to worry about where they might lead. No need to be rescued from drowning if you don't even approach the riverbank."

"I hadn't thought about that before. That would make you kind of lonely, wouldn't it?" The irony of who Madelyn was saying this to dawned on her. She reached over and put her arm around Mrs. Burnham. "I guess there are a lot of reasons to be lonely, aren't there?" she said.

Mrs. Burnham just nodded, but after a few quiet moments, she straightened up, wiping tears from her eyes. "I'm so sorry she can't read. What a burden that must be for her." She gave Madelyn a rueful smile. "I'd like to make things up to her, for not being the neighbor I could have been or should have been. Going your whole life without being able to enjoy books or even just get along in the world—that's tough." She was shaking her head. "She wouldn't have even been able to read you bedtime stories."

"Well, actually that's how I figured it out, but not in the way you might think," Madelyn laughed. "Dad used to read me stories until Mom memorized them. She's read—or whatever you want to call it—the same books to all three of us for years. If we hadn't liked those stories, it would have been tough luck for us. But the other day, she was reading to Jilly, only she was reading the story wrong. It's funny that the book she *could* read told me that she *couldn't*." Madelyn smiled at her neighbor. "You know, I wasn't planning on saying anything, but I'm glad I did."

"Me too."

"May I ask you something?"

"Sure. What is it?"

"Well, when I talked to my mom about not being able to read, she didn't say anything. She didn't respond in any way."

"Isn't that a response, in and of itself?"

"Yeah, I guess so. The problem is I want to help her learn, but I can't if she won't admit to it. What should I do?"

"Just be patient and wait. I imagine she'll come around."

1974

He expected the attic to smell musty, but the dry Colorado air had worked in William's favor, and dust was the only thing that assaulted his senses. Climbing the ladder had reminded him he wasn't a young man anymore, and he paused to rub his stiff joints before reaching up to pull the string for the single bulb suspended in the middle of the attic space. The dim light it gave out wasn't much, but at least he could see where to put his feet now. Reminders of Hazel were somewhere in this room. It's the only reason he was up here.

The attic had always been the place to arbitrarily drop things and, other than the Christmas decorations, promptly forget about them. But memories were what William was searching for this time around.

It was nearly midnight. He'd been unable to sleep—hadn't slept much actually since the car accident that took his Hazel only a couple months before—unless you counted the drunken stupor that often overcame him.

There was only one reason he was searching through the attic instead of drinking at this hour—Hazel. She never liked him drinking, and to keep the peace, he rarely drank when she was alive. She didn't like how easily he could get drunk, and when he was drunk, he was a different person, according to Hazel. He had to take her word for it—he didn't usually remember much afterward.

But something had been different earlier that day. He'd had lunch and reached for a beer, but he could have sworn Hazel wouldn't let him—it was like she was pulling his hand back and whispering in his ear. He kept himself busy all afternoon—whether to avoid thinking about alcohol or to avoid trying to understand what had happened, he couldn't be sure. When the same experience replayed itself at dinner, he couldn't ignore it any longer. Hazel was still around, and she must love him enough to care what happened to him—or more likely, what he did to himself.

The attic was finally the idea that hit him as he lay in bed staring at a ceiling that for once in so many days wasn't shifting erratically before his eyes. He wasn't certain, but he had a vague recollection of Hazel gathering pictures over the years. He thought they were for photo albums—not so much when Tommy was younger, but as he got older and could do more for himself, allowing time for other things like taking pictures.

Past the forgotten toys and the record player, William found a particularly old box. He sat down on the floor next to it then brushed the dust off before opening it to see what was inside. He'd been wrong—at least in part. There was no photo album, but in a shaft of light, he saw a pile of photographs.

William picked up the first one, holding it up to view it in the bulb's glare. It was Hazel—young, with a smile on her face. It was the day after he'd returned from the war. He'd been too busy holding her and the kids, in turn, to snap a photo the first day. A tear trickled down his cheek. They'd had their disagreements over the years, some of them intense, but if it hadn't been for Hazel, he'd never have felt intensely about anything.

At first, he only lingered on the pictures of Hazel, but soon all of them made him stop. Tommy had blossomed over the years—with Hazel refusing to believe he was as incapable of progress as all the doctors declared. And, of course, Rachel had been her stalwart helper in all things Tommy.

The group home had been a godsend. It's not that they needed to be free of Tommy's care, but he needed to be free of them. Hazel had said, "I'm not going to be around forever. We need to make sure he can live on his own and do for himself, within limits, of course." The work he could do at the sheltered workshop the group home arranged had turned out to be the solution they'd been seeking. Even still, William and Hazel looked forward to their regular visits with their son.

When William went to visit Tommy after Hazel's death, Rachel went with him. She'd always been a great strength. Her own little family kept her *plenty busy, but if ever he or Tommy needed anything, she'd drop everything and be there for them.*

William set down the pictures he'd been collecting in his hands so he could wipe away his tears. Reaching into the box again, his fingers touched something unusual. He picked up the object to examine it in the light. It was a tightly wrapped parcel, cylindrical, like the contents inside had been rolled up.

Something about it seemed familiar, but he couldn't place why. Turning it over and over in his hands, he searched his memory for the lost connection to this item. It was the feel of the fabric wrapping that finally evoked the memory. There was a French priest, he remembered. The cloth probably came from one of his own robes—durable, practical, yet somehow holy. The French priest had given him this for safekeeping on D-day, to keep it away from a ruthless, retreating German army.

After carefully climbing down the attic ladder, he almost reverently carried the mysterious parcel to the kitchen table. He flipped on the light, and for the first time, unwrapped what had been entrusted to his care.

"Oh, my goodness! Oh, wow!" was all William could say for some time. As uncertain as he was about how to proceed with life, he knew what to do with this—and he knew Hazel would approve. He looked up the number for his attorney and scribbled it down. William would call him first thing in the morning.

If only he hadn't started drinking again.

week six – summer 1975

SUNDaY

The next day when Madelyn talked to Dad on the phone, she almost said something about Mom, only she didn't know what exactly to say. So, instead, she chatted with him about what was happening in *The Hobbit*, as if nothing else mattered in the world.

She'd talked to Zane on the phone the night before. He had called wanting to know what was happening with her mom. "Nothing," wasn't much of a response, but it was the truth, unfortunately. During her call with Dad, she kept thinking about that previous phone call and had trouble suppressing a smile as she did so.

"Are you there, Madelyn?"

"Oh, yeah, I'm here."

She didn't even mind so much when it was time to hand the phone over to Mom. And it wasn't until that evening as she was playing a board game with Daniel and Jillian that she realized she'd forgotten to mark off another week. When she pulled out her pad of paper, she was surprised to see that five weeks were over with only five more to go.

MONDAY

Waking up early, Madelyn picked up her copy of *The Hobbit* to read in bed. She thought for a moment about tiptoeing into Dad's study, but the comfort of her blankets won her over. As she read, she couldn't help but think about Mom. It turns out Bilbo was the one to discover the hidden keyhole into the Lonely Mountain where the dragon lay watching over his stolen treasure. There was far too much of the book left for the dwarves to recover their treasure easily, but it seemed like such an important step forward. Likewise, Madelyn thought, if only Mom could admit to her illiteracy, then the rest of everything would fall into place, and life would be better. Surely, it could be that simple, couldn't it?

Despite Madelyn's concerns about her mother, once she got out of bed her day appeared normal in every way—typical breakfast, usual chatter from her siblings—everything mundane and ordinary. Her mother still wasn't talking to her much, but she'd come to expect that over the last few days.

But everything changed in the afternoon.

When the mail came, Madelyn grabbed the usual assortment of bills and ads, but as she sorted through them, she came across a white envelope. It was addressed to Rachel Osborne. She stopped short. It reminded her of the other envelope addressed to her mother just the month before. Mom hadn't opened that letter to read it—which now, in hindsight, made perfect sense. So, the question was—what was it and who was it from?

Her heart was beating faster as she carried the mail into Dad's study, trying to appear as casual as possible. But what to do now?

Madelyn wrestled for several minutes with the temptation to rip the letter open right then and there, but she couldn't bring herself to do it. It was her mother's letter, not hers. And if she did open it, how would she explain herself when she eventually handed the letter over? Her guilt would be obvious.

Running her fingers over the envelope in her hands, she contemplated what to do. There were only two things on the letter—the postmark and her mother's name and address.

Something about both of them tugged at her mind, like she should know them somehow. The postmark said "Merek, Colorado." She'd heard of it before. It was a city a little distance away, but it wasn't very big. It was peculiar for some reason, but what it was wouldn't come to her mind, although it was on the tip of her tongue.

The handwriting of her mother's name was familiar in a more personal way. The "O" in "Osborne" kept drawing her eye. It was looped more like a spiral, the ends never quite touching to form a circle. She snickered a little because it reminded her of a quail with the curlicue on the top of his head.

Of course! How had she not seen it earlier? That's exactly the way her grandfather formed his "O's" on every birthday card she had ever received from him. They came in the mail like clockwork on her birthdays—Madelyn Osborne, with a quail-like "O" starting her last name.

It was a letter from her missing grandfather, and she knew where he was—Merek, Colorado. She said the name of it out loud, "Merek, Colorado," as if it would bring him closer. "Merek, Colorado ..." It all came in a flash. Merek, Colorado was known for one thing—the state penitentiary!

Madelyn sunk down in Dad's office chair, the envelope shaking in her hand. Everything was suddenly clear—but in a way that makes you want to turn away and shield your eyes. No wonder he was abruptly gone. No wonder he "couldn't" visit anymore. And no wonder they didn't want to tell her.

The reality of it washed over her like a muddy dam that had broken and was heading her way. It was dark and dirty and smelled disgusting. But why? What in the world had he done?

The temptation once again was to open the letter, to read what it said. Her mother need never know the letter had even come—unless ... well, unless it contained something she needed to know. And if it did, would that be something she Madelyn wanted to know?

"Hey, do you want to come outside for a water fight?" Daniel said from the doorway.

Startled, Madelyn straightened up, slipping her hand with the letter down by her side where it wouldn't be seen. "Um, sure. Just give me a minute."

When he'd left, she stuffed the envelope in her pocket, quickly dispatched the other mail to its appropriate pile or the garbage can, and hustled off to her room.

WEDNESDAY

"Hi, Madelyn." Mom's voice broke into her thoughts as she sat on the back steps. It took a minute to register that Mom was initiating a conversation with her, something that hadn't happened for several days.

"Hi," Madelyn said while thinking of the envelope folded and stuck in her back pocket.

Mom sat down beside her on the step. She reached down to a patch of lawn and plucked off a yellow dandelion top, twirling it in her hands for several minutes before speaking. "Do you have a plan for getting rid of the dandelions?"

The question took Madelyn by surprise. Since when did Mom talk about plans or being organized in any way? She shrugged her shoulders. "I guess I don't. I just weed wherever I feel like, but that's not really working, is it?"

"Probably not." Mom surveyed the dandelions around them. "You know, I think we should give up on the back, don't you?" The suggestion caught her off guard, but Madelyn nodded enthusiastically. "Maybe we can make the front look good for your dad's return—let him know we could handle things." She got a wicked twinkle in her eye. "He doesn't have to see the backyard that first day he's home, you know."

Madelyn chuckled. "I like the way you think." It dawned on her that Mom's take on the dandelions wasn't any more complicated than that. Mom was trying to deal with her own insecurities about being illiterate—trying to prove to Dad that she could do hard things—like survive the summer without him to lean on. "That's a great idea, Mom."

"Well, sometimes you have to cut your losses and focus on what you can do, over what you think you can do." She smiled then surprised Madelyn by very quietly adding, "And, Madelyn, you're right. I can't read." She took a deep breath. "Do you have a plan for that?"

"Yes, I do," Madelyn said, brightening up.

"You know, I've always thought that not being able to read only affected me. But you've seemed so down, especially the last few days, that I had to admit to myself maybe I was wrong about that. It has ripple effects, doesn't it?"

Madelyn nodded. If only Mom knew the real reason she was down, she thought, feeling the weight of the letter in her back pocket. For a passing second, she considered whipping it out but then thought better of it. This wasn't the time. Mom's admission was a gift, and she didn't want to spoil it, at least not yet. "Well," Madelyn said, "there's this teacher named Mrs. Cutler at the high school..."

"Really?" Mom said with a hopeful smile.

"Yes, and did you know that Mrs. Burnham used to teach elementary school and now she writes books?"

"I did not," she said, her smile wavering just a bit.

.　　.　　.

By the time Madelyn had finished tending to the garden and come back inside to call Mrs. Cutler, Mom's demeanor had changed dramatically. "You know, Madelyn, I appreciate your concern, but I've been rethinking things. This isn't really necessary."

"What? I don't understand. Just an hour ago you were all ready to go. What happened?"

"I ... I don't know. I got caught up in the idea, I guess, but the reality's different. Maybe it does affect you, but it's better the way it is. I'm sorry."

"What are you talking about? Don't you want to be able to read? It will open up the world to you. There's so much that you're missing out on. I want to help you find that."

Mom's shoulders were hunched over, and she wouldn't look at

Madelyn, preferring to use her toe to scrub at some imaginary scuff on the floor. She mumbled something that Madelyn couldn't make out.

"What did you say?" Madelyn put her hand on Mom's shoulder and softly said, "What is it, Mom?"

"I can't."

"Can't what? Meet the teacher? Go alone? What?"

"I can't learn to read. I tried when I was young, when you're supposed to be able to learn easily, but I couldn't do it then, and I certainly can't do it now."

"Yes, you can. I'm sure of it," Madelyn said, even though she wasn't in the slightest. "Mrs. Cutler said she could teach you, and Mrs. Burnham wants to help too."

"Well, Mrs. Cutler has never met me, and Dorothy doesn't like me." Without another word she turned and walked away.

. . .

By afternoon, Madelyn had decided on a brave—or stupid—course of action. The outcome would determine which it was. In Dad's study, with the door shut for privacy, Madelyn picked up the phone and dialed Mrs. Cutler's number. It turned out it was the school number, and they had to transfer her a couple times before Madelyn actually reached her, but too soon she was on the other end. "Yes, this is Mrs. Cutler."

Madelyn's knees were knocking together and her fingers shaking. In as calm a voice as she could muster, she said, "This is Madelyn Osborne. We met last week. I've talked with my mother, and I'm wondering when I might be able to bring her in to meet with you. She needs to learn to read because she can't. I mean she can't read right now."

"Okay. I can meet with her tomorrow at ten or Friday at the same time."

"Friday. Friday would be great. Thursdays we visit my uncle. He's got cerebral palsy, and he looks forward to our visits, so – well, anyway, Friday would work." Mom may not be able to read, but Madelyn felt like she'd lost the ability to talk coherently. She was relieved when the appointment for Friday was confirmed, and they hung up.

Now, how could she convince Mom to go?

Before she could ponder the question, two different sets of giggles filtered in from outside the study. As she approached the door, Madelyn noticed it was slightly ajar. When she swung it open, a pail full of confetti showered her from above. "Daniel! Jilly!"

Although she made them think it when she found them, Madelyn wasn't angry. She was actually grateful for the distraction.

THURSDAY

Madelyn still didn't have a solution the next morning as she got ready to visit Uncle Tommy. Eating breakfast, she hardly dared look Mom in the face, not knowing what to say, not knowing what look she'd get in return.

Madelyn shouldn't have been so concerned. As they all finished eating, a horn honked from outside. "Hurry up, you two," Mom said, sweeping Daniel and Jillian out the front door.

Mom answered the unspoken question as soon as the front door closed behind them. "I arranged for Delia to come take them. That way we can have the day to ourselves." She took a deep breath. "I am willing to try to learn to read." Madelyn jumped up and hugged her before she had a chance to continue. Mom pulled back to hold her at arm's length. "But Madelyn, I make no promises about the results."

"That's okay. I'll help you. We can do this, Mom. I know we can." Mom gave her a weary look but didn't object.

After that breakthrough, along with the arrangements for her siblings, Madelyn figured the ride to Uncle Tommy's would be full of talk. It wasn't. They both sat silently, staring at the familiar road ahead, but Madelyn couldn't help fidgeting.

By the time they reached the last, long stretch of road, Madelyn's fidgeting had taken on a life and sound of its own—snapping her fingers, drumming on her legs, bouncing her feet against the car floor. Mom let out an audible sigh. "Go ahead and ask."

"How? How did you make it through school without learning to read?

What happened?"

She nodded toward the road ahead in the direction of Tommy's workshop. "Tommy. It wasn't his fault, but he was my excuse." Madelyn didn't respond, just waiting to see if her mom would continue. A few minutes passed before she did.

"I didn't understand the words I was supposed to be reading. I tried, but the more I tried, the more confusing it became. I didn't want to tell my parents, they were already so worried about Tommy. Pop always called me his perfect child. I couldn't let them know I wasn't."

"They never knew?"

"Whenever a teacher would send a note home, I'd throw it away. If they asked about school, I always made something up then changed the topic to Tommy." She shrugged her shoulders. "I tried to compensate by listening carefully—whenever a friend read a passage in a book or to what the teacher was saying. I tried to memorize whatever I could. Although I wasn't very good at that either."

"But what about your teachers? Why didn't they hold you back or something?"

"That just wasn't done, Madelyn. You got passed on to the next grade regardless of what you could or couldn't do. I was usually in the slow classes—what I liked to think of as 'stupid class.' No one flunks out of 'stupid class.' Sometimes I was clever enough to fool them, and I'm sorry to say that I became very good at making friends and having them help me. We'd get together to do homework, and I'd talk and talk so it felt like I was part of the effort, but, in reality, I was there to listen, to glean as much as I could that way."

She hesitated before continuing. "Letters baffle me, Madelyn. Some letters are fine, but others are confusing. There were times when the only thing that worked was actually tracing over my friends' work, so I didn't write the letters wrong. They thought it was funny—like I was trying to mimic their handwriting. They never knew just how desperate I was." Her face wore the anguish of such memories. "I know it doesn't excuse the cheating, but I didn't know what else to do."

"I had no idea. That must have been horrible," Madelyn said. Mom nodded, wiping at her moist eyes as she did so. Madelyn hated to ask, but if she wanted to know, she figured there wouldn't be another time. "How did you handle tests? You must have cheated on those too." She tried to modulate her voice, softening it, attempting to remove any sound of condemnation.

"That's a fair question. Not as much as you might think. Thankfully I was usually in those slow classes. I wouldn't have survived otherwise. But, to answer your question, I could usually convince the teachers to give me oral tests. I told them I had troubles with my eyes. When I could verbally give my answers, I could pass my tests. It was that simple. And even though I had trouble writing, I perfected Pop's signature. That got me out of a lot of things." She laughed at the memory. "You know, I'm probably better at his signature than my own."

"Wow. I'm sorry, Mom." They drove silently for a few minutes. "I thought I'd be upset that you cheated your way through school, but I guess it was kind of scary, wasn't it?"

She nodded her head. "I was always afraid I'd be found out. When I had choices, I took gym classes or sewing. I made a point to help other students that were struggling with their projects. It seemed fair, like payback of some kind. You know, I couldn't believe it when I graduated from high school and no one knew I couldn't read."

"What about Dad? Didn't you meet him in high school? I mean, he's got to know, doesn't he?"

"Yes, he knows, but he didn't know then. We met in the lunch line one day. We never had any classes together, but he would always find me and come sit next to me during lunch. I told him the night of graduation. He was heading off to college, and I figured if he didn't want to see me again, it would be an easy way out for him." She smiled at the memory. "He was shocked, and I thought he was going to walk out on our date, but he didn't. That's the moment I knew I wanted to marry him. If he could still love me, even though I wasn't perfect, then I knew I could always depend on him."

"I didn't know that. It's kind of sweet. But didn't he try to help you learn?"

"He offered to, but I was certain I *couldn't* read. After he asked about it several times, I told him never to bring it up again—it just made me feel stupid. He promised he wouldn't. It's a promise he's kept," she said as they pulled into the parking lot. It was hard to fathom, and yet, at the same time, what Mom had told Madelyn made sense.

· · ·

When Madelyn greeted Uncle Tommy and his friends, the silent Annie was clearly in a good mood. She couldn't wait to show Madelyn the new bracelet she had on. She pulled Madelyn over to Eliza so she could see that Eliza had one too. They were simple macramé bracelets—Eliza's had red beads woven in with the knots, and Annie's had purple. When Annie smiled and patted her chest, Madelyn said, "You made them didn't you, Annie?" She just beamed.

"She made mine with red beads, 'cause that's my favorite color," Eliza said. She was holding her wrist with the bracelet right in front of her eyes so she could see it.

They invited Annie and Eliza to join them for a picnic lunch outside. Uncle Tommy walked between them, escorting them like a gentleman to the patio table.

Madelyn leaned over to Mom. "Those three may not be able to do things most people can, but they always seem happy. It's easy to love them, isn't it?" Mom nodded.

Later, when Madelyn was helping Tommy slowly gather up the picnic remnants and throw them away, she looked around to see that Mom was busy helping Annie and Eliza back inside. "Uncle Tommy, do you remember my mom—Sissy—from when you were growing up?"

His face lit up. "You bet, Madly. She's why I walk and why I talk."

Madelyn stopped. "What do you mean?"

"She helped me get strong enough and smart enough. Then she taught me how. It was my favorite bedtime story Mom and Pop Pop tell me."

"Really? Do you remember the story? Could you tell it to me?"

"Sure. But we have to sit down because it's for when we're resting."

When they were seated on a picnic bench, Uncle Tommy began. In a sing-song voice, he told the story. "Once there was a little girl, bright and beautiful and perfect. And there was a little boy, bright and beautiful too. One day, their mommy learned that the little boy might never be able to walk or to talk or to do things most people can. The mommy was sad and scared, but the little girl said, 'I can help you, Mommy.' The mommy showed the little girl how to exercise the little boy's muscles. He didn't like it when Mommy did it with him, but the little girl made it fun, and he would do anything Sissy asked. She helped him become stronger and stronger, and she talked and talked to him too. So, the little boy decided he could make sounds too. And he started to talk to Sissy. And he started to talk to Mommy and Pop Pop. One day, he even walked to Mommy and Pop Pop, all because Sissy taught him how. And they all lived happily ever after. The end."

Madelyn stared at him. "Is that true?" she whispered. "Did Sissy teach you to talk and to walk?"

"Yep. True as true. That's what Mom and Pop Pop always said—true as true. The doctors said I couldn't, but Mommy and Sissy said I could." Then he leaned close to her and whispered, "I don't think Sissy liked the bedtime story because she'd get embarrassed. But I asked her. She said it was true as true too."

When Mom came looking for them a short time later, Uncle Tommy and Madelyn were leaning against each other in a big, gentle, sideways hug. His face lit up when he saw her. Once again, she was a woman transforming before Madelyn's eyes.

.   .   .

Madelyn wanted to ask about it on the way home, but she was afraid Mom would try to downplay her involvement or contribution. She didn't want her to do that, for her to diminish what Madelyn had just learned to be "true as true," and instinctively knew to be such.

Instead, Madelyn brought up something else that had been on her mind. "May I ask you something?" Mom hesitated before answering. She had already laid herself bare, but she finally nodded. "Why now? Why did you agree to let me help you?"

Mom sighed before responding. "Believe it or not, it was your grandfather." Madelyn sat up straighter, immediately attentive. "When I first came to you in the yard, it was out of embarrassment, because of what you knew about me. But the sudden thought of how many people would have to know that I couldn't read … it was too much." She was shaking her head.

"What does this have to do with Grandpa?" Madelyn interrupted.

"Well, I received a letter from Pop last month. I don't suppose it's about much of anything. I've been so used to not being able to read that I just threw it in a drawer and didn't give it another thought. But I happened across it last night. You know, I'd like to be able to read that letter." Mom's voice was husky and choked with emotion. But Madelyn's face had grown red, the weight of the envelope she'd taken to carrying around in her back pocket calling to her.

"I … I don't know what to say. That sounds good, Mom."

Mom chuckled slightly and glanced in Madelyn's direction, unaware of her distress. "Even still, I was awake all night building up my courage. However, this morning, when I talked to you, I did it for the right reasons. I'm doing it for me … and maybe a little for your dad and Pop too."

"It's also for Jilly," Madelyn added quietly. "I don't want you to feel bad, but she knows you can't read. She actually figured it out a long time ago. She just kept it to herself—I think because it doesn't bother her. But she'll be proud of you, all the same."

"I guess I'm not surprised. Jilly is seven going on twenty sometimes."

"I know. She's so smart. Look how long it took me to figure things out."

"Well, I've gotten pretty good at hiding it, but you're more clever than you give yourself credit for. Do you think Daniel knows?"

"According to Jilly, no. Personally, I think Daniel's too busy channeling all his brain power into other pursuits to notice." They both laughed, remembering the waffles he'd made that morning. He'd taken Mom's waffle batter, mixed in jelly beans and then laid a slice of bologna on the top before closing the waffle iron. Mom made him eat three bites of his concoction before he was allowed to throw it away and eat a regular waffle.

When they got home, it dawned on Madelyn that she and Mom had never had such a serious discussion in their lives. Maybe Dad being gone wasn't such a bad thing after all.

Friday

It was hard to tell who was more nervous, Madelyn or Mom, when they went to meet with Mrs. Cutler the next morning. Mom didn't say much but spent extra time fixing her hair and straightening her skirt. If it weren't for Jillian scooting them out the door, they would have been late.

As for Madelyn, she hadn't been able to eat breakfast. The butterflies in her stomach felt more like a whole load of spinning laundry.

Mrs. Cutler called them into her classroom at 10:00 on the dot. She had raised her eyebrows when she saw them waiting in the hallway. Madelyn wondered if she expected them to be late and silently thanked Jillian.

"So, let's see what you can do," she said to Mom, indicating a chair by her desk. She ignored Madelyn who found an out-of-the-way corner with a chair to settle in. Occasional sounds came from their direction but little else.

After about a half an hour, Mrs. Cutler stood up and surprised Madelyn by marching over to where she sat. "Your mother can't read. And in cases like this, it's very difficult to teach someone to read once they've reached adulthood." She said it matter-of-factly, with no emotion of any kind.

"What?"

"When we can work with non-readers when they're young, well then it might be different. But there are clearly obstacles to overcome. The effort it would take at this point, on my end and on hers, is just too great. So, I suggest you just take her home and let her continue as she's done. With illiterate adults, I've found they've usually created a number of coping mechanisms. I'm sure she'll do just fine."

Madelyn could see past Mrs. Cutler to where Mom had come up behind her. The hurt etched in the lines of her face threatened to haunt Madelyn the rest of her life.

"Mrs. Cutler, why are you speaking to me about my mother as if she weren't here?" Her blood was beginning to boil, and she knew if she said another word there would be no stopping her. But one look at her mom and her course was set.

"You stand there in judgment of a woman you know nothing about. You even have the gall to imply she *can't* learn. Well, let me tell you something. She is an intelligent, amazing woman and certainly more caring and warm than the likes of you! How dare you speak about her to me as if she were nothing more than a household pet.

"Do you know what she's done? When she was just a small child, she taught her brother, who has cerebral palsy, how to walk and how to talk. The experts, people like you, said it couldn't be done, that he couldn't learn. But she worked with him every day until he could. She never gave up on him, and I'm never giving up on her."

Mrs. Cutler's eyes were open wide. It's doubtful anyone had ever spoken to her that way before, but Madelyn figured maybe it was about time. "You've been extremely rude and insensitive to my mom. I'm trying to help her, and all you can do is shoot her down. I'm sorry we ever came to you." Her anger was quickly threatening to turn to tears. In an effort to stave them off, she mustered her best mom-voice and said, "Before we leave, I would like you to turn around and speak *to* my mother, and it better be nothing short of a heartfelt apology."

Her mouth was agape, but Madelyn gave her a glare that closed it. She slowly turned to see an equally surprised woman directly behind her. "I didn't mean anything by that, I just –"

"Try again," Madelyn said, interrupting.

Without turning in her direction, Mrs. Cutler said, "I'm truly sorry. I wish you the best." She hadn't retracted her words, so Madelyn raised her eyebrows at Mom, silently asking her opinion. Mom nodded. They would declare it good enough. Then, as if they had practiced the move, they simultaneously turned toward the door and marched out without so much as a backward glance.

As they exited the school in silence, it dawned on Madelyn what she'd said, and to an adult authority figure to boot. "You know, Mom, if you can arrange it, I think it would be best if I don't have Mrs. Cutler as an English teacher at any point during high school," she said. They looked at each other and started giggling, the tension breaking and falling like bits of glass around them.

In between giggles, Mom said, "I'm guessing she would be in agreement."

The tears came to Madelyn's eyes now—a result of her giggles mixed with the stress of what she'd witnessed and participated in. She wiped them away, glad Mrs. Cutler wasn't there to see them. "I'm sorry, Mom. I love you."

"You don't have anything to apologize for. And I love you too, Madelyn."

"Thanks, Mom." She smiled and climbed into the car to head home. She didn't know what her next step was going to be, but she was certain they'd figure out something. Lost in her determined thoughts, Madelyn didn't notice Mom's silence or the single tear running down her cheek.

Mom pulled into the garage then turned off the car without making any move toward opening her door. After a minute she turned to Madelyn. "I appreciate what you did back there. Those were kind words. But she's right, you know. I really can't." And before Madelyn could reply, she slipped out of the car and into the house.

It was a long time before Madelyn moved from her seat. If it weren't for Daniel, she probably would have stayed there all day. He came into the garage poking around for something. When he noticed Madelyn, he knocked on the car door until she cranked down the window.

"Whatcha doin'?"

"Thinking."

"About Mom?"

"Um, yeah. How did you know?"

"Jilly told me. She figured I needed to know what was happening. How'd she get so smart anyway? She supposed to be my *little* sister, but she always seems to know more than I do."

"Yeah, I know what you mean."

"So, what's up?"

She debated how much to tell him, stalling while she opened the door and got out of the car. "The teacher thinks Mom can't learn to read."

"Are you kidding?"

"No, and what's worse, Mom believes her."

"Where does she live? We ought to toilet paper her house or something."

That at least made Madelyn smile just a little. "I don't think that would help. Besides, I already gave her a piece of my mind."

"You did? Good for you, Madelyn. I didn't know you could do that. I mean, stand up for Mom and all."

"What's that supposed to mean?"

"Well, we all know you'd do anything for Dad, but Mom's another story." Madelyn was taken aback and started unconsciously balling her fists. "Hey, don't punch me. It's a compliment."

It was a back-handed compliment if she'd ever heard one, but she decided to let it go. "Okay, but what do I do about Mom?"

He shrugged his shoulders. "Get a second opinion." He was right, of course. Only this time Madelyn needed to stack the deck in her favor.

•   •   •

Mrs. Burnham opened the door quickly after her heavy knocking. "What's wrong?"

"Am I that obvious?"

"Well, I don't remember such angry knocking from a friend, and your look could burn holes right through me."

Madelyn laughed, thinking of the "Burnham's burners" nickname they had given to Mrs. Burnham's looks, and now the shoe was on the other foot. But her expression was puzzled, so she stifled the remainder of her laughter. It wasn't until that moment that Madelyn realized Mrs. Burnham had called her a friend. She was touched but also ashamed of her earlier opinion of this lonely woman.

"I'm sorry. I've been rude," Madelyn said. Mrs. Burnham nodded her head and stepped back to invite her in. Madelyn knew the apology had come across as apologizing for laughing without explanation. Honestly, she wasn't sure how to appropriately apologize for the rest. How could she say she was sorry for having unkind thoughts without admitting what those unkind thoughts were? Surely that would hurt more than it would help.

Madelyn hadn't budged from the doorstep while those thoughts swirled, but when she opened her mouth, she knew what to say. "Mrs. Burnham, I mean to say that I'm sorry it took me so long to be your friend. I misjudged you, and I was wrong."

She nodded. "Well, apparently, there's a lot of that going around." She reached out and embraced Madelyn. "Now, what's on your mind?"

After they sat down in Mrs. Burnham's kitchen, it didn't take long for the story to spill out. When Madelyn told her about Mrs. Cutler's response, Mrs. Burnham started to make angry grunts, and actual steam nearly billowed from her head. "What a cowardly way to act. You never tell a child, or an adult for that matter, overtly or not, that she can't learn. That either gives them permission not to, or worse, defeats them, so they never try. I ought to ... I ..." Her face was scarlet red, and she was bunching up her kitchen tablecloth in her grasp.

Madelyn put her hand gently on top of Mrs. Burnham's. "I told her she was wrong and made her apologize to Mom. It wasn't much, but I couldn't leave it that way."

She relaxed her grip on the defenseless tablecloth. "That's good."

"Daniel suggested I get a second opinion, and I thought of you. Maybe you could evaluate her."

Her eyes opened in surprise, but then her demeanor changed as she sat taller and her eyes started to dance with thoughts and ideas, almost as if she were reading a book herself. Abruptly, she stood up. "Let's go, Madelyn. We don't have a moment to lose."

"But your hair ... your wig?" Madelyn started to say. She'd learned by now that while Mrs. Burnham might skip wearing a wig inside her house, she never did when she left it.

Mrs. Burnham dismissed the thought with a quick wave of her hand. Then, despite Madelyn's youth and Mrs. Burnham's middle age, Madelyn had a hard time keeping up with her as she made a determined beeline for their house. She only stopped to wait for Madelyn at the front door, decorum requiring she not barge on in.

Jillian glanced up from the couch when they came in. "Where's Mom?" Madelyn said.

"When you got home, she went straight to her room and shut the door. I haven't seen her since."

"Did she tell you what happened?"

"No, but Daniel did. What do we do now?"

Up until that point, Jillian hadn't seen who was standing behind Madelyn. "Look who I have," Madelyn said, moving to the side. "Mrs. Burnham wants to help. Do you think we could talk Mom into letting her?"

Jillian looked from Mrs. Burnham to Madelyn. "Let me go talk to her."

They could hear from the bottom of the stairs Jillian's side of the conversation.

"Mom, could you come out for a minute? ... Please?" She turned and shrugged her shoulders. "She didn't even answer," she mouthed. "Mom, this is Jillian," she said using her full name instead of her nickname, surprising the others with the sternness of her tone. "You're going to have to come out of there sometime, you know. It may as well be now. We need to talk." Even with the little adult Jillian, there was no response.

Just then, Daniel took matters into his own hands. The previous summer, Dad had made a traveling salesman very happy when he paid for fire alarms to be installed in their home. Apparently, a candle held very near one of them sets it off.

The jarring alarm bells spurred them all to scamper out of the house as quickly as possible before even considering it might be Daniel. Much to their surprise, Mom was right behind them. Daniel was last, laughing his heart out.

Madelyn thought Mom would ground him for a year, but she was wrong. Mom focused in on him then turned to take the others in, one by one. Her gaze settled on Mrs. Burnham. "Hello, Dorothy," she finally said. Her calm composure was unsettling.

No one knew what to do next. So, they all stood on the front lawn, pretending to busy themselves with the grass and the sky, feigning annoyance with the fire alarm still blaring inside.

After a minute or two—that felt like ten, the alarm abruptly stopped.

Mom turned to go back inside until Daniel spoke. "Mom, I'm sorry." An apology for a Daniel prank was a rare occurrence, and it stopped her short. He threw his arms around her. "I just had to get you out," he said. "Don't let that witchy teacher make you sad. She was wrong. You're the smartest Mom I have."

She returned the hug. "I'm also the only Mom you have, you know." He just nodded his head, but his face was buried in Mom's chest. His body started to shake. The devious genius was crying.

Mom reached up to wipe a tear from her eye. "Well, Madelyn," she said, "what now?"

They were still standing on the front lawn. Madelyn felt exposed to the eyes of the neighborhood even though it was unlikely anyone was watching. "Let's go inside and talk."

• • •

It wasn't clear whose argument won her over, but every one of them begged Mom to let Mrs. Burnham sit down with her for a few minutes. In the end, it was probably simply a desperate attempt to get them to leave her alone. Her capitulation, however, came with a stipulation. "Fine, but this is it. I won't speak with another teacher after this."

Mom, Mrs. Burnham, and for some reason, Jillian, settled in the kitchen with a few books Mrs. Burnham had scooped up on the way out of her house. Daniel settled on the couch while Madelyn took up pacing. Fifteen minutes into it, she realized Mom had played her. Mom truly believed Mrs. Burnham didn't like her. So, the next logical thought was that she would declare Mom incapable of learning, just as Mrs. Cutler had. That would be the end of it—at least in Mom's mind. Madelyn could only hope Mrs. Burnham was the ally she hoped she was, and that Mom would cooperate enough to let her be so.

Thirty minutes passed and then an hour. Madelyn poked her head into the kitchen, afraid of what she might find. It seems they had been having a grand old time and hadn't even bothered to consider those who were waiting for news. They were all smiling and chatting like old friends. Jillian was the first to notice Madelyn and her confused expression. She waved her in.

"What's going on?" Madelyn said, her brow still knit.

Mom turned to her with shining eyes. "It's not me! I'm not too stupid after all."

While Madelyn was glad to hear that, she was also quite skeptical at the transformation in her mom. Scrutinizing the gathering, she waited for a further explanation.

"We figured something out, your mother and I. She's likely dyslexic. Her mind mixes up b's and d's, words like was and saw. She just processes things differently. The school district should be able to test her, and then they can match her with a teacher who can help," Mrs. Burnham said.

Madelyn turned to Mom for confirmation. She was nodding her head. "Dorothy says I can be taught to read. Once they know the dyslexia exists, they can deal with it and teach me in different ways." She started to cry. "I'm not too stupid, Madelyn. I'm really not too stupid."

She couldn't believe what she was hearing. Madelyn looked around the room at everyone, including Daniel, who had followed her into the kitchen. There was not a dry eye among them.

SATURDAY

The next day they held a celebration picnic in the backyard. Mrs. Burnham was the guest of honor, but they all felt like Mom was the real hero.

As Madelyn was helping Mom carry food outside, she said, "Are you and Mrs. Burnham okay with each other now?"

Mom chuckled. "Yesterday, before you came into the kitchen, we talked about that—even apologized to each other. Then we tried to talk like friends, but we're not there yet. Anytime it got awkward, Jillian said something to smooth things over." She set down the potato salad along with the sliced cucumbers and tomatoes from their garden. "You know, we thought we knew what the other one was like, and now we're having to shed that image, while at the same time replacing it with something more accurate. It will take some time, but we've gotten off to a good start."

"That's good." Just then Madelyn spotted Mrs. Burnham making her way over to the picnic table. She wasn't wearing a wig, but had fixed her own hair up nicely, and she was wearing a cute outfit. She carried something in each hand. "Hi, Mrs. Burnham. You look nice. Do you need some help?"

"Thanks, and yes, why don't you take this watermelon? And why don't you call me Dory? Mrs. Burnham, while it may be respectful, makes me feel like an old lady." She winked when she said it.

"I couldn't call you that. You're my neighbor, you're at least my mom's age ..."

Mrs. Burnham laughed. "I understand. Why not Aunt Dory then?"

"All right, Aunt Dory. I like the sound of that. So, Aunt Dory, what's in your other hand?"

"This is my famous chocolate mahogany cake." She was bright and cheerful, with a bounce in her step none of them had seen before.

"I didn't know you had a famous cake," Mom said.

"Well, I haven't made it in years—no one around to bake it for." She shrugged her shoulders. "It's a secret recipe from my grandmother, so don't even bother to ask for it."

·   ·   ·

After they'd stuffed themselves on dinner, and then further stuffed themselves on cake, they sat on the back patio in lawn chairs, unable or unwilling to move. "Dorothy, that cake was delicious. You may not have made it in years, but it's clear you haven't lost your touch."

They all mumbled in agreement. "Well, Rachel, first off, you can call me Dory. And secondly, when you can read it, I'll hand over the recipe." She smiled at Mom. "That should be pretty soon I would think." Mom just beamed.

"You know, Rachel, I should have thought of dyslexia right off the bat, but I didn't. It's the bedtime stories you memorized that threw me."

"Oh, you know about that?"

"Madelyn told me. Usually, it's hard for someone with dyslexia to memorize."

"It is? Well, you're not wrong. It took me years to memorize them. Roger read those three books to Madelyn from the time she was probably two. I didn't take over for him until she was about five and Daniel was two. It made me feel like more of a mom." Aunt Dory reached over and squeezed Mom's hand.

WEEK SEVEN – SUMMER 1975

MONDAY

Madelyn's alarm woke her bright and early Monday morning. On Saturday, they'd figured out who she needed to call at the school district, even pulling out the phone book and writing down the appropriate numbers. With a plan in place, she couldn't wait to get started.

It had been hard not to spill everything to Dad during their Sunday phone call, but they had all decided to keep it a surprise. An excitement was building with this step forward Mom was taking. It would make the greatest surprise ever if they could just hold onto it. So, if anything, their conversations with Dad tended toward boring and uneventful—their only hope being to downplay everything so nothing seemed important, then nothing would slip out. However, the random stifled giggling from Jillian and Daniel when it was their turns made it clear it was going to be a difficult secret to keep. Madelyn at least had *The Hobbit* to fall back on for conversation ideas. But as soon as Dad hung up, the whoops, hollers, and high fives had been rampant.

Now it was time to get down to work. Madelyn fidgeted through breakfast, waiting for the clock to register 8:00 when the school district office would be open. Right on the dot, she picked up the phone receiver and began to dial.

She was transferred several times before her call landed at the desk of

Mr. Henry Davis, head of something or other she didn't quite hear. "What can I help you with?"

"Well, we think my mom has dyslexia. So, I was wondering how we could get her tested."

He didn't respond at first. Then he said, "Okay, why exactly do you want to have her tested?"

"Because she can't read, but she wants to learn—only the dyslexia is getting in the way. I figured, or we figured, that if we could get the dyslexia diagnosed, then we could get her the right teacher to help her learn to read."

It all seemed pretty straightforward to Madelyn. Only it didn't strike Mr. Davis the same way. "Hmm ... well, that's kind of an unusual request. We have limited resources, and I'm not sure we'll be able to help you."

"Why not? Don't you want people to learn to read?"

"Well, of course we do." He was getting annoyed. "But it's not that simple."

"Why not?"

"Well, because it takes money to do those kinds of things." He was raising his voice, and while Madelyn knew she had a point, she also knew she needed him as an ally.

"So, what do you suggest I do?" She tried to say it gently, but bits of frustration were leaking through. "Is there anyone who knows about dyslexia? Is there someone I can talk to for help?"

"Well, ..." Madelyn was getting tired of that word, but she held her tongue. "You could try talking with the public library. They might know where to direct you." And then without even so much as a goodbye, he hung up the phone.

Madelyn slammed the receiver down in response. Some little old man sitting atop his power heap at the school district office was not going to stop her. She picked up the phone and dialed again.

"Hello, Stewart residence."

"Is Zane there? This is Madelyn."

"Sure. Just a minute."

She found herself twirling her fingers in the phone cord while waiting for him. She may be nervous, but she was even more determined.

"Hi, Madelyn. What's up?"

"I need your help. Would you mind meeting me at the library?"

. . .

When they entered the library, Zane grabbed her hand. It wasn't a romantic gesture—or at least she didn't think so. It was more like an I've-got-your-back kind of gesture. He was now up to date on her mom's reading situation—or lack thereof, and he was just as angry and determined as she was.

Stepping up to the checkout counter, Madelyn said, "I wonder if there's a librarian who I can speak to about illiteracy or dyslexia." The woman on the other side of the desk acted as if she hadn't heard her, but if she just wanted Madelyn to slink away, she was mistaken. Madelyn simply smiled at her and refused to budge an inch.

"Well ..." There was that word again. Madelyn could tell once again it was going to be used to put her off. "I don't know that we do much with that."

Madelyn stood up straight. "Well," she said purposely, "could I just speak with the head librarian?"

The librarian stood up while glaring at her. Madelyn just smiled in return, but she was gripping Zane's hand like a vice at the same time.

"You're doing great," he whispered in her ear, and she relaxed her hold on his hand.

A few minutes later they were seated in the office of Mrs. Laura Larsen. Madelyn was thinking she should have thought twice before marrying someone with that last name, but, then again, there's no accounting for love. "Thank you, Mrs. Larsen. My mother, it appears, is dyslexic. I'm trying to find a way for her to be tested to verify that. Then with that knowledge, I'm hoping she can find the right teacher to help her learn to read."

"Your mother can't read?" She acted appalled.

"No, she can't. I'm sure you can understand that this is a difficult situation for her, to come forward now and admit this, and be willing to accept help. It's not really her fault that she can't read. Besides the supposed dyslexia, there were other extenuating circumstances."

"Oh, what circumstances?"

Madelyn knit her brow and turned, puzzled, to Zane. Did she need to explain to everyone the circumstances of Mom's growing up and convince them of all that she was, what she had done, how intelligent she was? Turning back to Mrs. Larsen, she said, "I'm not –"

Zane cut her off. "I think what she's trying to tell you is that we're wasting time with these details when we should be working on getting her mother the guidance she needs. When someone wants to learn and is willing to put in the effort, even when she knows that effort will be great, then we should jump at the chance. Isn't that right?" Then without pausing for her response, he continued. "Can you test her for dyslexia? That's the first step we need to take."

"Well ..." Zane had to hold Madelyn down. "Well, we don't actually do any testing here. Generally, the school district does that. We're just a small library, and we don't have the resources for that kind of thing."

"Then why did you just waste our time?" Madelyn said. "Can you offer us any help at all?" She was standing by now, glaring down at Mrs. Larsen.

She cowered but gratefully spoke. "There is a woman I know at the high school." Madelyn's immediate thought was, please don't let it be Mrs. Cutler, please not Mrs. Cutler. "Her name is Miss Zimmerman. I know she's arranged for some dyslexia testing before."

"Thank you. Do you know where I might find her?"

"She should be at the high school now. She teaches summer school, I believe."

"Thanks," Madelyn said, even though she was squeezing Zane's hand again.

•   •   •

"Man, do you feel like we're on a scavenger hunt, only we're not able to collect anything along the way?" Zane said to her as they parked their bikes outside the high school.

"Yeah, I do. Why can't this be easy?" He just shrugged his shoulders in response.

When they found Miss Zimmerman's classroom, they poked their heads inside, only to discover she was teaching a group of students. "Did you need something? We'll be finished in 15 minutes."

Fifteen minutes didn't seem to be much time to wait, so they sat down on the floor outside her door.

"Thanks for coming with me, Zane."

"Hey, not a problem."

"I'm a little scared, to be honest. I opened up this door with Mom, and I'm not quite sure what I'll do if I can't help her walk through it."

He reached over and once again held her hand in his. It was warm, and for a moment all thoughts of her mother left. "Just keep at it. You'll figure it out," he said.

"How can you be so calm?"

"Well …" He covered his mouth to cover his laughter. "Sorry, that wasn't nice, was it?" She shook her head. "Madelyn," he turned so he could face her, "it's a journey. None of these people represent the end or the goal, they're just steps along the way."

"More like roadblocks, I'd say."

He laughed. "Probably."

They were quiet for a while after that, silently entwining their fingers. Madelyn glanced around the hallway. Outside her classroom, Miss Zimmerman had various posters of books—some of them she had read, and others she hadn't.

"Zane, do you like to read?" Madelyn whispered the question, almost afraid of the answer. It shouldn't matter, especially with her mom not even able to read, but he was helping on this crusade to make it possible for her to do so. And Madelyn realized she needed to know. If he didn't like to read, then he was just humoring her. But if he really did like to read, then she could trust him, knowing he did want to help her, to help her mom, that they weren't just fools. He didn't answer right away, and Madelyn found herself holding her breath.

He finally responded without actually answering the question. "Did you ever wonder how I got a name like Zane?"

She didn't want to be sidetracked, but his question intrigued her. "I guess not. You're the only Zane I've ever known, but I've known you since I was little, so it just seemed like a normal name to me."

"I've never met another Zane either, but I know of one—Zane Grey. Do you know who that is?"

"No, but it does sound vaguely familiar."

"He's an author. He died a long time ago, I think around the start of World War II. He wrote stories about the American West."

"I didn't know that."

"Yeah. Anyway, my grandpa loved Zane Grey novels, and so my dad read them as a kid too. It was a connection they had. Whenever they might have disagreements about something, they could always repair things by talking about Zane Grey. It's something that kept them close over the years. My dad wanted to name me Zane because of that father-son bond that he wanted to continue, and I guess Mom relented."

"That's cool. Did he tell you all that?"

He laughed out loud. "Of course not. He probably did it without even thinking about it. My mom figured it out and told me. She actually swore me to secrecy because Dad would probably be embarrassed. But, yeah, I think it's cool too."

"So, do you like Zane Grey novels?"

"No," he said, laughing and shaking his head. "I don't. They're just not my thing. Isn't that terrible?"

They were both stifling laughter when Miss Zimmerman's door opened.

•   •   •

"You know, I'd love to help you," she said after they'd explained the situation. "I've never diagnosed an adult before, but the process would be the same as for a child. I just don't have a lot of leeway with the district watching over my shoulder."

Madelyn was about to object when Miss Zimmerman continued, "I'm not saying no. It's just a matter of timing. We're getting geared up for the new school year, and I'm up to my eyeballs in testing that needs to be done at all different levels within the school district. That should continue into the first several weeks of school. I'll get in all kinds of trouble if I deviate from that. However," she flashed them a smile, "once that's done, I'm sure I could sneak her in. It just won't be until late September or October."

It was good news, it really was, Madelyn kept telling herself. "Thanks. It's not what I was hoping for, but it's the first good news all day." They exchanged numbers and agreed to keep in touch. As they left the room, Madelyn thought of one more thing, "Oh, Miss Zimmerman, do you teach freshman English? I'd kind of like to avoid ending up in Mrs. Cutler's class."

"As a matter of fact, I do. I'll take care of it. Zane? How about you?" He nodded his head.

After collecting their bikes, they rode over to the park. Madelyn knew she should go home and report what had happened, but she was still trying to process it. And, besides, she didn't mind in the least spending more time with Zane.

Lying down on the grass, she said, "So, you never actually answered my question earlier. Do you like to read?"

"Yes, I love to read. I may not like the same books as my dad, but with an author for a namesake, I couldn't exactly *not* like to read, could I?"

"Yeah, I guess not." She was smiling in relief. "Have you ever read *The Hobbit?*"

"No, I haven't. Is it good?"

"Yeah, it is. I'm not finished with it yet. My dad and I are reading it together over the summer. He has a copy and I have one. It's ... I suppose it's our version of Zane Grey—only we don't usually fight."

"I'll have to read it when you're done. I mean if I can borrow your copy?"

She rolled onto her side so she could see his face. "As long as you don't dog-ear any pages, I'm fine with that."

He matched her feigned serious stare. "All right. I'm reading *Watership Down* right now. We'll swap. You can hold my book hostage until I return yours—unscathed."

"Okay, it's a deal. Let's shake on it. What's it about, anyway?"

"Rabbits."

"Rabbits? You're kidding, right?"

"No, seriously, it's about rabbits and a journey they make."

"A journey? There seems to be a lot of that these days. You know, *The Hobbit* is about one too."

It wasn't until they had gathered their bikes that Madelyn realized *Where the Wild Things Are* involved a journey as well, even if you could argue about whether Max ever left home.

·   ·   ·

"The car's in the garage. Where did they go?" Madelyn said as the two of them searched an empty house upon their return.

"They're not out back," Zane said, shrugging his shoulders.

"It's not like them to just take off without leaving a note or something."

Before she could say another word, a chorus of voices reached them, coming in through the front door. Aunt Dory, Mom, Jillian, and Daniel spilled inside. They were talking and laughing, only stopping when they saw Madelyn and Zane looking puzzled in front of them.

"You're back. That's great," Mom said.

"Not as great as you might think," Madelyn was quick to say. "You won't believe what we've run up against. After that disastrous phone call this morning, we went to the library, like I told you we were going to, but it didn't stop there –"

"Madelyn, it's okay," Mom said, interrupting.

"No, it's not. You don't understand. The librarians can't or won't help. So, then we ended up back at the high school and waited to talk to –"

"No, Madelyn, I'm telling you it's okay. Just listen to me for a minute."

"What? What are you talking about?"

"I saw how determined you were this morning. I appreciate that more than you know. It also got me thinking. I know having a dyslexia diagnosis will be beneficial in the end, but that doesn't mean we can't get started now."

"Yeah, I guess you're right." Madelyn was nodding her head. "We could –"

"Hold on. We've already figured it out. I've been talking with Dory. She's going to help me. I needed the push from you, Madelyn; I really did. But if I could teach my little brother how to walk and talk, maybe I can learn to read too—with help, of course," she said, nodding in Aunt Dory's direction.

"Wow! That's great, Mom. And thanks, Aunt Dory." She turned to Zane, "I'd like you to meet Aunt Dory. She lives next door. Aunt Dory, this is Zane."

"Nice to meet you," Aunt Dory said.

Zane, on the other hand, was bewildered. "Your aunt lives next door?"

"Sorry," Madelyn said, laughing. "She's our neighbor, Mrs. Burnham, but we've just decided to adopt her into the family." He still wore a confused expression, so she added, "I'll explain it all later." He nodded, willing to accept it for what it was.

"So, you can teach her to read? Even with the dyslexia?" Zane said.

"Yes. The school district might be willing to supply tutors once she's diagnosed, but I can get started right away." Then she winked. "And you know what? I know quite a few retired teachers, and a lot of them would welcome something to fill their time."

"That's what we've been trying to tell you," Mom said. "We've been on the phone all morning. Everything is set up."

Madelyn looked at each of them. They were all nodding in agreement. She turned to Zane. "I guess our work here is done." He smiled in response.

· · ·

When Zane left to go home later, Madelyn walked him out. "Thanks for everything, Zane." He just nodded. "Hey, can I ask you something?"

"Anything," he said.

"You like to read, and your family clearly likes to read, but you didn't judge my mom."

"Is that a question?"

"Yeah, I guess it is."

"Well, it's not like we're out there reading classic literature. What we read and enjoy isn't exactly high-brow."

"So? Still, you didn't ..."

He shrugged his shoulders. "Why would I?"

She gazed deep into Zane's eyes. A few years down the road who knew what might happen between the two of them—maybe something, maybe nothing. But one thing Madelyn knew for sure—she would be forever grateful for those three words.

TUESDAY

Mom came home from her first real tutoring session looking like nothing Madelyn had ever seen before. Her eyes were on fire. Her jaw was set, and if it was possible, Madelyn could have sworn she was taller.

"So, how was it?" Madelyn said.

"Hard. Probably harder than anything I've ever done before." Madelyn's face fell, until Mom continued, "But it's also the most amazing experience. Letters ... well, they're not just random shapes to me anymore. That's all they've ever been. How could you make sense out of a line of shapes, like seeing a circle, followed by a tree, followed by a mountain? And then sometimes the mountain would move in front of the tree." She was shaking her head. "But Dory is teaching me with things I already understand."

"Like what?"

"Well, she pulled out yarn, for example. I use that in my craft projects all the time. So, she had me use pieces of yarn to form the different letters. I used red yarn to write 'red,' and brown yarn to write 'cat,' which is fuzzy and brown like the yarn. She kept saying the words as I wrote them. You know, Madelyn, she even told me that tracing the letters is a good idea. I just laughed and told her I've been doing that for years, but it never helped. She pointed out, rightly so, that I wasn't tracing them so I could learn the words. I was only doing it so I could turn in assignments. I suppose I've already got the skill, now I just need to focus on why I'm doing it."

"That's kind of funny, Mom."

"Yes, somewhat ironic, I know. Madelyn, the letters are more than individual letters. I can see how they're part of something bigger. It's like all the pieces I gather to make an art project. Together they make something interesting or amazing. You look at it, and you don't see the individual parts, only the whole. That's the way words are. I just never understood that before." She was gesturing with her hands, and her voice was animated, even when she added, "It is still hard, so hard, but I'm not afraid of the work—at least not when I can see that it *will* work. We can do this, Madelyn. We can do this."

Madelyn almost couldn't get the words out, "Yes, we can."

FRIDAY

They soon settled into a routine, one that would have taken them to the end of the summer—if things hadn't conspired to change it. The routine was simple enough. Right after breakfast, Mom would go to Aunt Dory's or she would come over to their house to work for a couple hours. Then most afternoons, Mom would spend about an hour reading with a different retired teacher, usually in their homes. She finished both of these exhausted, but she never backed away, and the newfound light in her eyes never dimmed. If she wasn't too tired at night, all the kids would take turns reading bedtime stories with her—something other than what she had memorized.

With all the warm weather they'd been having, they were reaping a bountiful harvest from their garden. As often as Madelyn could, she'd take a basket of fresh vegetables over to Aunt Dory's house to share.

"Thank you, Madelyn," she'd always say, but she was thanking Madelyn for more than the vegetables. Helping Mom to read was clearly the highlight of her day. Becoming an honorary member of their family didn't hurt either.

Despite all the good news—and Mom's determined efforts were definitely good news—it had not escaped Madelyn's notice that even though Mom said she wanted to read her father's letter, she'd never mentioned it again. With that gnawing at her, the second letter riding around in Madelyn's back pocket ate at her even more.

Working outside on the yard, or at least pretending to, became an escape. She was proud of her mom, but at the same time, she was uncomfortable with the closely-guarded secrets, fearing they would come between them.

Half-heartedly, Madelyn dug up a few dandelions in the side yard. If she were determined, the lawn would be green with no yellow polka dots by the time Dad returned. That was the only motivational thought she could come up with.

"Hey, how's it going? Can you use some help?" Zane had appeared out of nowhere, moving in close enough to block the sun.

Madelyn's day was immediately better. "Hey, yourself. I'm not sure you want to dig up dandelions, but be my guest."

"All right," Zane said, sitting on the ground beside her, without making any real overtures toward the dandelions.

Madelyn had been kneeling over her work but sat back when he joined her. She was certain he could hear the slight crinkly sound of paper from her back pocket as she did so, but his face betrayed nothing. She sighed. "Zane, read this," she said, pulling the now opened letter from its hiding place.

"What is it?"

"It's from my grandpa to my mom." He raised his eyes but didn't ask the obvious question, much to her relief. He spread it out on the grass in front of them, silently reading the words, while she reread them for the tenth time.

Dear Rachel,

I hope you're doing well. I know you haven't responded to the other letter I wrote, but I thought I would reach out to you one more time. If what I asked is too much, then please don't worry about it. But if not, I could use your help. Would you please come visit?

I don't blame you for not coming to see me. I completely understand. But I hope you will reconsider and that I might see you soon. Please watch over Tommy for me.

Love,
Pop

"What is it?" Zane said.

"I'm not sure." She started picking at the grass around her. Afraid to meet his eyes, she spoke to the dirt instead. "He's in prison. I don't know why, but that's where this letter came from. It fits too. He hasn't been around. We haven't seen him for quite a while, and Mom gets evasive if I ask where he is."

Zane was silent, but when she dared look up to see his expression, it was sad and full of concern, not repulsion, like she had feared. "I found the letter in the mailbox last week. I haven't given it to my mom yet. There was another letter from him at the beginning of the summer, only I didn't realize it at the time. But now ... well, his home was broken into, and it was clear he wasn't living there. I tried to ask about it, but I couldn't get a straight answer. This letter, or at least the postmark, have given me more information than I had before."

"Why did you open it? It doesn't say much."

She let out a sigh. "Yeah, I know. I wasn't going to open it, but everything seems to be going so well. Everyone's so happy about Mom—and I am too—but there's still something wrong, something missing. And no one else seems to care or notice. I thought maybe if I opened it, I'd find some answers. But all I have is more questions."

"Well, then we'll just have to find the answers on our own then."

It took Madelyn a minute to register that he had used the plural form— that he was offering to find the answers with her. She wrinkled her brow. "Why are you so nice to me? My life is nothing but a mess, and you keep helping me with it. Why?"

He shrugged his shoulders. "I guess it's nice to be needed, to feel like what you do might make a difference." He got a wicked twinkle in his eye. "And besides, I like hanging out with Daniel and Jillian."

She punched him in the ribs. Then they got down to the business of how they could go about learning the truth.

1974

When the phone rang, Rachel picked it up. It was certainly a phone call she'd never expected to receive. It was late at night, so Roger and Rachel quickly discussed what should be done. Fortunately, the driving directions weren't complicated. It was a straight shot once she made it to the freeway. So, Rachel figured she could handle it alone.

"I'll get the kids off to school in the morning if you're not back," Roger said. "Do you want me to stay home from work tomorrow?"

"I don't know. I don't really understand what's going on yet. If there are any papers, I'll bring them back with me for you to go over, but I can't imagine anything has actually been drawn up yet—it's too early." She shook her head, "This just can't be real. It has to be a mistake."

"Well, go talk to your pop. I'm sure he can explain. You're right. It's probably all a simple mistake."

●   ●   ●

It took her over an hour to get there, and by the time she arrived, Rachel was wishing Roger could have come with her. It had started to snow almost as soon as she left the house, and while she was comfortable driving in snow, it didn't help her nerves any. Maybe they should have waited until morning when the kids were at school, then they could have come together. The driving itself was straight-forward enough, but following the directions once she walked into the building threw her for a loop. In answer to her questions, the receptionist just pointed to a sign without looking up. Rachel wasn't sure what to do, and the strain of the whole thing brought tears to her eyes.

A kindly-looking man was filling out some paperwork nearby. He noticed her tears and walked up to her. "Can I help you?"

She let a sob escape. "I'm so sorry. I just want to see my father, but I don't even know what to do."

"Is he inside?"

"Yes. I just got a phone call from him."

"This is new to you, isn't it?" When she nodded, he smiled sympathetically. "I'll walk you through it."

True to his word, he did exactly that—helping her fill out a visitation form and even physically walking her into the room where she would be able to talk with her father face to face. Then he quickly retreated so she could have her privacy.

After an interminable wait, her father was finally brought to her. His head was down, his hair unkempt, and he shuffled reluctantly to the table where Rachel waited. While their visit was lengthy, their conversation was short. Her father kept repeating the same thing. "I just don't remember. I'm so sorry, Rachel."

"But what happened, Pop?"

"I went out drinking with my friend George. I thought it was just an ordinary night, but ... I just don't remember. I was drunk. I'm so sorry, Rachel. I just can't believe what happened." He let out a sound of anguish and pain like Rachel had never heard before as he buried his head in his hands.

She reached over and patted his arm. "It will be all right. We'll figure this out. There has to be a different explanation. You're not a violent man," and then she added, "even when you're drunk."

His head came up at that, and he looked her in the eye. "I don't know. I wouldn't have thought so, but I've been thinking about the war lately. It wasn't good to be at war. I don't know what I'm capable of anymore," and then he burst into sobs. "Your mother would be so disappointed in me. She never liked me drinking, and since she's been gone, that's all I've really known how to do. I'm so sorry. I'm so sorry."

By the time Rachel returned home, she was shaking all over. Roger greeted her at the door of their home, but one look at her and he called into work saying he wouldn't be in until the next day.

They decided early on—Roger, Rachel, and her father—that it was too much for the kids and especially Tommy to understand. Rachel was certain, anyway, that it would all blow over, that nothing would really come of it.

Time turned out to prove Rachel wrong.

WEEK EIGHT – SUMMER 1975

MONDAY

When Aunt Dory showed up Monday morning to tutor Mom, Madelyn darted past the two of them as they were hunched over the kitchen table. "I'm meeting Zane for a bike ride if that's all right. I'll be back soon."

Mom was distracted trying to decipher the words in front of her, but she nodded her head all the same. It was the response Madelyn was hoping for, and she hurried out the door before Mom could change her mind.

Zane was waiting at the end of the driveway. "How did it go?"

"Fine. I'm not completely sure she heard me, but that's okay too."

"I called the newspaper this morning. We can search through their archives as much as we want."

"Great," Madelyn said. Then they rode in silence to the center of town.

The newspaper office was glad to help them, although it took a little longer than they had thought it would. "What dates did you want to see?" the receptionist, a Miss Harriet Webster, asked.

Madelyn looked at Zane, unsure how to answer. "Just a minute. We'll be right back," he said as he led her to one of the nearby seats. "I know you don't know what happened, but do you have any idea when whatever it is might have happened?"

"Well, Mom told me that we wouldn't be seeing Grandpa for a while right around my birthday at the end of March, but we hadn't seen him much anyway, now that I think about it. I know we saw him at Christmas time, but something was off with him. I figured it was because of Grandma dying. She was killed in a car accident in September." Laying out the timing gave Madelyn pause. "But, come to think of it, after she died, he was sad. At Christmas, it's more like he was nervous."

"Okay. So, I'm guessing it happened before Christmas. Was there a time when your mom seemed to get more stressed than normal?"

"The first few months after Grandma died were really hard on her. I can't think of anything that stands out." Then a light went on. "Wait a minute! I remember getting up one morning for school, and she was gone, but Dad was home. He said that Grandpa wasn't doing well and that Mom was off helping him. But when I got home from school that day, I asked Mom if Grandpa was still sick, and she stared at me like I was crazy. Then she finally said something like, 'I don't know.' I thought it was strange at the time, but then I forgot about it."

"Great. Do you know when that was?"

"Well, it was a Monday. I know that because I remember it being the start of a school week. It was cold and snowy that morning, and I had to help Dad pull out the snow boots. He didn't know where they were."

"You were in the winter play at school. Did you have play practice after school?"

Madelyn tried to mentally retrace her steps, envisioning asking Mom about Grandpa's illness and attempting to conjure the events that just proceeded it. "Yes, I did, but we were just starting to read through the script, so it must have been early in November. I remember wanting to tell Mom about the script and my part, but then I saw her face—she looked awful. That's what reminded me to ask about Grandpa."

They jumped back up to Miss Webster's desk and asked her for a calendar. Before long, they'd come up with two possibilities: November 4th or 11th. "Madelyn, do you think it was right before the election or after?"

"I hadn't even thought about that. I think the election was already over because my parents talked a lot about it right around when it happened, and then they just didn't anymore. So, let's try November 11th."

Miss Webster showed them to a room where they could view microfilm copies of the newspaper from November 1974. In Friday's edition on

November 15th, Zane found the mention of Madelyn's grandfather. It was a small note in the police blotter. Zane read it out loud.

The man police arrested early Sunday morning has been identified as William Knight, 57. The victim has also been identified. He is one George Holliwell, 66. Both men are of Freeborne, Colorado.

"What does it mean victim?" Madelyn was shaking. This was worse than she had thought.

"I don't know. There must be an earlier article that explains what happened. Let's work backwards in the paper, looking for a crime but without the names." He turned back to the microfilm, but Madelyn was staring straight ahead, horrified.

"I know that name."

Zane startled at her icy tone. "George Holliwell? Who is he?"

"He was my grandpa's neighbor. We talked to Mrs. Holliwell after Grandpa's house got broken into. She seemed really sad, only I didn't know why. But you know what? Mr. Holliwell wasn't there when we were talking to her, even though he's retired." Madelyn looked down at her hands, her voice barely a whisper. "Zane, he wasn't there because he's dead. My grandpa killed his friend. He's in prison for murdering his best friend."

Zane hesitated. "Well, that might be what victim means, but maybe he just robbed him or beat him up or something." He shrugged his shoulders, but neither of them was buying the alternative explanation.

They returned with vigor to their search, now knowing the incident had happened early Sunday morning. Madelyn found the article in Tuesday's paper.

Local man arrested on manslaughter charges

In the early hours of Sunday, November 10th, police responded to reports of a fight in the alleyway behind the Last Call bar and grill. Two men, who have not yet been identified, were found in the alley. A male in his 60s was pronounced dead at the scene. Another male, allegedly covered in blood, was taken into custody.

According to a police spokesman, witnesses at the scene say the two men got into an argument after walking out of the bar. Things escalated quickly, and before they could call the authorities, witnesses say the one man pulled out a knife and stabbed the other man until he stopped moving. When police found them, the alleged perpetrator was passed out drunk, but the knife was nearby with his bloody fingerprints all over it. Sources close to the investigation say he will be charged with involuntary manslaughter later today.

"Wow! No wonder Mom didn't want to tell me anything." For once, Zane didn't have anything to say. He just reached over and grabbed Madelyn's hand and held it tight.

TUESDAY

Madelyn was up early the next morning. She had a phone call to make. When Delia honked her horn soon afterward, Madelyn raced outside. Zane had suggested telling Delia what was going on. It's always nice to have an ally, but more importantly, they needed someone who could drive. Madelyn agreed—as long as she didn't have to be the one to tell Delia about her grandpa.

"How are you?" Delia said when Madelyn got in the car.

"Well, obviously I've been better. Mom's good, though. She was actually reading to Jilly last night. It was so cute. Oh! Did you know my mom can't read? Or at least couldn't?" She was surprised how little the illiteracy bothered her now.

"Um, well. Zane told me ... along with the other stuff. I hope that's okay."

"Yeah, it's okay. I'm glad you know. Anyway, she's so excited about starting to read, even though it's hard work. I guess that's why she didn't notice that, you know ...," Madelyn shrugged her shoulders, "that I'm not really talking to her."

"Because of your grandpa," Delia said. It was a statement more than a question. "Are you mad at her?"

"No, not really. I want to be, but I understand why she didn't tell me. You know, in some ways I wish I never knew."

"You'd have found out eventually. It couldn't have stayed a secret forever," Zane said.

"Yeah, you're right. It's strange because now that I do know, I want to know everything—even if it's ugly."

The car grew silent until Delia turned on the radio. Music carried them to Grandpa's neighborhood where his home lay empty. Delia drove past his house and turned into the Holliwell's driveway next door.

"Are you ready for this?" Zane said.

She shrugged her shoulders. He reached for her hand and held it until they stepped onto the doorstep.

"Hello, come on in," Mrs. Holliwell said when she answered the door.

The three teenagers nodded in greeting and followed her to the living room.

"I'll admit I was surprised by your phone call," Mrs. Holliwell said. "What can I do for you?"

All eyes fell on Madelyn. "I'm so sorry your husband's gone ... and that it's because of my grandpa.

She nodded an acknowledgment. "I lost my husband and a good neighbor at the same time. I've honestly tried to be angry at William, your grandfather, but I just haven't been able to muster enough steam to do it. He was always such a good friend to George."

All they could do was nod their agreement. "I'm not very good at this," Madelyn said. "Maybe if I were older, I'd know what to say. Sorry just doesn't seem like enough."

"Age, I'm afraid, doesn't help, Madelyn. You're braver than most by just being here, and saying sorry is so much better than saying nothing. Few people know what to say, so they avoid talking to me at all. They stay away. I can tell you, that does no good."

"If you don't want to talk about it, I understand. But, if it's all right, I want to know what happened. I want to know why my grandpa would do such a thing. You probably don't have any good reason to help us, but I'm trying to find some answers."

"About that night?"

"Yes, and before that or after that. I'm sorry to bring this up and make you relive it, and if you'd like us to leave, we will." When she didn't respond, Madelyn added, "But, there's got to be more to the story—even just something so I can understand why."

"I'm afraid I'm not going to be much help because I don't understand it myself, and believe me, I've tried. One minute William had invited George to go out for a drink, and the next I'm getting a knock on the door from a very nervous policeman. It didn't seem real. It couldn't be—yet it was.

"I told you I'm not angry at your grandfather, but the whole thing isn't easy. I miss my George." She was fighting back the tears. They all sat quietly, giving her time to collect her thoughts, time to decide what she wanted to say and what she didn't. When the words did come, they were almost lost in the telling—coming out so softly, being swallowed up in the memories and echoes of her lonely home. "I want to understand why too. It keeps me up at night, but I've never told anyone that part before."

Madelyn moved over to sit on the couch beside Mrs. Holliwell and wrapped her arms around the widow. In return, she reached out and patted Madelyn's leg as she began to tell her story.

"I've thought about this long and hard—wondering when or how things changed between them. And, to be honest, I never noticed anything different about the two of them. They were simply friends. They shared everything across the side fence—hedge clippers, cigarettes, gardening advice. If anything, they were talking more, being even friendlier. They'd had several rather animated conversations shortly before that night."

"Animated? Like they were angry?" Madelyn said.

"No. Animated, like they were talking about something interesting. But that's the way they were. They could get excited over the silliest thing, like a new garden hose or college football."

She lowered her voice like she was about to tell them a secret. "The only thing that stands out happened about a week before. William invited George over to his house. He wanted to show him something. That was unusual. They were outside types. When the weather turned bad, they may not see each other for weeks at a time because they weren't outside themselves. It's just the way it was."

"Yeah, my dad has a neighbor like that," Delia said.

"That's how men are," Mrs. Holliwell said. "It's the yard, the garden, the grill, the mailbox full of bills—they need a reason to talk, an excuse, and those excuses typically happen when they cross paths out of doors. It's not like that with women. We may chat over the garden fence, but we're just as comfortable visiting while cooking a pot of stew or mending a shirt. Or we'll call on the phone just to talk—about something in particular or about nothing at all. Talking itself is the excuse, any activity going on at the same time is completely irrelevant."

Delia laughed. "You're right. My mom is just like that with her sister and a friend of hers down the street." Zane was rolling his eyes while also nodding his agreement.

The comment struck Madelyn very differently. They were here to talk about Grandpa, but it hit home that her mom didn't interact with other women that way. It's what Mrs. Burnham, or Aunt Dory, had mentioned. Her mom had become guarded, too afraid someone would learn she couldn't read. Until that moment, Madelyn hadn't realized what courage it must have taken on her mother's part to march over and enlist Mrs. Burnham's help. Even the other retired teachers, other women, were tutoring her as if they were friends. It was new territory for Mom—a place she knew women went, only not women like her. Madelyn couldn't help but feel a hint of pride in her mother.

Delia's voice brought Madelyn's focus back to the task at hand. "So, what did he show your husband?"

"I have no idea. George never told me. I didn't ask, but the more I think about it, he didn't actually give me the chance. He kept bringing different things up in conversation until I forgot to ask. I'm pretty sure he didn't want to talk about it." The memories started to shine in her eyes, and she turned away for a moment but reached over to pat Madelyn's leg again.

"That night was supposed to be a celebration, you know," she said when she'd collected herself. "William came over to invite George for drinks, like I told you before. William was in a great mood. For what it's worth, I think he said something like, 'Everything's getting worked out.' " She shook her head. "I'm sorry, but that's all I know. I wish it were more, but I've gone memory shopping in this old head of mine, and those are the only packages I've been able to purchase."

"But then what were they arguing about outside the bar?" Madelyn said without thinking.

"That's the thing. They never argued. I was at the trial too. The witnesses both said William and George were arguing, but they couldn't say about what. I can't imagine what it could have been. I guess drunk men do things we may never understand." She hadn't meant the comment to hurt, but it did all the same. "I'm sorry. I ...," she quickly added.

"No, it's okay," Madelyn said, "the truth isn't always pretty."

Mrs. Holliwell nodded. "I hope you find more answers. We could all use them. I only wish I could help you more."

"It's enough," Madelyn said. "It will be enough." She wasn't sure it actually was, but it was clearly all Mrs. Holliwell had to offer. She just didn't know where they were going to find the rest.

On the drive back home, Madelyn said, "If they were such good buddies going drinking, I'm with Mrs. Holliwell, what were they arguing about? And for that matter, why did my grandpa have a knife?"

"Good question," Zane said.

WEDNESDAY

There had been no new plan formulated after their visit to Mrs. Holliwell. Instead, they parted with even more questions than before, any kind of answers being elusive.

Just as Madelyn was clearing her breakfast dishes the next day, the phone rang. It was Zane. Madelyn extended the long phone cord into the living room, away from the kitchen windows, and out of earshot of her family relaxing on the back porch.

"What should we do now?" Madelyn said.

"I don't know."

"I know this may not sound right, but after talking to Mrs. Holliwell, I feel like we're getting closer," Madelyn said.

"Closer to the truth? I don't know. All it seems like to me is we're collecting more questions. Do you think your grandpa would tell us what he showed George Holliwell?"

"I doubt it. George didn't even tell his wife. He was keeping the secret safe, for sure. That's not something my grandpa's going to talk about easily."

"You're probably right."

"I mean, it might be possible. But I'm going to have to tell my mom what I know first. After that maybe we can –" Madelyn stopped abruptly. She'd heard the back door open and close. "Hey, I've got to go. Someone's coming. I want to keep this a secret until I figure out the right way to bring it up."

"All right. I'll talk to you later."

What Madelyn didn't know was that someone was listening in on her side of the conversation.

•   •   •

Madelyn ran into her mom in the kitchen as she was hanging up the phone. "Hey, Madelyn, Dory is busy today. How about I help you with some dandelions."

"Thanks, Mom. That would be great. I've sort of been neglecting them."

"Well, we've been a little preoccupied," Mom said with a smile, "thanks to you."

The comment made Madelyn worry Mom was onto her and her detective work, but then she realized Mom was just giving her credit for the reading efforts. "No problem," she replied.

They were soon outside, both of them pretending they could actually get rid of the remaining dandelions in the lawn by working as hard as they could on them. Madelyn didn't know if their efforts were valiant or futile.

Mom was a real trooper through it all, but she got tired out in the sun, even after only an hour. Stopping for a breather, she wiped the sweat off her brow, leaving a large smudge of dirt behind. "You know, Madelyn, I think I'd like to tell your dad about my reading."

"Really? Now? I thought you were going to wait for him to come home. It's not that far away."

"I know, but after all this time, I think he'd like to know. And to be honest, I'm tired of hiding things from people. I'm not sure I'm ready to tell the whole world that I've been illiterate most of my life, but I like the idea of telling people when it's appropriate. It feels like I'm taking back my life—I'm the one in control now."

Madelyn found it slightly ironic that Mom was still hiding everything about Grandpa from her, but she also understood it was done out of kindness, in an effort to spare her. "I like that, Mom. Then tell him."

"I will." Then satisfied that her break should be over, Mom returned to the task at hand, digging up another dandelion. They were too hot to talk much after that.

Madelyn did notice one thing about their conversation, however. Even though Mom wanted to come clean with Dad, she didn't mention telling him about their dandelion crusade. It took the rest of their time outside for her to figure out why. Reading was important. Mom was doing something Dad had hoped she would do for longer than they'd been married. Finally tackling that would be a sign to him that she could do it, she could succeed.

But the dandelions were something he didn't expect. They were a project Mom chose, a symbol, to him and to her, that she could not only succeed, but she could choose on her own how to define that success. She would always need him, just as he needed her, but he didn't have to carry all the weight. She could be an equal partner.

"I'm proud of you, Mom," Madelyn said as they were putting away their weeding supplies.

The words took her by surprise. "Well, thanks, Madelyn. Because of the reading?"

"Well, that, and just everything." Mom was smiling, but her head was cocked to the side, clearly not understanding the sudden adoration. Madelyn motioned to the yard. "Trying to be Dad and Mom, showing Dad what you can do."

Mom blushed and glanced down at her feet. "I made some goals at the beginning of the summer, and I have to admit most of those have flown the coop by now. But I can't seem to let go of this one. Dandelions have become my nemesis. I figure if I can conquer them, then I can conquer anything."

She was standing tall and strong, almost regal, except for one thing. "You're probably right, Mom, but you might want to wash your forehead first." Mom reached up to wipe her forehead but only succeeded in smearing the dirt that was there even more.

Madelyn couldn't help herself and burst out laughing. Mom bent over next to the car to look at herself in the side mirror. All she could do was join in.

•　　•　　•

Madelyn had been trying to find a good time all day to call Zane. She was hoping he had some new ideas because she was fresh out. Finally, as evening fell, she made her way to Dad's study. The others were reading in the living room, and with the study door closed, Madelyn thought she would have the privacy she needed.

"Stewart's," Zane answered, his voice bringing an involuntary twinkle to her eyes.

"Hi, Zane. It's Madelyn. I finally got a chance to call you back." She was met with silence. "Is there something wrong?" Again, nothing—no response, but also no noise of any kind, no background sounds. "Hello? Hello?" She clicked down the receiver. When she let up, she should have heard a dial tone, but there was nothing.

"Mom," Madelyn called as she walked down the hall to the living room, "what's up with the phone? I was making a call, and it just went dead. There's no dial tone or anything."

Mom looked up from her book. "That's odd."

"Shh. What's that?" Daniel whispered. Footsteps could be heard coming up the front steps.

An unseen gathering storm was closing in upon them. Madelyn watched as if in slow motion as Mom swiftly rose from the couch scooping up Jillian and Daniel as she did so, one in each arm, alarm spreading across her face.

Quick as a mother hen, Mom herded them all to the back door off the kitchen. They were stumbling over each other when Jillian abruptly stopped in front of them. She was holding out her finger, pointing at the back door. The handle was slowly turning.

In a split second, like a wave changing direction, Mom hustled everyone into Dad's study, shutting the door behind them just as they heard an outside door creak open.

"Hurry, hurry, out the window," she whispered.

Daniel had the window open and lifted the screen out in no time. He helped Jillian out then quickly followed. "Run to Aunt Dory's house," Mom ordered.

As Madelyn was about to step out, two voices came clearly from the hall. "You really screwed up the first time, you know. They weren't home. You could have ransacked the place like I did the old man's. Then we wouldn't have had to come back."

"Yeah, but that might have tipped them off. They don't actually know anything yet."

"Not yet. But you heard them, they're getting closer. They're suspicious. It's only a matter of time."

"Well, see, me coming back to plant that bug was a good thing, after all. That's better than having trashed the joint. It gave us information."

There was a sound of disgust. "Information? Our boss isn't paying us for information. We have to find it before they figure anything out. So, start looking."

Madelyn and her mom didn't need any further encouragement to hustle out the window. They hit the ground outside one right after the other. A small sound drew their attention to the dark yard in front of them. They could just make out the figure of Jillian sprawled on the ground where she must have tripped. But a moment later, they saw what must have been Daniel picking her up and running next door.

Just as they were about to flee, through the window came the sound of a door opening, startling them. "You're right, they were here. See, they took the screen off and climbed out the window." Whoever it was, was right on their heels. Mom grabbed Madelyn's hand and they ran and dove behind a bush at the edge of their yard, afraid to cover the open ground to Aunt Dory's house.

They lay still and breathless, watching as the men climbed out the same window. Portions of words reached them on the night breeze. "... go after them ... the boss ... force him to talk ... look around." All other words were lost to them. Thankfully, the men shifted directions, moving back toward the house.

"Do you think they know where we are?" Madelyn whispered. Mom didn't answer, but it didn't matter. Neither of them could take their eyes off the flashlight beams, still so close they could almost feel their heat, bouncing up and down with the men's steps and swinging from side to side, searching, searching for something—only they had no idea what.

"What was that all about?" Mom said.

Madelyn didn't respond, but she was beginning to know exactly *who* it was about, even if she didn't *what* yet.

• • •

When Mom and Madelyn finally made it safely to Aunt Dory's, they discovered she'd already called the police. However, by the time the police arrived, even with lights and sirens, the invaders were long gone.

Madelyn and Mom only entered their house, what no longer felt like a home, with the officers who responded. Things were in disarray, but less so than at Grandpa's. It was clear they knew time was limited. As near as Madelyn could tell, nothing had been taken, even though much had been disturbed.

"Do you know what they might have been looking for, Ma'am?"

"No. That's the problem. We have no idea. Although, we're pretty certain now that at least one of them has been here before."

"Oh, and when was that?"

"Last month. We dismissed it at the time, but I guess we shouldn't have. It was late at night, and my daughter and I were still up. We heard the front door open, and I'm fairly certain we heard a man clear his throat." The police officer raised his eyebrows, but it wasn't clear if it was because he found the information interesting or didn't believe it. Madelyn nodded her head in agreement with Mom's words.

"And then what happened?"

"We think he ran out, but if what we heard him say last night was true, he was just here to plant a bug."

"He planted a listening device in your house?" He was clearly incredulous.

"Well, yes, officer. That's what we overheard them talking about. In fact, they also mentioned that he'd been here before then too."

With realization dawning, Madelyn said, "It must have been the day we came back from the store, and the front door was unlocked. Remember that, Mom? I'd forgotten about it, but it makes sense now. The house was kind of messy too, but I just figured it was us, you know." She shrugged her shoulders.

The officer's partner came up behind him, having overheard the conversation. It was two on two—two disbelieving officers and two who knew they sounded crazy but weren't. "Why don't we look around to see if there is a bug? It would have to be here in the living room because he didn't go anywhere else in the house that night," Mom said.

"Plus, the men talked about overhearing us. It had to have been things we said sometime before they showed up, things we said in this very room," Madelyn added, realizing at that moment that her short conversation with Zane that morning must have been the trigger. Then she had another thought. Whispering, she said, "If the bug's still here, won't they be hearing everything we're saying right now? Will that make things worse?" The officers ignored her comment, but Mom shrugged her shoulders then put an arm around Madelyn.

Begrudgingly, the officers helped search. On the bottom of an end table, they didn't find a bug, but they did find a dangling piece of tape. Mom and Madelyn felt vindicated, even if the officers weren't entirely convinced. They did soften a little, apparently at least entertaining the possibility of a bug. "Do you have somewhere else to stay until this blows over?"

"Yes, they do." It was Aunt Dory, watching from the doorway. "I just came over to suggest you gather what you might need for the four of you. I've already set up beds and Jillian and Daniel are playing checkers and eating ice cream. I want to get right back to them, unless you need help carrying anything."

Mom went to her and gave her a hug. "You're an angel. We'll be over soon. And I'm sure we can manage."

There wasn't much more the police could do that night. Before they left, one of the officers showed them where the phone line had been cut— right outside the back door. Chills went through Madelyn as she thought of how close the two men had been and how fortunate they were not to have come face to face with them.

"Thanks for everything, Officer," Mom said.

"No problem, Ma'am. Put a call into the phone company first thing in the morning. I don't know how long it will take, but they can repair the damage. If they have any questions, they can contact us. We'll assure them this was not your fault."

Madelyn bristled, wondering how it could possibly have been their fault, but Mom caught her eye and smiled. She was right. The officer was just trying to help. It wasn't meant as an insult.

When the police finally pulled away, Madelyn helped Mom gather the things they might need. "How come you're so calm?" Madelyn said.

"Calm?" Mom let out a short laugh. "My insides are jelly. I've never been so scared in my life."

"Really? That makes me feel better. I can't seem to stop shaking."

Mom grabbed Madelyn's hands in her own. "If those two had done anything to one of my children ... well, they would just wish they were dead by the time I got through with them."

"Wow. Thanks, Mom." They embraced, holding each other for a long time, long enough for the shaking to subside.

They worked silently after that—rounding up clothes and toothbrushes, carrying them next door, climbing into the sofa bed Aunt Dory had fixed up, and all without even so much as a glance at the clock. Exhaustion overcame the last bits of residual agitation from the evening, and they slept. But not before they spoke the final words of the day.

"I love you, Mom."

"I love you, Madelyn."

They were just a few simple words, but they followed an evening that was anything but simple. And that evening had come on the heels of a complicated summer. It was a turning point, a beginning. The feeling of it was palpable and beyond explanation. It was the moment when Madelyn's story and Mom's became one.

ParT 3

Madelyn couldn't remember the first dandelion she'd ever seen. It's not like witnessing the eruption of a geyser or seeing the ocean for the first time. Those things are rare, and dandelions—well, they're certainly not. But she did remember wondering how they changed over time. She never could capture that moment when yellow became white, when bloom became seed. It just happened They were one or the other, but never something in between—or so it seemed.

Maybe if she'd paid more attention, she would have seen the closed-up blossom as a portent of things to come—closed before opening into bright yellow sunshine and closed again before displaying its lifeblood of seeds. If you looked for the signs, they were there, unlike life with its absence of road signs along the way warning of what's ahead. But then again, sometimes the signs were there all along.

THURSDAY

The next morning dawned far too bright and early. Everyone was happy to hunker down at Aunt Dory's, too shaken to want to leave its safety. Jillian was acting like a skittish cat, ready to bolt at the slightest sound. Daniel was trying to act tough, but all attempts at practical jokes had ceased, and he was particularly kind to Aunt Dory. It appeared he was trying to crawl under her protective wing as much as the rest of them.

Mom was the surprising one. Finding her reading voice had done something to her. The more challenging life got, the more she stood up to it—something she never would have done even two months before. And having men threaten the safety of her children didn't intimidate her, it motivated her. A simmering anger ran through her veins, but it was coupled with a desire and will to act—and no one better tell her she couldn't.

As soon as Madelyn saw her at the breakfast table, she knew it was time, time to talk to Mom about Grandpa. Everything tied back to him. She waited until Jillian and Daniel had wandered off to find a game to play then she opened her mouth to speak.

Mom beat her to it. "Madelyn, I've been thinking this morning. You've shown yourself to be more of an adult than a lot of adults I know. If you'd like to know everything about your grandfather, I'll tell you. But I'll warn you, it's not pretty."

Madelyn was surprised but pleased. "It's all right. I already know. Or at least I know some of it."

"You do? How do you know?"

"He sent a letter. Well, I mean he sent *you* a letter." Madelyn pulled the crumpled letter from the back pocket of her jeans. "I figured out that he's in prison from the postmark. I'm sorry, I read the letter."

"Wow. Okay. What did it say?"

"Not much. But he does mention he needs your help with something, only he doesn't say what."

Mom was lost in thought. "I got a letter from him at the beginning of the summer. I would have had Roger read it to me, but it came after he'd left. It's the one I told you about, that I wanted to be able to read."

"I remember. How'd you know it was from him? It didn't have a return address or even a name. Oh, and for that matter, you couldn't read then anyway."

Mom chuckled. "I may not have been able to read, but I did learn a thing or two along the way. You have to be pretty clever to avoid detection as long as I did." There was a twinkle in her eye. "I've practiced my dad's handwriting so much I could recognize it blindfolded."

"Okay, maybe I didn't give you enough credit."

Mom could have rubbed it in more, but she didn't. "Anyway, initially I put the letter aside, figuring I'd wait 'til your dad got home. But the thought of reading it on my own was pretty appealing. I've just been waiting until I was certain I could read all the words. I'd assumed it was Pop saying he was sorry and that he loved me."

"Well, it wasn't," Madelyn said.

"What? You read it?"

"No, I didn't. It's just the letter I did read talked about something he'd already asked you to do, something from a previous letter. That's how I know."

"Well, that's interesting." Mom thought for a minute then shook her head as if to clear it. "We'll have to figure out what it all means. I'll get the letter from the house so we can read it. But, I'm afraid, what you know is just the half of it, Madelyn. He's in prison for-"

"I know. For murdering his friend George. Zane and I ... well, we went and looked it up in the newspaper."

"Oh," was all Mom had to say.

"Are you mad?"

"Well, no, just surprised. Was the newspaper ... well, were they kind? I didn't read it—obviously, and your dad never told me."

"Well, they weren't mean. They just stated the facts."

Mom breathed a sigh of relief. "You've been busy."

Madelyn winced. "And that's not all. We—Zane, Delia, and I—went and talked to Mrs. Holliwell, George's widow, a couple days ago. I was talking to Zane about it on the phone yesterday. I think that's why those men came and broke into the house. They heard what we were talking about. It's the only thing that makes sense." Mom was nodding, understanding dawning. "And at the same time, it doesn't make any sense at all. What did they want? What were they looking for?"

"That's the question, isn't it?" Mom's eyes had hardened, turning smoky gray. It wasn't an angry look, rather a determined one, with a brooding warning for anyone who got in her way. "So, Zane and Delia know? About your grandpa?"

Madelyn nodded, worried she was in trouble. She shouldn't have been.

"Good. We'll need all the help we can get. Do you think they can come over? I think it's time we had a conference and got to the bottom of what's going on."

Relieved, Madelyn said, "I'll call them right now."

Zane answered the phone on the second ring. "Stewart's"

"Hi, Zane. I-"

"Hey, Madelyn. Are you okay? I tried to call you back last night after we got cut off, but the phone wouldn't even ring. What happened?"

She tried to quiet the panic that threatened to rise with the memories of last night. "Actually, a lot happened." Just as she finished telling Zane about the night before, Mom burst into the kitchen where she was on the phone.

"Hold on, Madelyn. Can they come over this afternoon instead of now? We need to visit Tommy today. I forgot all about it. It's his Thursday. He'd never understand if we didn't show up."

"You're right," Madelyn said, realizing Uncle Tommy had been the furthest thing from her mind.

•   •   •

With plans made for the afternoon, everyone piled into the car to go visit Uncle Tommy. Leaving the comfort of Aunt Dory's wasn't exactly what they wanted to do, but Uncle Tommy's workshop was a warm and inviting place. It would be all right.

It wasn't really a surprise to Madelyn that she'd forgotten about visiting him. She didn't even remember that it was a Thursday. The two weeks since their last visit felt like ages ago, so much had happened in the meantime. And yet, it also felt like no time at all, she'd been so busy with other concerns.

Mom, on the other hand, wasn't quite so forgiving of herself. "I can't believe I almost forgot Tommy." She was mumbling to herself as she drove. "He would have been devastated if we didn't show up, especially since Pop's gone. Pop trusted me to keep watching over him." She continued berating herself the whole way to Uncle Tommy's. Occasionally, Jillian and Daniel glanced at Madelyn as if they were expecting her to bring up the issue of where Grandpa was now that Mom was talking about it too. But she wouldn't meet their gaze, not certain how to respond.

Over lunch, Mom made a point to tell Tommy, "You know I love you, Tommy, right?"

"Yep. I love you too, Sissy."

"And Pop Pop loves you. You know that too, don't you?"

He looked at her sideways. "Course I do. Besides, he told me himself."

"Really?" Mom was surprised. "He doesn't usually ... I mean he's not one to say that very often with ... well, with words."

"Sissy, you're funny. He only said it once, the last time he came and saw me."

Mom wrinkled up her forehead, "He did? I don't remember that."

"Well, he did, when he came to see me before he went away, when he came without you."

"Tommy, Pop Pop never came without me."

"He did then," Tommy insisted.

"Oh, of course he did." Mom shrugged her shoulders, not sure what to make of his comment.

After lunch, Mom pulled a small children's book out of her purse and haltingly read it to her brother. It only had a few words on each page. She'd been practicing those words with Jillian just for this moment.

Madelyn had been impatient to get home and talk over the situation surrounding Grandpa, but this slight pause while Mom read to Uncle Tommy made waiting worth it. She was so proud of her mom.

They stayed a little longer—watching Tommy at work, "talking" with Annie despite her usual silence, even laughing with Eliza as they tried to play "I Spy" although she couldn't "spy" anything, even if she wanted to. The events of the previous evening, while making them anxious for answers, also filled them with a profound gratitude for the important things, or people, in their lives.

. . .

As soon as they got home, to Aunt Dory's home, they called Zane and Delia. While Jillian and Daniel played checkers in the back room, the others gathered in the living room. No one seemed to mind the extra clothing and belongings littered about the room since this was now doubling as a bedroom.

Aunt Dory was the only one unaware of why this little meeting had been convened. "Dory, I suppose I need to explain," Mom said. "We think last night had some connection to my father, to Pop. There's no easy way to say this, but he's in prison ... for murder, or technically involuntary manslaughter. He killed his neighbor, his friend George Holliwell." Aunt Dory's eyes got big, but Mom tried her best to ignore the reaction and get the story out. "They started going drinking together—after my mother died, anyway. I don't know what happened that night. Pop was drunk. I doubt he knew what he was doing, but that doesn't excuse what he did. Pop changed after Mom died. I don't remember him ever drinking before that, but after ..." She trailed off while shaking her head. "She was his rock—with Tommy, with everything. It was rough after she was gone."

"I'm so sorry, Rachel. How's he doing in prison?"

"I'm not sure. I visited him in jail when he was first arrested. After that, he was released on bond. But once he was sentenced ... I haven't been to see him. I guess I should have."

Madelyn moved beside her mom and put an arm around her. One person's actions can affect so many. "Are you mad at Grandpa? Is that why you haven't visited him?"

A tear was trickling down the side of Mom's face. "No, I don't suppose so. It just makes me sad—so much heartache, so much loss—for George's family, for ours. I stayed away because I couldn't make sense of it. I asked him to explain, but he was so passed out drunk that he doesn't even remember. You know, I've gotten pretty good over the years at burying problems rather than dealing with them." She gave Madelyn a half smile. "I have to admit, it feels better getting them out in the open. Thanks, Madelyn." She let out a big sigh, "I suppose it's time to go see him."

"That's a good idea," Aunt Dory said. "I mean it's good in the sense of reconnecting with him. But you said last night had something to do with him. What was that about?"

Madelyn was the one to answer. "The two guys that broke in—we overheard them talking. They'd bugged our house. I think they heard me talking to Zane about Grandpa. And last month I'm guessing the same guys broke into Grandpa's house and Mrs. Holliwell's house too. There's got to be more to this story."

"Mrs. Osborne," Delia said, "do you know anything about what happened the night of the ... the night George died? Mrs. Holliwell said the two of them went out drinking to celebrate something. Do you know what they were celebrating?"

Mom was shaking her head. "I don't. Something may have been said about that at the trial, but I don't remember. I just assumed they were going drinking like they always did."

"She also told us that William, your dad, showed her husband something over at his house," Zane said. "She didn't know what it was, but she seemed to think it was some big secret."

"I don't know about that either. Did she have any idea what it might have been?"

It was now their turn to shake their heads. "No. She was completely in the dark," Madelyn said.

They grew quiet, thinking through the possibilities, but Madelyn was fidgety, knowing she had one more question. "Mom, the paper said Grandpa stabbed his friend. Do you know why he had a knife or where it came from?"

Mom didn't shake her head this time but cast her eyes down instead. "I don't know why he had it with him. Believe me, I've tried to understand that one. But it came out in the trial that the knife was his. It was a switchblade. I even recognized it. He'd had it for as long as I can remember."

"Oh," Madelyn said, "I'm sorry. I guess it could be one of those things he just carried around with him."

"The thing that doesn't seem clear here is his motive," Aunt Dory chimed in. "Why would he kill his friend? When they prosecuted him, did they mention what his motive was? It seems like that would have come out in the trial."

"I don't remember any motive ever being mentioned. Of course, I was in a daze through most of the trial. It was all such a shock. I think they felt they had enough evidence to convict him without a motive, or they decided being drunk was enough of a reason. The trial didn't finish anyway. Part way through his lawyer convinced him to take a plea deal. The verdict seemed like a foregone conclusion."

"What did your dad say about it? Did he ever say why he did it or if he thought it was fair for him to go to jail?" Aunt Dory was speaking softly, trying to gently deal with this horrible subject.

"He never denied anything, but he also didn't have much to say about it."

"That doesn't help us much."

"Why don't we read the transcript of the trial?" Zane said. "He'd have to tell his story there. Maybe there's something we're missing—something you didn't even know you needed to pay attention to back then. These break-ins change everything, don't they?"

"That's a great idea," Mom said. "I honestly don't remember much of the trial. Seeing the knife really shook me. Everything after that is a blur."

"Then it wouldn't hurt to look it over, would it?" Zane said. "Delia, do you think Dad might be able to help us get a copy of the transcript from the trial?"

"He's a patent attorney, not a trial lawyer, but someone at his firm should know who to ask at the clerk's office. It's worth a try," she said.

"We'll see what we can do then," Zane said.

"Good. I'll go visit Pop in prison. It'll be good to see him. And maybe now he'll be willing to talk to me about it. He may not remember what happened after he got drunk, but there are plenty of questions that he *can* answer from before then."

Madelyn was happy with all the progress they were making, except for one little detail. "What should I do then?"

Mom turned to her. "You're going with me, of course. Did you think I was going to leave you behind?"

"Well, yeah, I guess so."

"No, not anymore. How about first thing tomorrow morning?"

"That just leaves me," Aunt Dory said. "I'll gladly keep an eye on Jillian and Daniel."

"Oh, and we forgot one other thing," Madelyn said, "the letter. We need to read that first letter."

"You're right. I can go get it right now." Mom hesitated a moment. "I don't suppose there's anyone who would want to go with me?"

•   •   •

When they'd gathered once again in the living room, Madelyn encouraged her mother to read the letter from Pop out loud. Mom opened it then perused it with dismay. "It's in cursive. I can copy his cursive, but I can't decipher it. You read it, Madelyn. One step at a time here."

"Okay. I've got it," Madelyn said while giving her mother an encouraging squeeze.

The letter read:

My Dearest Rachel,

I'm sorry for all that has happened, but I know I can't possibly put that into words in any kind of adequate way. So, I'll save that for a time when we can talk in person.

I understand why you don't come to see me. I miss you, but I have no one to blame but myself for where I am. How are the kids? I know it's best they not see me like this, but it doesn't mean I don't miss them too.

I hate to bring it up, but I need your help. I have a loose end to tie up. It's weighing on my conscience. That may sound strange given where I'm sitting, but I'm trying to fix the things I can fix.

I made a mistake a long time ago. It was inadvertent, but a mistake all the same. Something was entrusted into my care during the war. I'd always intended to return it to its rightful owner, but I simply forgot about it. And now I can't do it on my own. I need your help.

I've put it in a safe place. The alcohol may have been making me a little paranoid, but I think someone was after it. Before all this happened with George, I was being followed, and my house may have been bugged. Writing this down, sober as I am, it sounds nuts. Maybe I am, but I still need to make this right, regardless.

Please come visit me and I'll explain. (The only one visiting me now is my family lawyer, and he's not as charming as you are.)

Love,

Pop

Madelyn stopped reading and was met with stunned silence. Aunt Dory got up and locked the front door. The others shifted in their seats, moving closer to one another.

"You were right, Madelyn. All of this traces back to Pop," Mom finally said.

"What he mentioned—that's got to be what he showed George. What do you think it is?" Zane said.

"I don't know, but I'm hoping Pop will tell us tomorrow."

Friday

Madelyn was up early the next morning, eager to visit Grandpa and hopefully get some answers to their questions. When she sat up, she noticed the other side of the sofa bed was already empty. She found Mom in the kitchen eating a bowl of cereal, the cardboard kind an older widow might have around her house.

"Any good?" Madelyn asked, nodding toward the cereal.

"It's okay. I like it, but you probably won't. Don't worry. There's leftover pizza in the fridge."

As she helped herself to a slice of pizza, Madelyn started to formulate a plan in her head. What would they ask Grandpa, and how would they go about it? She glanced over at her mom, ready to ask for her opinion, when it dawned on her it was unnecessary. Mom had a far-off look and her eyes were dancing. This was about more than getting answers—it was about a father and daughter seeing each other for the first time since he was sent away. The questions would come, and the answers would flow, but the reunion was more important.

Breaking out of her reverie, Mom said, "What do you think we should tell Jilly and Daniel?"

"I hadn't thought of that. Can we tell them we're trying to figure things out—with the break-in?" Madelyn appreciated knowing the truth, but it carried a weight with it as well.

"I think that sounds like a great idea. I'm afraid we're going to need to tell them sooner rather than later, but maybe we can ease our way into it."

Aunt Dory poked her head into the kitchen. "Good luck today. I hope you find some answers."

"Me too," Mom said, "and if it's all right with you, could we work on some reading this afternoon? I don't want to neglect that, but I've got to do this first."

"Of course," Aunt Dory replied.

Madelyn hadn't even considered that, but she was glad her mother had.

• • •

"Do you realize it's August? Today is August 1st," Mom said as she drove the two of them to the prison.

"I didn't. I kind of lost track of time." She regarded her mom, a woman she had come to know more in the last month than in the first 14 years of her life. "You know, I broke the summer down into ten weeks. I figured I could mark off the weeks that Dad was gone and count it down. But I've been forgetting about my countdown. This must be week eight, which means he'll be home in just over two weeks." Mom nodded. "I don't think about Dad as much as I used to. Is that bad? Does it mean I don't love him as much as I thought I did?"

Mom reached over and patted Madelyn's leg. "Not at all. It just means you're growing up. You're learning that you have to be patient and wait for some things. And, I suppose it also means that you're learning that little setbacks aren't the end of the world."

"Thanks, Mom. I love you."

"I love you too, Madelyn. And I'm proud of you."

They settled into a comfortable silence after that, only broken by Madelyn's exclamation, "There it is! That's the sign for the prison." She was excited to see her grandpa after all this time, but not just a little scared about the thought of all the other criminals living within those walls.

It turned out none of their expectations were met that day—all of them negated by the bureaucratic policies of the prison system. Visiting day, it turns out, was Monday.

"But you can fill out this paperwork ahead of time if you like," the clerk told Mom. "It will save you time come Monday morning." Mom nodded, staring at all the lines that needed to be filled in. "Is there a problem?" the clerk asked.

"No, not really. Is it all right if my daughter fills this out? I'm just now learning to read." Madelyn was shocked at her mother's admission but incredibly pleased as well.

The clerk, on the other hand, didn't seem to be fazed at all. "No problem. I'm glad you're learning. Too many never do."

When Mom turned to hand the paperwork to Madelyn, she was beaming.

•   •   •

Back in the car, Madelyn said, "That was great, Mom. I'm so proud of you." Mom just grinned in response. "I mean, other than not being able to see Grandpa."

The smile faded but only a little. "Yes, well, I guess we know what we'll be doing on Monday. And now we know the way and what to do, so no more reason to be nervous."

"Oh, I didn't know you were nervous. Because it's a prison?"

Mom shook her head. "Not really. Madelyn, every time I go somewhere new, I'm nervous. I never know when not being able to read is going to rear its ugly head and make something harder than it ought to be." Focused on the road ahead, she added, "But I'm happy to say, I actually was able to read quite a bit of that form."

"What? Then why did I have to fill it out?"

"Well, I couldn't be sure," Mom said while suppressing a grin.

"Okay, you got me." Madelyn grew thoughtful for a minute. "Is it getting better?"

Without looking in her direction, Mom said, "It is, but I have a lot of work ahead of me, and I know it. Even as I learn, it's going to be a while before I'm confident in what I know. I've been making excuses for so long, it's hard to think that I don't still need them."

Madelyn nodded. "I can't say I know what that's like completely, but I understand what you're saying. In a way, it's how I feel about high school. I'm afraid of what I don't know—what will my classes and my teachers be like, will I have friends. I wonder if people will like me once they get to know me. Maybe it's not the same thing, though."

"It's not a bad comparison. The biggest difference is that with a little time, you should be able to answer those questions. And I'm pretty sure you'll find your place. Lori may have moved away, but there are other kids you know, even if there are a lot you don't, at least not yet. And of course, you'll have Zane to hang out with." Madelyn colored at the suggestion, but it wasn't an unpleasant thought.

"What I don't think you realize, Madelyn, is that until this summer, the concerns I had always hung over me. They followed me wherever I went, without any chance of being resolved."

"I'm sorry, Mom."

"Don't be. I'm not sorry for myself. I'm realizing that I dealt with life the best way I knew how. And now, I have a different option, thanks to you. For the first time, I can do something about those nagging questions. It makes for some scary and wobbly first steps, but it's nice to have some control, even if I know it'll take time."

"That's good. I never knew it was like that for you," Madelyn said, then added, "Thanks."

"For what?"

"For telling me. For trusting me." It was still new territory for the two of them, and they grew quiet contemplating it.

"Mom, can I ask you more about Grandpa?" Madelyn finally ventured. Mom nodded. "What was his trial like? You said you were there."

"Yes. It was awful. Do you remember all those days we ate out or Dad brought home pizza or chicken?"

"I'd forgotten about that, but now that you mention it ... I just figured Dad had gotten a raise or something."

"Nope. Thankfully it wasn't very long. The two witnesses testified against him. Your grandfather only testified briefly in his own defense. Saying you were so stupid drunk that you don't remember anything isn't something that's bound to help your case. His lawyer actually stopped the trial part way through Pop's testimony and convinced him to take a plea deal. It wasn't a hard sell. I don't know what they would have said if they'd continued with a defense anyway." She was shaking her head, trying to wipe the past from her mind, but it was clear the memory was there to stay.

"I remember right before the judge was going to sentence him, Pop's defense attorney was handed a note. It passed right in front of me, and I stared at it, so hopeful that it might be about some key piece of evidence they'd just found that would clear his name. But I couldn't read it, and it didn't matter anyway. The only thing left to do was figure out the terms of where he would carry out his sentence." The defeat of not having a last-minute reprieve washed across her.

"I'm sorry," Madelyn whispered.

"Thanks. It's okay. At least it's over. But I am looking forward to seeing the transcript. It's not such a shock anymore. And it's easy to imagine I missed things."

.   .   .

Much as they wanted to know what the transcript contained, it also was going to have to wait. As soon as they returned to Aunt Dory's, Madelyn called Zane.

"I have good news and bad news," she reported to Mom and Aunt Dory after hanging up. "Zane's dad found someone that can help us. But the first he can get to it is Monday."

Mom nodded, and then said what they were all thinking. "This is going to be a long weekend."

"Well, then why don't we read a good book or two?" Aunt Dory cheerfully replied.

SATURDAY

The next day thankfully came and went without much fanfare and also without much turmoil either. Mom woke up determined to go about the day as normally as possible. "Why don't we grab a few groceries." It was a statement, not a question, and they were all happy for the distraction.

They went without a list, instead wandering up and down the aisles, adding anything that sounded good to the cart. Mom couldn't deny them these simple requests after the week they'd had, and to be honest, she was glad they were finding comfort in something. A tentative peace was settling over them.

It lasted until they pulled into their own driveway. No one moved to get out of the car. It felt safe, where their home did not. With a sigh, Mom said, "Well, the phone lines have been fixed. So, our phone service is back on. We're good to go. Everyone grab a bag, and let's take it inside."

With as little talking as possible, they carried the groceries in to the kitchen counter. Anything that needed refrigeration immediately went into the fridge, still in the brown grocery bags from the store. Everything else remained on the counter.

The four of them stood still, not sure what to do next. Mechanically, following Madelyn's lead, they opened some bread and slapped peanut butter and jelly down, eating the resulting sandwiches quickly and with little to no conversation. Without bothering to return the peanut butter to the cupboard or even wash the knife, Mom said, "Madelyn, why don't we go work on the yard. Jilly, you and Daniel can go play out back if you want."

There were chores that needed to be done—the typical vacuuming and dusting, and it was time to mow the lawn again—but no one minded that they weren't getting done. Silently, Mom and Madelyn gathered some tools for weeding and made their way to the side yard. They dug up one dandelion after another, but their work was slow and haphazard at best.

"Do you still want to tell Dad about your reading?" Madelyn said as she sat up from where she'd been bent over her work.

Mom sat down on the grass and wiped her brow. "I think so. He's waited a long time for this. He shouldn't be made to wait anymore. But I don't know if I want to tell him about the other stuff." Madelyn nodded in understanding. Mom got a twinkle in her eye. "And besides, I want him to be happy about my reading. News about the break-in would ruin that surprise." She laughed a genuine laugh. "No one should steal my thunder."

Madelyn was relieved that her mother could still joke around given the circumstances. She picked up her weeding tools again, but then said, "Can we quit for now?"

"That's the best idea you've had all day," Mom said. They stood up, gathering their supplies, but stopped once they turned to view the house. It was still theirs, still looked the same, yet everything was different.

Standing frozen to the spot, a warm voice enveloped them. "What are you two doing? It's time you came back inside. Your sheets are all washed, and I've got a pot of stew on for dinner."

Mom and Madelyn turned into the welcome embrace of Aunt Dory. "Thank you," they said in unison.

"Despite your intentions, you didn't think I was going to let you sleep back in your house just yet, did you?"

"Well, I thought –," Mom said.

"I'm sorry, but you thought wrong in this case. Come along. And grab whatever cookies you bought at the store. I just hope you bought some chocolate chip," Aunt Dory said as she retreated to her house.

With a lightness to their steps, they returned their tools to the garage and collected Daniel and Jillian along with their indulgent purchases. The remainder of the day was spent putting together a jigsaw puzzle while chowing down on homemade stew and store-bought cookies.

WEEK NINE – SUMMER 1975

SUNDAY

The trouble with discovering Mom's illiteracy followed so closely by all the mess with Grandpa was that Madelyn's favorite thing to do got lost in the mix—reading. She simply forgot to do it. Sunday morning rolled around and with it the startling realization that she hadn't read anything at all in *The Hobbit* during the past week, even though she'd remembered to grab it from home and bring it over to Aunt Dory's.

Madelyn hurriedly dressed for church then started reading the allotted two chapters while downing a bowl of cereal—thankfully a sugary cereal they'd bought at the store the day before. In so many ways things were going well for Madelyn's literary friend Bilbo. The dragon guarding the treasure was dead, and he had found the desired Arkenstone, but it was clear all was not well. She continued to read in the car on the way to church about the alarming battle of the five armies that ensued. Mom had to nearly pry the book from her hands as they entered the chapel.

With a sigh, she not only realized she wanted to find out what would happen to Bilbo and the others, but she'd also enjoyed the escape reading gave her from the troubles around her. Dad had been right to send her the book, even if the concerns she'd started the summer with no longer followed her.

Daniel interrupted Madelyn's thoughts when out of the corner of her eye she caught him aiming a paper airplane at the back of the head of a cute girl in front of him. When she grabbed and crumpled his would-be weapon, Mom gave Madelyn a dirty look with a shush.

Daniel's stifled laughter at Madelyn being the one in trouble was meant to further goad her, but she surprised him by putting her arm around him and pulling him in for a hug instead. Not unexpectedly, he initially resisted before settling peacefully into her embrace.

Madelyn turned and whispered, "Jilly," while motioning with her head for her little sister to come closer. Jillian was on the other side of Mom but snuck over her to sit beside Madelyn. With an arm around each of her siblings, all felt right with the world.

.   .   .

When they got home, they still had a little time before their weekly phone call to Dad. With the excitement of *The Hobbit* still on her mind, Madelyn had a stroke of inspiration. There was no reason Mom couldn't enjoy a book just because she couldn't read it yet.

"Jilly, tell Mom I'll be right back, okay?" she said as she headed out on her bike, not even waiting for a reply.

Zane, it turns out, had been spending more time reading than Madelyn had. He'd long since finished reading *Watership Down* and was more than willing to lend it to her.

Until it was time for their phone call, Madelyn gathered all of them—Mom, Daniel, Jillian, even Aunt Dory—and read aloud the story of the rabbit brothers, Fiver and Hazel. It was an escape for all of them except Mom, who was watching the clock.

As Madelyn finished a chapter, Mom broke in with, "Well, it's just about time to call Dad. Dory," she said, acknowledging her with a nod, "has kindly offered to let us make that long-distance phone call from her house. But I don't want us to dawdle when it's on her nickel. So, we need to decide what we're going to tell him."

She took a breath before continuing. "I talked to Madelyn about telling him I'm learning to read. Is that okay with everyone? We'd decided together to make it a surprise. So, what do you all think?"

"Tell him! Tell him!" they all said together, including Aunt Dory.

"All right then," she said, smiling. "But what about the break-in? I think we should tell him, but I don't want to scare him."

"Why?" said Jillian.

"Because he'll either want to rush home right away before his training is done, or he'll be worried and stressed about us—only unable to do anything about it. That will make it even worse for him."

"I have an idea," Madelyn said quietly. "I've been thinking about it. Why don't you tell him about reading, and then tell him how Mrs. Burnham became Aunt Dory? Tell him we have family we didn't even know we had—right here. And that there have been unexpected challenges, ones we'll tell him all about once he's back, but that we're good right now because of family."

It was a toss-up who would hug her first, Mom or Aunt Dory. "I think that's a perfect idea. Thank you, Madelyn," Mom said.

· · ·

Despite the trauma they had so recently been through, the excitement of telling Dad about Mom and all she was accomplishing took over. It felt like Christmas Eve waiting until they could get Dad on the phone. Aunt Dory had three phone extensions in her house, so it was agreed that Jillian and Madelyn would listen in on one together, while Daniel and Mom took the other two.

The phone rang twice before Dad picked it up. Then the four of them tried to say "hi" all at the same time.

"Whoa! How did I get so lucky to get all of you at once?"

Much as each of them wanted to blurt everything out, they had agreed to let Mom be the one to speak. "Honey, I hope you're sitting down."

"Yes, I am," he said hesitantly.

"Well, I wanted to tell you about the way things have been going lately with you being gone. We've been learning a lot from each other. The kids have been great. Madelyn has really stepped up to the plate. Today she even started reading a book to all of us. It's kind of fun."

"That sounds great."

"And I've been reading books to Jilly, and sometimes the others."

"Good."

"No. I don't think you understand. I've been reading *new* books to the kids."

"You mean …"

"Yes, books other than those three."

There was complete silence on the other end. Then they heard a sound they'd never heard before. Dad was weeping, weeping for all he was worth. He tried a few times to form words but failed, collapsing into sounds of sobbing.

Madelyn and Jillian quietly hung up then went to find Daniel. When he saw them, he hung up too.

Forty-five minutes later, Mom found them playing board games with Aunt Dory. Her face was shimmering—wet with tear stains and completely aglow. She went around the table, in turn hugging each of them. It was more than words could have expressed.

MONDAY

Madelyn and her mom were just walking out the door to visit Grandpa when Daniel passed by. "Where are you going?" He was still rubbing the sleep out of his eyes.

Mom opened her mouth to offer a quick explanation then stopped herself. Instead, she turned around and crouched down so she could look Daniel in the eye. "Madelyn and I are trying to figure out what's going on around here. So, we're off to visit your grandpa. Daniel, he's in prison. I'm sorry the truth of it isn't pretty, but I suppose it's time you knew."

His eyes grew big, but he said nothing.

"He's in prison?" It was Jillian. No one had noticed her figure down the hall by the entrance to the kitchen.

Mom straightened up so she could see her youngest. "Yes, Jilly. He is. I didn't think you would want to know, but ..." She shrugged her shoulders. "You'd find out soon enough."

Jillian ran down the hall and hugged Mom. Daniel, needing the same comfort and unwilling to wait his turn, reached over and surprised Madelyn with a big squeeze around her middle.

Aunt Dory came across the scene a minute later. "Oh, so that's where you all got to. I'm guessing these aren't happy hugs?" she said, noting the somber mood.

"Mom just told us Grandpa's in prison. I've never known anyone in prison before," Daniel said.

"Well, now you do. It's not something to brag about, but it's not something to be ashamed of either," Aunt Dory said. "You can't make choices for someone else, but you can make choices for yourself. And despite everything, I'm sure your grandpa loves you."

"Thank you," Mom mouthed to her.

"Now, get along you two," Aunt Dory said, "We've got some breakfast waiting for us in the kitchen. I made fresh pancakes." And just like that, Jillian and Daniel were smiling, racing down the hallway to the kitchen, and Mom and Madelyn were heading out the doorway.

• • •

Visiting the inside of the prison was a new experience for Madelyn. Being in the outer office a few days before didn't even compare to walking down the concrete hallway to the visitor's room. What stood out to her was how loud it was—no background music to cushion the sharpness and starkness that surrounded them, just one long metallic, icy sound and sensation after another. Even her mouth was awash with the iron-steel taste, just like the taste of a bloody lip.

Most of the people filing in for visiting day were adults. Even though Madelyn was on the list, the man checking them in was hesitant to let her in. Mom straightened her back, looked him square in the face, and said, "This is his oldest granddaughter. He hasn't seen her, nor she him in some time. You're not actually suggesting they be kept from each other, are you?"

For a man working in the toughened environment of a prison, his reaction wasn't what they'd expected. He apologized and gave them no further trouble. When Madelyn peered into the faces of the other visitors, however, she understood better. They were the type he must normally deal with. Beaten, discouraged, tired, and defeated described every one of them—until the prisoner they were waiting for arrived through the far door, progressing toward the plexiglass partition. Then smiles formed on their faces—only they weren't fooling anyone that their supposed happiness was genuine.

Madelyn was so busy watching the people around her that she missed seeing Grandpa come through that same door. Her back was turned to him until she noticed that same fake smile paste itself on her mother's face. She turned, and they saw each other at the same moment. His shock mirrored her own.

He had aged and not in a gracious way. His hair, what little was left now, was grayer than before, his eyes sunken and lifeless, his walk a hesitant shuffle. He grabbed the back of the chair that was placed in front of the plexiglass with an iron grip. Snatching the phone with his free hand, he spoke through gritted teeth to Mom while never taking his eyes off Madelyn. "Why is she here?" His words came to Madelyn's ears cold and harsh through the receiver Mom was clutching with both hands. Madelyn's stomach sank, and she felt like she was about to lose her breakfast.

"Pop –"

He turned at the sound of Mom's voice. "She shouldn't see me like this. I thought we agreed the kids would never know. Why did you bring her?"

"She's old enough to know the truth. Maybe she wasn't a few months ago, but she's shown herself to be worthy of our trust—of our honesty." She stared him down while he seemed to decide what to do. Eventually, he dropped into the chair, still gripping the phone in his hand as if it was a crutch.

"Okay," he said, but he refused to look at Madelyn again. "Thanks for coming, Rachel. I wanted to see you, but ... but I understood why you didn't come."

Mom nodded and placed her free hand on the glass, fighting to hold back the tears. Grandpa was slow to respond, but eventually, he brought his hand up to match hers on the other side. "Why now? Why did you come?"

"Your last letter. I didn't read the first one, not until a couple days ago. I'm sorry. I ..." She glanced at Madelyn who could see the question written across her face. *Do I tell him why I didn't—couldn't—read it earlier?* Madelyn simply shrugged her shoulders in response, knowing it was Mom's history, Mom's decision whether to share or not. Mom fiddled nervously, peering down at her shoes, stalling. With a sigh, she said, "Anyway, I'm here now, and it is good to see you, Pop."

He nodded his acknowledgment then his voice cracked as he said, "It's good to see you too, Rachel. I've always depended on you."

"I know," Mom said. Madelyn reached over to squeeze her hand, knowing now how that view of her mother had been a double-edged sword.

Mom glanced up to give her a knowing smile before continuing. "So, Pop, what did you need me to do? What's the loose end you mentioned?"

He drew in a deep breath. "I should have told you about it sooner, but everything got so complicated." His head dropped in shame, seemingly reluctant to share the reason he'd summoned Mom in the first place.

"What is it?" Mom prompted. "What do you need returned?"

He was starting to form words when Madelyn said, "Was it the same thing you showed your neighbor, Mr. Holliwell?"

His head came up sharply, "What did you say?"

Madelyn took the receiver and repeated, "Was it the same thing you showed Mr. Holliwell?"

"How did you know about that?"

Madelyn realized her mistake and handed the receiver back to Mom as if it were a snake about to strike. "Well, something strange has been going on. So, we ... uh, we, started asking around. Lydia, I understand, said you showed George something," Mom said.

Grandpa's eyes narrowed. "What do you mean strange?"

Mom and Madelyn looked at each other. "There was a break-in at your house," Mom finally said, and Madelyn nodded, understanding that wouldn't sound as bad as the two intruders at their own home.

Instead of responding, Grandpa dropped the phone and put his head in his hands and began to shake his head back and forth. "Pop? Pop, what is it?"

He picked up the phone again, "When was the break-in? What was taken?"

Mom was slightly taken aback. "Last month. We couldn't find anything missing, but the place was pretty trashed—furniture turned over, closets ripped apart, that kind of thing."

"No, oh no. It couldn't be. I was afraid this might happen, but I don't know how ..." He was agitated and talking to himself.

"Pop. I'm sorry. It wasn't that bad. I think it was just a neighborhood thing. The Holliwell's house was broken into too."

At that, he suddenly sat up, terror masking his face. "George's house? Was Lydia hurt?"

"No, she was fine, a little shaken up, but otherwise okay. It's really nothing to worry about. So, what was with the letter? What did you want me to do?"

"No, no, nothing now. You don't need any more trouble. I wanted you to help, but I'll figure it out on my own. Just … nothing, do nothing."

"What are you talking about? It's no trouble. I'll help in whatever way I can. Just tell me what you need."

"No!" His tone startled both of them. "I don't need anything." He regained his composure before continuing. "Now, why don't we enjoy our visit. How's your family doing? How's Tommy?"

"But Grandpa, we already are involved. Just tell us what's going on," Madelyn said. He didn't respond. He may not have heard her since Madelyn wasn't holding the receiver, but she was pretty sure he had. He'd flinched at her words, but that was it, not even looking in her direction. Madelyn's shoulders slumped in defeat. She turned to her mom and shook her head. He was going to tell them nothing.

Mom held her gaze for a minute before turning back to Pop. Her voice was small as she answered his questions, telling him about her little family.

Near the end of their conversation, he snuck a peek at Madelyn, one that seemed genuine, like he wanted to take her in—how she'd grown, what she looked like now. She loved him, but her disappointment kept coming out on top. They desperately needed his help, and he was unwilling to give it. So, she folded her arms and glared at him instead.

She didn't know what she was hoping for—a sudden confession, breaking down and asking their forgiveness? Whatever it was, he wasn't about to oblige. He turned his head, never so much as glancing her way again.

With his last words to Mom, he brought up the topic he had so deftly steered away from earlier. "Rachel, before you go, just know that I'm glad to see you. I didn't really need you to do anything other than come see me. Just forget I said anything. Seeing you is enough. And I'm sorry I was upset about you bringing Madelyn. You were right to tell her." And even though he mentioned her name, he refused to turn so he could view her disapproval once again.

．　　　．　　　．

When they got home, Jillian and Daniel peppered them with questions. "How was Grandpa?" "Did he ask about me?" "How far away is the prison?" They were asking everything except what they truly wanted to know—why was Grandpa in prison in the first place.

"Whoa, wait a minute. Let me set my purse down at least," Mom said, knowing what she needed to tell them. "Okay. Let's go sit down in the living room, and I'll answer your questions."

When they were all settled, she held up her hand. "Before you say another word, let me tell you something. Jilly and Daniel, your grandpa is in prison for involuntary manslaughter."

"Wow!" they both said.

"What does that mean?" Jillian said.

"It means he killed a man, but he didn't really mean to." Mom let the words hang in the air, gradually falling to the ground around their feet, like a muddy quagmire.

After a full minute passed, Daniel whispered, "Who did he kill?"

"His neighbor, George Holliwell."

"Why'd he do it?" Jillian's little voice squeaked out.

"I don't know. I don't think he meant to, but someone is gone, regardless. So, he's in prison to pay for it."

All of them were nodding their heads, accepting but not possibly processing all that meant. Aunt Dory voiced it best. "Jillian, Daniel, I don't know your grandfather, but that doesn't matter. It's a devastating thing to have happened—for the victim, his family, for your grandpa, for you. I know this is hard. I'm guessing you're not sure what to say or even what to think, but it does seem like there's something to *do*—a mystery of sorts that we're trying to sort out. So, for the meantime, let's focus on that. I imagine, over time, you'll come to grips with the facts at hand."

And just like that, more truth was out. It was horrible and freeing at the same time. Relief washed over Mom's face. "Okay then. Let me tell you what's been happening."

By the time Mom was done explaining things to Jillian and Daniel, everyone was eager to move forward, to find what answers they could. "Can we listen to the transcript too?" Jillian wanted to know.

Mom looked over at Madelyn and Aunt Dory. "I think we'll read through it and share anything we think is important," she said. "I don't want this to be harder than it already is. So, if there are some details that I think are too much, we won't share them. Got it?" Jillian and Daniel both nodded their agreement.

"Let me go call Zane to see if they were able to get the transcript yet," Madelyn said. But before she could do so, there was a knock at the door.

"Zane!" Madelyn said when she answered the door.

"Hi. Delia's coming in too. She's just parking the car."

By now everyone had gathered around the door, looking at him expectantly. "Well?"

"We got the transcript. It took us all morning to track it down, but Delia's bringing it in."

"Have you read it? What does it say? Is there anything that stands out?" Questions were coming from several people at once.

He laughed. "Hold on. One question at a time, okay? I haven't read it. I figured we should all read it together. That only seems fair and decent."

"Thanks, I appreciate that," Mom said. "And where are our manners. Come in, come in."

A few minutes later, they were all gathered in Aunt Dory's living room, eager to learn what the pages of transcript might reveal. They started by dividing it up between the fastest readers—Delia, Zane, Aunt Dory, and Madelyn. It was quiet while the four of them read, except for the anxious pacing of the others.

"This doesn't strike me as that unusual," Aunt Dory said at last. "My part is about the two witnesses. They both said they were at the bar and saw your father drinking heavily. This one, a Mr. Tony Garfield, said, 'The two of them left the bar together. Mr. Knight could hardly walk. Then a few minutes later we heard a lot of arguing. So, I went running out. I got there just in time to see Mr. Knight repeatedly stabbing Mr. Holliwell. I yelled for him to stop, but it was just too late.'" Aunt Dory let out a gasp. "Oh, Rachel, I'm sorry," she said, looking at Jillian. "I probably shouldn't have read that." Jillian's eyes were as big as pancakes.

Mom shook her head. "I don't know what I was thinking letting them be here, but I guess it's too late now. Go ahead. What else does it say?"

Aunt Dory had to regain her composure. "Well, Mr. Garfield goes on to say, 'My friend, Jake Downey, came running out after me. He's the one that ran back inside to call the police.'

"Then the attorney asked, 'What did Mr. Knight do then?' and the witness responded, 'He just passed out on top of the other man. He was like that when the police arrived.'

"That's the gist of the testimony. The other witness was Jake Downey. He told the exact same story," Aunt Dory concluded.

"I read the part where your grandfather testified," Zane said. "It's not very long. His own attorney asked him just a few questions. Here's what it says:"

Attorney Peter Bruce: You just heard these two men testify against you. Do you remember them in the bar?

William Knight: Yes. I hadn't met them before, but they were in the bar. They bought us, George and me, some drinks.

Bruce: Just stick with the question at hand. Now, did they seem like the type that would come running if they heard screams or a scuffle?

Knight: Well, sure, I suppose so.

Bruce: Why did you go out drinking that night? Were you trying to settle a fight with your friend George?

Knight: No, not at all. My lawyer—not you—my other lawyer invited the two of us to meet him for drinks that night.

Bruce: Why did he invite you?

Knight: We were celebrating.

Bruce: What were you celebrating?

Knight: Well ... It's kind of like we'd just worked out some details of my wife's will.

Bruce: But your lawyer wasn't at the bar. How can you explain that?

Knight: When we got to the bar, he wasn't there, but he'd left a message with the bartender. He's the one who passed it along to us that my lawyer couldn't make it after all, but that we were to enjoy a couple rounds on him.

Bruce: Was this a written note?

Knight: No, the bartender just relayed the message.

Bruce: Can you explain why the bartender doesn't remember any of that?

Knight: I guess you'd have to ask him that. I can't account for another man's memory.

Bruce: Your honor, I wonder if I might have a recess to confer with my client.

Zane set down the pages he'd been reading from. "That's basically it. The judge grants it, and next thing you know, they have a plea deal."

"I'm not too fond of that lawyer. He didn't sound like he was helping your dad's case," Aunt Dory said.

"No," Mom said, "but I'm not sure how he could have helped."

"What was that about Grandma's will? What details had to be worked out?" Madelyn said.

"I don't know. I didn't think there was much to it. It had been read long before then. So, I honestly don't know what he was talking about."

"And why would his lawyer invite both of them and then not show up? Even more than that, what did Mr. Holliwell have to do with Grandma's will?" No one had an answer to that.

"You know, Madelyn, I should probably ask the lawyer who handled

Mom's estate about that. He ought to know what they were celebrating, and he can tell us why George Holliwell was invited. It may have been just one of those 'bring a friend along' kind of things, but he could tell us either way."

"What I want to know," Daniel chimed in, "is about Grandpa being drunk. I've seen drunk people on TV. Sometimes they can't even stand up or hold a pen to write their own names. How could Grandpa hold a knife? And if he was so drunk, how would he be strong enough to stab his friend? Wouldn't he just fall over if he tried?"

Those were very good questions—ones they were surprised no one had thought to ask before.

It was a lot of food for thought, and they took their time chewing on it. The more they learned, the more questions they had, and the more questions they had, the more elusive the answers became.

Mom was the first to break the silence. "I wish I'd talked about this when it happened. I imagine it would have been easier to get to the bottom of it then. The trial, the testimony given, all of it, just flew right over my head." She was shaking her head. "It's not that I didn't understand what was going on, I just couldn't believe it was real. It felt like a horrible nightmare, and I was just certain I was going to wake up any minute."

"I can't begin to imagine how it made you feel, dear," said Aunt Dory. "Don't beat yourself up about it. I'm sure your reaction was normal. And it's not likely your father would have been any more eager to talk to you then than he is now."

"You're probably right."

"But that's not true, Mom," Madelyn said. "Grandpa decided not to talk to us when he heard about his house being broken into. Before that, I think he wanted to talk. That's why he sent the letters."

"Yeah, you're right."

"So, what next?" Madelyn said.

"Let's call that lawyer," Mom said.

TUESDAY

The next morning brought with it too much idle time. Mom had gone back to their house the previous afternoon and with Madelyn's help had looked up her father's lawyer, a Mr. Ross Musil. His secretary had been happy to set up an appointment for them. They would be visiting with him later in the afternoon.

Breakfast had concluded all too soon, and everyone appeared weary in waiting, wanting to move forward in understanding and unable to focus on the typical distractions of toys and games. Even Daniel seemed unable to devise any form of mischief.

Mom was the only one who seemed energetic. Madelyn couldn't help but notice the recent changes in her. She was gaining confidence in her world and her apparent place in it. Despite the concerns about Grandpa and the troubles swirling around them, there was a new spring to her step and a determination in her look and bearing. She was smiling more, talking more, doing everything more. A few days before, she'd even carried on a conversation with the store clerk who bagged her groceries instead of the hasty, "Thank you," as she scooped up her bags to leave. Like a newfound butterfly, she was emerging from her forgotten chrysalis.

While Mom and Aunt Dory finished up the breakfast dishes, Daniel had been tasked with washing the kitchen table. He was swirling the washcloth around in lazy circles, if anything, spreading the mess instead of cleaning it up. Jillian was sitting at the table while Madelyn braided Jillian's hair

"Dory, do you think I could read some of those children's books you wrote?" Mom said once they finished. The early reading books around their house had gained new life. Mom couldn't get enough of them and had taken to gathering the books along with one or more of her children to read them to.

"I might be able to find a few," Aunt Dory said with a twinkle. "Come with me."

"Would you three like to join me?" Mom said.

Daniel didn't need to be asked twice, quickly dropping his washcloth and leaving the room all in the same motion.

"I'll just finish Jilly's hair. We'll be there in a second," Madelyn said.

But it was only a few moments later when Daniel burst back into the kitchen. "You gotta come here. Mom's trying to figure something out."

Mom was sitting on the couch, a book open in her lap. Biting her lip and twirling a finger in her hair, she glanced up as they came in. "I remembered something, only I can't remember all of it." She pointed to the page she was reading. "This word—keep—it was on that note."

"What note?" Madelyn said.

"The note that was passed to my father's defense attorney at the end of his trial. Maybe it doesn't mean anything, but one of the words was *keep*."

"Really? What else did it say?" Mom raised her eyebrows at Madelyn. "Oh, sorry. Dumb question. Do you know how many words it had on it?"

Mom paused, trying to piece it together in her mind. "Keep was the first word," she finally said, "and I'm pretty sure there were two more words. It wasn't much of a note, now that I think of it. What can you say in three words? I should have realized it wasn't about any new evidence, but ..." She shrugged her shoulders. "I just didn't."

"It's okay, Mom," Jillian said. "I wouldn't have thought so either." She probably didn't have a clue what they were talking about, but she was trying to make Mom feel better.

Mom was thinking hard and started to mumble to herself then inexplicably got up and walked out of the room. They could hear her calling, "Dory, I need you to help me figure something out."

When Mom didn't return, they went searching for her. Mom and Aunt Dory were huddled over the kitchen table, talking back and forth about ways to decipher the note. Aunt Dory was writing different letters in various ways to see if they jogged a memory. When she showed Mom a lower case "m", Mom grabbed her hand. "Stop! I remember the mountains, at least that's what the 'm' looked like to me."

"I can see that. You wouldn't have been thinking in terms of letters."

"Yes, there was definitely an 'm' in the second word, but I'm not sure what else went with it."

"Well, what about the last word?"

"I think it started or ended with one of those hand letters," Mom said.

Madelyn had no clue what she was talking about, but Aunt Dory apparently understood. She had Mom hold her hands out in front of her and make them into fists with her thumbs pointing upwards then turned the hands inward toward each other. With her left hand, she'd formed a "b" while her right hand looked like a "d."

"What are you doing?" Madelyn said.

"Her brain mixes up letters like b and d, but if you recite the alphabet in order, you get 'a' then 'b,' " Aunt Dory said, pointing to Mom's left hand. "Then 'c' and the other hand, 'd.' This is just a way to visualize the letters and keep them straight." Turning back to Mom, she said, "Okay, Rachel, picture the word in your mind. Which hand looks like the right letter?"

Mom stared at her hands then gradually lifted her right hand. "It was definitely this one. It was a 'd.' I'm sure of it. And there was a circle, I mean an 'o' and a snake, an 's.' I think there was another letter too—like a circle, but not quite."

"How about an 'e?' " Aunt Dory said, writing it for Mom to see.

"Yeah, that would fit."

"That might make *does* or even *dose*." Aunt Dory wrote out the words. "Is it one of these?"

"It could be. But what does it mean? Keep ... something ... does or dose? Keep my dose, maybe? That doesn't make any sense." She was shaking her head. "But you know, I can't get rid of the feeling it's important."

"Why?" Daniel said.

"I don't know. It's something in the way the note was passed, I think. It was furtive, sly almost. That's why I took notice. It was around the time of sentencing, but it wasn't the normal shuffling of paper. This was off. You know, now that I think of it, it didn't even come from anyone at the table with him. The note came from the public area, from the area where I sat."

"Like a spectator?"

"Yes, I think so, but I'm assuming not some idle observer."

"Do you know who it was? The person who gave him the note?" Daniel said.

"I don't. I was so surprised, or more likely hopeful about the note, that I only remember the hand reaching forward. I must have seen the person, but I don't remember him." Everyone sat silently thinking. "I wish I knew what it meant." They all nodded, feeling exactly the same way.

•　　•　　•

The one thing trying to decipher the note had accomplished was helping time pass. Before they knew it, it was lunchtime and then time for Mom and Madelyn to leave. As they were heading out the door, Zane called Madelyn to wish them luck.

They arrived right on time at the red brick law offices of Mr. Musil and his partners. Stepping into the brightly-lit interior, his secretary immediately ushered them back to his office. He stood up to greet them from behind his mahogany desk with a big smile on his face—as if his old client wasn't wasting away in jail. "What can I do for you today?" he said, motioning them to sit in the two leather chairs facing his desk.

"We're here about my father." A cloud passed across his features, but only momentarily. "We just have a few questions, if you don't mind."

"About what?"

"Well, I've been thinking about my dad, his trial, and such. I didn't really process it at the time, but now ... well, I'm trying to understand it. I should have asked you sooner, but in his trial, he mentioned going out to celebrate something getting resolved with my mother's will. What was the trouble? I thought everything was straightforward with her will."

"Well, yes, it was." He shifted uncomfortably. "I'm not sure what he was referring to. Everything with the will was resolved right away. There were no issues with it."

"That's strange. Then why did you invite him out for drinks that night?"

"The night George was killed?"

"Yes, that night. What other night would I be talking about."

"But I didn't. I don't know anything about that."

"But my father said –"

"I don't know what he said. I wasn't at the trial. Honestly, William is my friend. All I know is I didn't invite him out that night."

"But there was a message from you at the bar and everything," Madelyn interjected. "He said you were celebrating something, and that Mr. Holliwell was invited too. You must know something. You just called him George. So, you knew his neighbor."

Mr. Musil didn't have a response right away. His eyes darted from Madelyn to her mom and back again. "That has nothing to do with this. That's between me and William."

"We're not so sure about that," Mom said. "Can you tell us what he might have been celebrating?"

"I'm sorry. I can't."

"Can't or won't?" Madelyn said, standing up from her chair.

When he remained silent, Mom said, "Well, we appreciate your time. Is there anything else you can tell us?" When he simply shook his head in response, Mom said, "Thank you." She stood up to join Madelyn. "Oh, by the way, do you happen to know anything about his defense attorney, Mr. Peter Bruce?"

"I only know of him in passing. He works around the corner from here, so we run into each other on occasion." Mr. Musil was breathing easier and had settled comfortably back into his office chair.

"Did you recommend him?"

"I imagine I did."

"What does that mean?"

"Well, my secretary has a list of criminal defense attorneys that I hand out when needed. He must be on the list. Probably just picked the first one off the top."

"Okay. Well, thank you for your concern," Mom said.

When they'd made it out to the hallway, Madelyn pulled her mother aside. "What do you mean, 'Thank you for your concern.'? He didn't seem to care much at all."

"He's been friends with your grandpa for a long time. I'm sure he does care in his own way." Then Mom moved past her down the hall, leaving Madelyn unconvinced, but powerless to argue.

As Madelyn reluctantly followed, she was surprised to see her mother stop at his secretary's desk. "Hello. Daphne, is it?"

"Yes," his secretary replied.

"We were just in Mr. Musil's office. He said he would have given my father a list of defense attorneys. Do you happen to have a copy of that list?"

"Of course." She pulled open a filing cabinet behind her and located the paper she was looking for. "Here's a copy. Is there anything else you need?"

"No, that should be everything. Thank you so much."

· · ·

"Why did you want that?" Madelyn said once they were outside.

"I'm just trying to examine every detail. Here," she said, handing the paper to Madelyn, "Pop's defense attorney was named Mr. Bruce. Can you see that name anywhere? I'm sure you can find it faster than I can."

Madelyn took the paper and quickly scanned it. "Well, he's certainly not at the top of the list. If it were in alphabetical order, he might be, but it isn't. Oh, here he is, on the second page."

"I wonder why Pop picked him." She was deep in thought. "Maybe Mr. Bruce knows. Let's go ask him," she said. "If his office is just around the corner, which way do you think we should go?"

Madelyn located the address from the paper they'd been given, and in a few minutes they were standing outside a dilapidated building. Its masonry was cracking, and some of the brick facing had fallen to the ground where it lay in broken pieces at their feet. Weeds were pushing their way through the brick remnants and other cracks in the cement. In front of them was a door with number 312 painted in fading letters on the glass. No name accompanied it, but the number matched the address from the sheet. It stood in stark contrast to the offices they'd just left. The cold exterior did nothing to encourage them to enter.

Mom took a deep breath and pulled on the door. It stuck, but eventually creaked open. Tentatively, they stepped inside. The air was stale with the smell of cigarettes, alcohol, and sweat—a sense of desperation accompanying it. "Haven't you been here before?" Madelyn was whispering without knowing why she did so.

"No. Pop didn't want me to be part of any of his meetings. He was fine with my attending the trial, but that's as far as he wanted me involved. I'm wishing now that hadn't been the case, although I doubt it would have made a difference."

Gingerly they moved down the shadowy corridor toward the door at the end with light escaping around its edges. As they drew closer, they could make out the nameplate beside it: Peter Bruce, Attorney-at-Law.

As Mom reached for the door handle, it unexpectedly opened, almost knocking her over. "Oh, excuse me," she said, flustered.

"No bother," a scantily-clad woman said, brushing past her, the tinkling of her cheap jewelry and earrings calling back to them as she made her way outside.

Madelyn's eyes were wide. "Are you sure we want to talk to him?" Mom simply nodded in reply as she entered the law office of Peter Bruce.

Inside, it appeared empty. "Hello? Anyone here?"

After a few minutes, a man came out from an office at the back. "Do I know you?"

"Um, well, maybe. I'm William Knight's daughter."

"Who?"

"William Knight, you defended him in his murder trial."

"Oh, yeah. What do you want?" It wasn't a gruff statement, just an uninterested one.

"Well, I wanted to know more about my father's trial."

"What about it?" He had yet to offer them a seat, so they all stood uncomfortably in the open space in front of what had to be his office.

"For starters, do you know why he chose you to defend him?"

"No." He stood with his arms crossed, clearly not planning to elaborate.

"Didn't he say something when he first set up the appointment? Anything to tell you why he chose you?"

"Not that I recall."

"Do you have any notes from that first meeting, perchance then?"

"If I do, that would be privileged information."

"I see. Well, would you care to –"

"No," he said, cutting her off before she had a chance to finish, "I wouldn't care to anything. Now, there's such a thing as attorney-client privilege. I don't *care* to break that."

"Yeah, you don't seem to *care* much about anything, do you?" Madelyn said, tired of keeping her mouth shut. "Why didn't you mount a better defense for my grandpa? We read the transcript. You didn't seem to be on his side."

He shifted uncomfortably for the first time. "You know, he didn't help much in his own defense."

"So what! That's your job!" Madelyn said.

"And who are you, little girl, to be questioning me?"

"That's my daughter," Mom piped up, "and I suggest you take a different tone."

"Fine. You try to mount a defense when two eyewitnesses tell the exact same story. They were ironclad. All I could hope to do was keep your father alive. I succeeded." He had regained his composure and taken complete control of the situation.

The problem was, neither Mom nor Madelyn could argue with his logic. Defeated, they fell silent.

"Now, if you don't have any further questions ..." They shook their heads. "Good. Then I'll be getting back to work." As he turned back to his office, he threw parting words over his shoulder. "Have a nice day," as if they could.

WEDNESDAY

"So, what do we actually know?" Aunt Dory said the next morning. Zane and Delia had joined them for a conference to help decide what they should do now. They were all gathered around the kitchen table. On the edge of it, Aunt Dory was balancing a dusty chalkboard she'd retrieved from her garage.

"Well, Grandpa said he was celebrating something the night Mr. Holliwell was killed, but we're not sure what."

"Right. It included Pop and George and maybe the lawyer, Ross Musil," Mom said.

"And was it really about his wife's will?" Aunt Dory said. On the chalkboard, she wrote with squeaky chalk:

CELEBRATION
– William, George, Lawyer?
– Wife's will?

"Well, and there's the mysterious item that he wanted help taking care of," Zane offered. "That must be what he showed Mr. Holliwell."

To the chalkboard, Aunt Dory added:

VALUABLE ITEM
– Wanted Rachel's help with it
– Showed to George

Daniel piped up with, "That must be what someone was looking for when they broke into Grandpa's house and then our house."

"You're right," said Aunt Dory, as she added:

– Men searching for it at both houses

As everyone studied the board, trying to make sense of it, Aunt Dory propped it up against the wall. "Would anyone like something to eat?" Without waiting for a reply, she started cutting up some apples. She set down a bowl of apple slices on the table for everyone then moved to wash her knife.

Mom had been watching her movements. She spoke so quietly, it took a moment for the others to register she had spoken.

"What did you say, Mom?"

She turned at Madelyn's voice. Her face was pale but etched with hope. "He's innocent. I know all the things that have been said, but for the first time, I believe he didn't do it."

"Why?" Aunt Dory said.

"The knife. Dory, I saw you with the knife. Daniel wondered before about that, about how he could possibly wield a knife when he was so drunk. I can't believe I didn't see it before. Everything was there, but I didn't understand it. But it all fits now."

"What? What are you talking about?"

"There was never a motive. Why would he kill his friend? But if there was something valuable at stake ... then someone else would have a good reason to commit murder."

Everyone in the room started to nod, even Jillian understood what her mother was talking about, except for one thing. "But why wouldn't whoever wanted it, kill Grandpa? Why did his friend get killed instead?"

"I don't know."

"If that's true, that means people are lying. What about the two witnesses?" Delia said.

They all sat contemplating that for a moment. Then a big smile spread across Aunt Dory's face. "Madelyn, tell me about the break-in at your house. What did the intruders say? Who came into your dad's office first? That kind of thing."

That seemed a strange thing to ask at that moment. "Don't you already know all about it?"

"Yes. But I'd like you to tell me again—not everything, just some of the details."

"Okay. Well, I remember them saying they'd planted a bug and heard what I'd said that morning on the phone with Zane. I think they both came into Dad's office at the same time, just as we slipped out the window."

"Is that the way you remember it, Rachel?"

"Basically."

"No, I mean specifically. What do you remember?"

"I don't think they said anything about overhearing a phone conversation. They did mention a bug being planted. We overheard them talking, but they were out in the hallway when we made it out the window. Then one of them came into Roger's office and called the other one to come join him."

"That's not right," Madelyn started to argue.

Aunt Dory waved them both aside. "Don't worry about it. That doesn't matter. You just illustrated exactly what I thought." Everyone stared at her, lost and confused. "I knew something was bothering me, but I couldn't put my finger on it. You see, people's memories aren't exact. You were both there, and you remember it differently. I think that would be especially true in a stressful situation ... like when you witness a murder."

They quietly contemplated what that could mean. "What are you talking about?" Daniel asked, still confused by the situation.

"You probably don't remember this from the transcript, but I do because I read the witness testimonies. The two witnesses at your Grandpa's trial told the *exact* same story. They were identical. Every detail—the order of things, what was said, who did what—those were all exactly the same. It's almost as if they memorized the same script."

Mom nodded then walked over to the phone. After dialing, she said, "Is Mr. Musil available? I need to speak to him." After a moment's pause, she said, "Hello, Ross Musil? ... This is Rachel Osborne, William Knight's daughter, again. I just have a quick question. I know you're not a trial attorney, but with witnesses, would it be likely that they would tell the *exact* same story as each other." She was nodding. "Thanks, that's what we thought. ... Yes, that's right. The two witnesses that put my father away gave identical testimonies about what happened."

She turned the phone, and they all heard his excited voice. "You mean he might be innocent? I couldn't bring myself to attend his trial. It was too hard to stomach what I thought my friend must have done. Generally, when prosecutors say they have a solid case, they're right—the accused is guilty. But, oh my ..."

"Yes, I have to admit a little guilt in that department too," Mom reassured him. "Thanks, again. I imagine I'll be in touch later."

"It's all starting to make sense, isn't it?" Madelyn said.

"I think so," Mom said. The problem was, despite things coming together, no one was sure what to do with what they thought they knew.

"Well," Delia said, "Zane and I can talk to our dad again. I'd like to find out more about that defense attorney. From everything I've heard so far, I don't trust him. I doubt our dad knows him personally, but he probably knows someone who does. We can come back tomorrow. Hopefully, we can tell you something by then." It was the best idea anyone had, and when no one offered anything else, Zane and Delia made their excuses, leaving the others to stew in their juices.

· · ·

Lunch was carried off with a minimum of talking, even their chewing was done with mouths closed, making it quieter than normal. Daniel finished first then took to staring at the chalkboard they'd written on that morning. "Boy, whatever Grandpa had must have been pretty valuable to kill somebody over it," he said. "What do you think it might be worth, whatever it is?"

Mom visibly startled. "What did you say?"

Daniel shrugged his shoulders. "I just asked what it might be worth."

Mom's eyes were wide. "Do you kids remember having Grandpa over for dinner often after Grandma died?" They nodded their heads. "Well, one time he asked Roger, your dad, for help finding out what something might be worth."

"Do you think he showed it to Dad?" Madelyn was alarmed. "Is Dad in danger now?"

"No, no, it's not that. Pop was seeking advice. I remember now that he wanted to know the name of an appraiser, but he wouldn't say what it was he wanted the appraiser to examine. Roger told him that made it kind of tough to point him in the right direction, but he gave him the name of someone anyway. He assumed Pop had something old of my mother's that he wanted to put a value on, that was all." Mom's brow was knit while she was pulling the rest of the memory out of the recesses of her mind.

"Pop said he'd explain later. I was curious, but I must have forgotten about it once he was arrested for murder."

"That certainly would overshadow something as trivial as an appraiser," Aunt Dory said. "Do you think Roger would remember who he sent your father to?"

"I would think so. As I recall, he only gave Pop one name, so I'm guessing that would be the same appraiser he would recommend today as well. I'll call him tonight after he's done with training. I'll see what he can tell us."

• • •

"Hi, Roger," Mom said when he answered the phone. "I know this is unusual, calling you in the middle of the week, but I had a question for you. Do you remember giving Pop the name of an appraiser for something? ... You do? Do you remember his name? I'm just trying to tie up a loose end for Pop, nothing to worry about." She motioned for a piece of paper then wrote down: Howard Cramer.

"Thanks. Did he ever tell you why he wanted the name of an appraiser? ... Me neither. Oh, and I wanted to tell you how my reading's going."

Madelyn and Aunt Dory smiled at Mom's deft change of topics. They corralled the others out of the room to let Mom share more about her newfound reading with Dad.

• • •

It wasn't until Madelyn climbed into her side of the sofa bed that night that she realized a phone call had occurred with Dad without her talking to him too. For all her angst and anger when he left, life had managed to go on. She'd survived without him—even found new ways to thrive, new ways to be involved and help. If she was honest with herself, she hadn't had time to miss him lately. It's not that she wouldn't be glad when he finally returned, it's just that she didn't think about it all the time. Sometimes, she even forgot he was gone, forgot about the things that tied her to him, like neglecting to read *Hobbit* chapters until the last second or even trying to corral those pesky dandelions. With everything that had been happening, both of those things had fallen by the wayside.

He must be coming home soon, but she'd lost all track of time. Lately, she was lucky to keep track of what day of the week it was, the actual date was another matter entirely. She climbed back out of bed to find the calendar in Aunt Dory's kitchen. It was the 6th of August. That meant it was week nine of Dad being gone. One more full week after this one and Dad would be home. It was hard to imagine.

Madelyn climbed back into bed, thinking of the upcoming reunion. It made her smile. But those thoughts were soon eclipsed by other concerns— ones about the dangers swirling ever closer. They'd need to move back into their house before Dad returned, but that idea made her shiver. She didn't feel safe there yet. "Please," she prayed, "help us figure out what's going on before it's too late."

THURSDAY

By mid-morning on Thursday, they'd set up an appointment to meet with the appraiser for 2:30 that afternoon, and Zane had called saying his father was asking around. They agreed to all meet up at Aunt Dory's in the late afternoon.

Despite their great desire to get to the bottom of the mysteries surrounding Grandpa, mundane things needed to be taken care of. Everyone gathered clothes and bedding to go into the wash, and Jillian pointed out they needed to go grocery shopping.

"Could we get some more cereal, please?"

"Sure, Jilly. Let's put together a list. Madelyn, would you write it down for me?" Madelyn raised her eyebrows at Mom. "Yes, I could probably start writing it myself, but, if you haven't noticed, we're all a little stressed right now."

"That's fair enough. What do we need?"

With Aunt Dory and Jillian's help, Mom began to dictate a list that included milk, toilet paper, apples and everything in between.

"Would you mind stopping at the drugstore?" Aunt Dory said, "I could use some office supplies—some paper, paper clips, and even some staples."

"Sure," Mom said while Madelyn added those things to her list.

"What are paper dips?" Jillian said. She was peering over Madelyn's shoulder and pointing to one of the last items.

"Silly, that's paper clips, can't you tell?" Then Madelyn caught herself. Of course she couldn't tell. Her writing had gotten sloppier and sloppier as her list went on. The "cl" in "clips" had run together. It looked just like a "d."

"Mom, your note!"

"What? What about my note?" Mom said, clearly lost.

"The last word of the note you saw. It didn't start with *d*. It was probably just a sloppy *cl*. How about the word *close*?"

"You're right," Mom said, "it could be that. Like *keep me close*."

"Or *keep him close*," Daniel said from the doorway. "They were deciding where to put him in prison about then, weren't they?"

"Yes."

"Well, that would make sense then."

"But what does it mean? Why would they want that?" Mom said.

"Mom, did you ask his lawyer to make sure he was in a prison close by? You know, so it would be easier to visit him?" Madelyn said.

"No. I never even thought about it, and his lawyer certainly never suggested anything along those lines."

"So why would anyone care if he was close by or not?" Once again, Daniel was voicing the question they all had.

"I don't know."

After a moment's hesitation, Aunt Dory spoke up. "Rachel, I know your father wouldn't tell you anything before, but he's the one person who knows what's going on, or at least what the fuss is about. Do you think maybe you should try again?"

"I suppose so. But how can I change his mind?"

"You could tell him all the things we've learned so far," Daniel said.

"Maybe if you told him you think he's innocent, that might convince him to cooperate," Madelyn added.

Mom was nodding. "Sounds good, and I think I might have another ace up my sleeve." Then without explaining what it was, she made another phone call.

"Mr. Musil, please?"

"His lawyer again?" Madelyn whispered.

Mom nodded. "I don't trust the other one, and I'm hoping he can get me in to see Pop without waiting until next Monday's visiting day."

"Hello? ... This is Rachel Osborne again. I'm sorry to trouble you, but it's urgent that I speak with my father. I remember him mentioning that you had visited him in prison. Is there any way you can get me in to see him right away? I don't think this can wait. ... Yes, I know Monday is just a few days away, but I think that will be too late. This is a matter of great importance, and it's dangerous to wait. ... Yes, you heard me right." Mom looked at the others around her. She lifted her hand and crossed her fingers for them to see.

"Thanks, I appreciate that."

Mom put her hand over the receiver. "He's going to call the prison and see if he can make arrangements, but he's not making any promises."

Removing her hand, she spoke to Ross Musil once more. "I did have another question. When someone is being sentenced, can you choose where he does his time? I mean, could you ask to have him stay close by?" She nodded. "Thank you very much. ... Yes, I'll wait for your call."

"What did he say?"

Her brow was knit. "It's like we thought. The judge could choose to be lenient at sentencing. If, for instance, it would be a hardship on the family to get to a prison farther away, he could have him locked up in a prison closer to home. But no one mentioned that to me, so it doesn't make sense." She shrugged her shoulders. "Hopefully we can get in to see him soon. I'll ask him if he knows what that was about."

"Sounds good. But, Mom, why did you want to see him now? It's only a few days until Monday. Why not just wait?" Madelyn said.

Mom brushed a hand across her daughter's hair. "Because something's wrong. I have a bad feeling about all of this, and I don't think we should wait."

·　　·　　·

Just before they left to meet the appraiser, Mr. Musil called back. Mom was nodding and smiling throughout the conversation. "Thank you. I appreciate it," she said before hanging up the phone.

"We can get in to see him?"

"Yes," Mom said with a sigh of relief, "tomorrow morning. Everything is arranged. He said he had to pull some strings and we're not likely to be able to do it a second time, but yes, we can see him."

"Is that soon enough, Mom?" Madelyn had been ill at ease ever since her mother's statement that morning.

Mom pondered for a moment. "Yes, I think that will be fine. However, we need to be careful. Someone is very serious about this. We don't know who they are, but we're beginning to understand the lengths they'll go to to get what they want."

A shiver ran up Madelyn's spine. She knew her mom was right.

. . .

The appraiser's office was downtown off the main street and down a dimly-lit alley. The door had the name of Howard Cramer on it but no window for seeing in. Mom opened the door slowly, but as soon as she did, a man jumped up from a desk.

"Hi. Welcome. You must be Mrs. Osborne, and is this your daughter?" He was full of energy and had a big smile for them. He was young with an athletic physique—not at all what Madelyn thought an appraiser would look like. She had imagined him to be an older man wearing glasses, huddled in an office with books and magnifying glasses. The reality was vastly different. "So, how can I help you today?"

"My father, I believe, came to you to have something appraised. His name is William Knight. I wonder if you could tell us more about it."

His face clouded and he physically pulled back. "Why do you want to know?"

"Well, he *is* my father," Mom said. "And he needs my help with it."

He stared at her for a moment, deciding how to respond. "It seems to me, if he was so interested in your help, he would have told you all about it himself."

Mom put her hands on her hips. "You'd think so, wouldn't you? But something has him spooked. He asked for my help, and then he suddenly won't talk about it anymore. Now, what would you do in my situation?"

Her words rattled him a bit. "Okay, I understand, but I've had others come around asking about it too. How do I know you're who you say you are? I wouldn't tell them anything because it was your father's wish that I tell no one. And I'm going to have to continue keeping my mouth shut. This is my business, how I earn my livelihood. If someone can't trust me, then I have no business."

It became a standoff—each staring down the other, but Mr. Cramer's physical size made it an unbalanced standoff—not to mention he was holding all the cards. Mom finally let out a sigh and slumped her shoulders.

"Mr. Cramer, can I ask you something?" Madelyn ventured. He didn't answer but turned to look at her, which gave her enough encouragement to continue. "Could you at least tell us who else came to ask about it?"

"You can ask, but I can't tell you much. It was a couple—a husband and wife, or so I thought. They were a bit subtler than you two. They started by bringing me a diamond ring to evaluate—it was a phony. Then they mentioned that their 'father' had been in to see me. So, are there more siblings in your family, or is at least one of you lying?" he said, directing his comments back to Mom.

"She's not lying," Madelyn said before Mom had a chance to comment. "But could you tell us what the couple looked like?"

He glanced between the two of them, apparently deciding whether to trust them with further information. "I imagine you're who you say you are," he finally conceded. "However, I could describe them for you, but it wouldn't help. Later that day I found wigs in the garbage along with a plastic nose. For all I know, the woman wasn't even a woman." He threw up his hands. "I wasn't exactly studying them like I'd need to remember what they looked like."

"Why are you trusting us then?"

He shrugged. "Since they were frauds, I'm guessing that makes you real. Call me a fool, but I like to trust people. Maybe I shouldn't."

The one question Madelyn had, that she kept to herself, was could they trust him?

•　　•　　•

Gathering their family along with Aunt Dory, Zane, and Delia was getting to be a regular occurrence. To Madelyn, it had the feel of the familiar, bringing comfort to her unsettled mind.

"Our dad asked around about Mr. Bruce. The impression he got was that Mr. Bruce works by himself and not with a larger firm because no one really wants to work with him. He likes doing things his own way," Delia said.

"Yeah, and Dad said people told him, that as a lawyer Mr. Bruce is sloppy, but he's basically harmless other than that," Zane added.

"Well, it's not that I want to find a rotten apple here, but someone's got to be the bad guy," Madelyn said in exasperation.

"I know what you mean," said Mom. "So, whatever Pop has or had seems to be the biggest problem. Who knew about it besides himself?"

"George."

"And the appraiser, of course," Aunt Dory said.

Madelyn quickly added, "An appraiser who now knows we're snooping around."

FRIDAY

The drive to the prison was a quiet one. They had so many questions but didn't know which ones Grandpa could answer, or for that matter, which ones he would.

The paperwork was all in order, and before they knew it, they were sitting in front of Grandpa again. He was all smiles this time. "I'm so glad to see you again. This is wonderful."

"I'm happy to see you too," Mom said, "but this isn't a normal visit." His face fell, uncertain what was next. "We're here because we need some answers." He physically pulled back then stiffened when Mom added, "We visited the appraiser. We *will* find out what's going on, but we'd rather have your help."

He wrinkled his brow, seeming to consider her words, but he said nothing. Mom was not to be deterred. "I walked away last time and let you hold your peace, but I'm going to make you a deal this time. I'm going to tell you something I haven't wanted to tell you, and then you tell me whatever it is you haven't wanted to tell me." She didn't even wait for his agreement, she just plowed forward.

"Pop, I never learned to read. I tried when I was little, but everything got mixed up in my head. So, I quit trying. Instead, I worked hard at hiding it." His hand went to his mouth, covering it like the say-no-evil monkey. He was in complete disbelief.

"It turns out I'm dyslexic, that's why I couldn't sort out the words the same way normal people can. But I've found someone to teach me, and this summer, for the first time, I'm actually learning to read. It's never too late." She reached over to squeeze Madelyn's hand. "My daughter taught me that." Grandpa looked from Madelyn to Mom and back again.

"I never knew. I can't believe I never knew. With Tommy, I ... Oh, Rachel, I'm so sorry. I never knew."

"It's okay, Pop. I was the 'perfect' one. I couldn't let you down."

"But ... Oh, I'm so sorry."

"All right. Now it's your turn. What were the letters about?"

He seemed at a loss for words, fighting an inner battle with himself then seemingly changing the topic. "Have I ever told you about the war?"

Mom and Madelyn exchanged glances. What had prison done to him? "Well, not that I remember," Mom finally responded.

"I was a paratrooper on D-Day. And ..." He peered around nervously then lowered his voice. "I mailed home something priceless to your mother. Something I got that day."

"How did you come to own this priceless item?" Mom was sounding skeptical of his story.

"Shhh. It's not mine."

"That's not making me feel any better about it."

"No. I didn't steal it. It was given to me for safe-keeping. A priest on D-Day gave it to me because he didn't want it to fall into German hands. It was all wrapped up. I didn't even know what it was. He just thrust it into my hands. I shipped it home, figuring I'd deal with it after the war."

"Okay," Mom said, the skepticism leaving her voice. Madelyn was leaning in, intrigued.

"When I got home, there was so much to do. It was great to be home, but Tommy ..."

"I know. I love him dearly, but there was always something with Tommy," Mom said as they both nodded. Madelyn could see the connection they were making with each other as if it were a visible, silken thread. It was a connection they hadn't had before, one with no regrets, just newfound understanding.

"I forgot all about it. I found the trussed-up package after your mom died. It was in a box shoved into a corner of the attic. When I pulled it out, I recognized it and opened it for the first time."

"Wow," Madelyn said, loud enough that Grandpa heard it through Mom's receiver. "What was it?"

"Shh," he said, flitting his eyes around. Then abruptly he sat up and said, "Do you remember the big coffee table books we had when you were growing up?"

Mom stared at him. "You're asking that?"

"Yes. Do you remember them?"

"Sure I do. They were books with lots of pictures. I didn't need to read to appreciate them."

"I'd never thought about that before. I remember how you loved them, but I never made the connection." Mom waved his thoughts aside. "Rachel, do you remember what the largest book was about?"

"Yes. It was about Renaissance art, wasn't it? And wasn't it mostly paintings?" He just nodded in response. "I fell in love with those paintings— the Mona Lisa, anything by Raphael. Mom used to tell me the names. But, Pop, what does this have to do with –"

"I *am* telling you my story. What I unwrapped was a painting, a piece of priceless Renaissance art." His voice had dropped to a whisper, such that they weren't sure they'd heard him correctly.

"Are you serious? A piece of Renaissance –"

He cut her off. "Hush. Yes, I'm serious. I was just beginning to figure out how to return it to its rightful owner, the church where it was handed to me ... when all this happened."

"So, is that what you need us to do? Return it?"

"Yes, but I still need to figure out a few things first."

"Where is it now?" Mom asked, but Grandpa shook his head. "What?"

"It's safe. That's all you need to know now."

"Then what do you want us to do?"

"Just sit tight. Let me think it through, okay. Can you come back next week?"

"No, we can't!" Mom's words startled him. "Don't you understand? That's *why* all this happened. We need some answers. We made special arrangements to see you today. Didn't you wonder why we were visiting you when it's not even visiting day?"

"I guess I didn't." He looked sheepishly at the two of them. "I was just glad to see you again."

"So, where is it, Pop?"

He shook his head. "No, I've got to think this through carefully. It would put you in too much danger."

Mom and Madelyn both let out exasperated sighs. "Okay," Mom said, throwing up her hands, "I'll leave that alone for now, but then we have some other questions." He nodded but didn't commit to answering them.

"Why did you pick Peter Bruce as your defense attorney?"

The question clearly caught him off guard. "What?"

"Why did you pick that particular attorney?"

"Ross recommended him."

"Ross Musil, your family lawyer?"

"Yes, of course."

"You picked that name from the list he gave you?"

"No. I was just given the one name."

"That's –" Madelyn started to say when her mother cut her off with a warning glance.

"On to the next question," she said with a false calm in her voice. Madelyn nodded that she understood. Grandpa might just stop talking if he knew all the red flags he was raising.

"Pop, at the end of your trial, your attorney Mr. Bruce was handed a note. It said, 'keep him close.' Do you know what that was about?"

"It was talking about me?"

"Yes, I think so. It was right before they worked out your sentencing. Was there a reason someone would want to keep you close by? Did you ask them to keep you close so it would be easier for us to visit?"

"No. Honestly, I didn't even know I could ask something like that. My attorney never mentioned it."

"Then why do you think the note said, 'keep him close'?"

He just shook his head. "I have no idea."

·   ·   ·

They had more questions for him, but he waved off any other attempts to ask. He was processing the nature of their questions, clearly wondering why there was a need to ask them. After a few minutes of neither side gaining any information from the other, Mom decided it was time to leave.

The two of them ended up in a dilapidated diner down the street from the prison. The guard, when asked for a recommendation for lunch, had apologetically told them this was the only place anywhere close by.

The door to the diner almost wouldn't allow them to enter, creaking on its hinges as if to say, "Go away." The interior wasn't much better. The colors of the tables, the chairs, the flooring, even the walls were so faded it was hard to tell what the original colors had been. Or maybe they were just coated in a layer of dust and despair.

Madelyn raised her eyebrows and stepped back, but her mom ignored the motion and marched to the counter. "Can we just sit anywhere?"

The cashier glanced up from her romance novel. "Yeah. Anywhere," she said while returning to her book. "I'll bring you some menus," she added without moving to do so.

Madelyn and Mom settled into a booth and found it to be surprisingly comfortable, the half walls warmly embracing them in this unfamiliar place. After they placed their orders, they relaxed. And since the diner was mostly empty, they started talking openly with each other.

"Can you believe the ... that thing ... was in your house the whole time you were growing up?"

"Not really. It's crazy to think about."

They grew silent when the waitress showed up with their food. Mom had insisted on attempting to order on her own. "Hot dog," it turns out, was easier to decipher than "Reuben sandwich," even though that was her favorite. Mom was eyeing the hot dog she'd managed on her own, weighing whether to be filled with regret or pride.

"Good job, Mom," Madelyn said, giving her a big smile. She beamed at the compliment, allowing the pride to win out.

In between bites, Madelyn said, "So, what do you think it looks like?"

"I have no idea," Mom laughed. "You'd have thought we would have asked. I can't believe we didn't."

Madelyn grew quiet. "There's a lot we didn't ask ... or get answered," she finally said.

"I know."

"We can't go home until we do, you know." Home was an interesting word. Right now, Aunt Dory's house was their home, but it wasn't their real home. Their own home wasn't safe until they had *all* the answers, not just a few.

"I'm beginning to hate it when you're right," Mom said.

• • •

The guard at the prison was surprised to see them back again. "I can't just go pull your father out again like that, you know."

But Mom was not in a mood to be deterred. "Young man, we were told we could visit today. So, it may not be the regular visiting day, but it is a visiting day for us. Isn't that right?"

"Well, kind of. But-"

"Right. It's not visiting hour or visiting morning, it's visiting day. So, we took a lunch break. Thank you for your recommendation, by the way. What a lovely place. So, now, if you'd be so kind, we're wasting daylight. We would like to visit with William Knight, my father."

Her self-assurance was disarming. The guard didn't say another word to her, just turned to his subordinate and requested they summon Grandpa to the visitor's room.

If they'd thought the guard was surprised, it was nothing compared to the look on Grandpa's face. He dutifully picked up his receiver, but said nothing, waiting for Mom's explanation.

"Pop, you don't want to put us in danger, but I hate to tell you, you already have. If you don't want to tell us where the 'item' is, that's fine. I won't ask for its location again. When all this blows over, you can decide when to tell me so we can return it to its rightful owner. But, in the meantime, we have a lot more questions, and we need the answers. I'm not leaving here today without them."

"But I don't have all the answers. I actually have more questions than I do answers."

"I understand. Just tell us the things you do know. To start with, tell me about the two witnesses who testified at your trial. Do you remember them?"

He registered surprise at the question but readily answered. "They were at the bar when we got there. They were really friendly. We struck up a conversation, just normal stuff."

"Did they have a reason to lie about what they may or may not have heard and seen?"

"Boy, not that I know of. Why would you ask?"

"I just need to know. Is there anything else you can tell me about them?"

"I don't think so. When they found out we were World War II vets, they started buying us drinks. They were just a couple of nice young men."

"Okay. Did you and George have any reason to argue?"

He was again taken by surprise but easily answered, "No. We never disagreed about anything other than sports teams."

"That's what I thought," Mom said, nodding. "Pop, why did you have a knife on you that night?"

"Wow, I could get whiplash from your sudden changes in direction." He paused waiting for Mom to laugh, but her face was like stone. "Well, all right. I don't know. It was my switchblade. I often carried it with me. It's a habit I developed from the war, you know, like putting my wallet in my pocket in the mornings. It's funny, though."

"What's funny?"

"I thought I had mislaid it a few weeks earlier. It seems like one morning I just couldn't find it. But when they brought it out as evidence at the trial, it was definitely my knife. I guess I was wrong. Maybe I'd left it in the pocket of those pants, or something." Then more quietly, he added, "Or maybe I was too drunk to know my right hand from my left."

Mom ignored the last comment and plowed on, determined. "If you thought it had gone missing, why didn't that come out at the trial?"

"My defense attorney said it didn't much matter. It was clearly my knife. I never tried to deny that. So, he said if we brought up anything about it ... well, it would draw more attention to it and would only make matters worse."

"Really," Madelyn whispered to her mom, "a missing knife didn't strike him as important?"

Mom rolled her eyes and covered her receiver so Pop couldn't hear her. "I know. Let me just keep going and see what we can learn."

Turning back to face her father through the plexiglass, she said, "Pop, with any murder, there's usually a motive. That didn't come out in your trial. Why kill him? Why kill George?"

He started shaking his head, his calm demeanor from a moment ago evaporating. "I don't know. I don't remember. I don't remember anything."

"Are you sure you did it?"

His head came up, and he stared into Mom's eyes like he was deciding if she was serious or not. She returned his steady gaze. "Two people saw me do it. Two people who weren't drunk as a skunk like I was." The tears he'd been holding back for a long time started to silently trickle down his cheek, but he didn't turn away. "I'm so sorry I was drinking—so sorry I ever started drinking again. I don't know what happened that night, but if I hadn't been a sad drunk, nothing would have happened."

Mom slowly nodded. "I suppose so, and I guess that's something you have to live with, but I'm not sure you need to live with it in here." He glanced over at Madelyn for confirmation of what Mom was saying to him. She gave him a faint smile—hopeful, but not certain.

"I have another question for you, Pop. Who did you tell about the painting? Did you tell George? Is that what you showed him?"

His face went white, but he nodded.

"Don't you find it curious that he ended up dead?"

He was slow to respond. "So, even if I didn't kill him, I'm still the reason he's dead?"

"No. I don't see it that way. Whoever killed him is the reason he's dead. It's like saying you're responsible for Tommy's cerebral palsy. Sure, if you'd never fathered him, he wouldn't have cerebral palsy, but that's because he wouldn't exist."

He gave a derisive laugh. "Don't think I haven't been down that road a few times."

"And it didn't lead anywhere, did it?"

"No, you're right. Your mother used to tell me that too. She'd add that if I spent too much time looking back, asking 'what if,' that I wouldn't have eyes to see how to navigate the road in front of me." He shrugged his shoulders. "She was right too."

"Hey, Grandpa," Madelyn said, taking the phone receiver from Mom, "What was with Grandma's will? You said you were celebrating something about her will that night."

He got a sheepish grin. "That was technically perjury. We were celebrating the artwork heading back to Europe. I had contacted my lawyer,

Ross Musil, about finding a way to get the painting back where it belonged."

"So, Mr. Musil knew about it too?"

"Of course he did. He'd been working on it for a bit, and he called to let me know they'd found its home and we could send it on its way. It was a win. It seemed reasonable to celebrate."

"Did a whole bunch of people know about the painting, Grandpa?"

"No. George, Ross, and I suppose the appraiser. That's it. That's why I lied about it in court. I didn't think anyone else needed to know. Ross had reached out to people in France—to track down the right church, but I don't think he told them what it was actually about. All the same, I was a little worried. It seemed like suspicious things had started to happen."

"Was that what you were talking about in your letter—people following you, that kind of thing?"

"Yes. I thought I must be imagining things at first, but when it keeps happening, you stop second-guessing and just get scared."

"Did you tell your defense attorney, Mr. Bruce, about any of it?"

"No, I didn't. I didn't want to tell anyone else. If I told him about those strange things, I figured I'd also have to tell him about the painting. I didn't want to do that."

Mom took the receiver back. "Pop, did Ross Musil invite you out that night, the night of George's death?"

"Yes, he did. I thought you knew that."

"I thought I did too, but he claims he didn't."

"Why would he deny that?"

"That's a good question."

"Pop, I truly think things are not as they appear. We're going to find out who's behind this. I just need to know, is the art safe? Could they have found it when they broke into your home?"

He shook his head. "It's safe. They wouldn't have found it."

"All right."

Madelyn took the receiver again. "Grandpa, I have one more question. Why isn't the painting already back in France?"

"I wanted to return it myself—hand it directly back to a priest in that church at the same place it had been handed to me. Ross learned that the church was still standing. Somehow, it just seemed fitting." He shrugged his shoulders. "Then all this happened, and it wasn't possible for me to leave the country. Now it's not possible to even leave these walls. Ross offered to take care of it for me, but I declined. It was too personal."

"That makes sense."

"This is such a mess. I should have taken care of it years ago. I just forgot, and now I'm stuck here where it will haunt me forever. I'll never be able to forget again." He put his head in his hands.

Mom reached out and put her hand on the glass. "I love you, Pop."

He lifted his head then matched his hand with hers on the other side of the glass.

·　　·　　·

It was strange driving home, covering the same territory they had just a few hours earlier. Yet it felt like forever ago with all the new pieces they'd added to their puzzle—only they weren't sure how they all fit together.

Madelyn shivered to think about everything that had happened to Grandpa once he'd found the art. "You know, Mom, all this talk makes me nervous. I keep looking around, waiting for someone to jump out of the bushes or something. I've even imagined we're being followed. Isn't that silly?"

"You saw the brown car too?"

Madelyn's eyes got big. "You mean I'm not imagining things?"

"Well, I thought *I* was, until you said that. If we both noticed the same thing, I think we better take it seriously. But why don't we check to be sure."

"How?"

"Just keep an eye out, and see what happens."

Mom took the next exit off the freeway. It led to a small town, but rather than following the road into town, she pulled into the gas station.

A brown car pulled up to another pump on the other side.

This station still offered the service of pumping the gas for you, if you wished, and Mom signaled the attendant for his help. As he pumped, she reached across the seat and grabbed hold of Madelyn's hand. It was hard to tell who was shaking the most.

"Thank you," Mom told the attendant when he was done. She pulled forward, but instead of pulling out of the station, she turned into a parking spot by the convenience store.

"Let's go in and grab a candy bar, shall we?" She was smiling, speaking cheerfully, but Madelyn knew she was anything but.

When they came out, they both scanned the area around them. No brown car was in sight. With a new spring to their step, they climbed in to head home.

Pulling back onto the highway, a brown sedan eased out of the shadows and entered the highway right behind them. It was only a moment before Mom spied him in her rear-view mirror.

"Don't look back, but we're not alone, Madelyn. Just stay calm and start praying." Madelyn had to fight the urge to whip her head around to see for herself. She started to wring her hands while closing her eyes in silent pleadings.

Home was only three exits away. Mom changed lanes, moving to the left. The brown car followed. She sped up and slowed down, but nothing changed. They tried to sneak a peek at the driver, but he wore a hat that put his face in shadow.

At the last minute, Mom dangerously veered across traffic to the right to take her exit. The move was too quick for their pursuer. They could see him turn his head to watch as they exited the highway.

Mom paused at the stop sign at the end of the offramp to catch her breath. "Wow. That was close." But her relief was short-lived. Above them on the highway, a car pulled off to the shoulder and began to slowly back up to the exit.

"Mom, look!" In response, Mom swiftly turned right, even though home was left. "Mom, I thought if someone was following you, he tried to hide it, so you didn't know he was there. But we know he's there, and he knows we know."

"Yeah. It's not like I have a lot of experience with this," Mom said as she took a quick right followed by another quick left, "but I think he wants us to see him. He's trying to scare us."

"Well, he's doing a pretty good job of it," Madelyn said.

They grew silent as Mom did her best to shake him, turning down one street after another. Then she mumbled to herself, "I should have thought of this sooner." Then without explanation, she set out on a decided course.

"Where are we going?" Madelyn asked after a few minutes.

"Right there," Mom said, pointing at the city police station. She pulled into the parking lot. They watched as the brown sedan paused at the entrance then sped away.

"Madelyn, did you get his license plate number? I was too busy driving to catch it."

"I tried, but it was covered in mud. I couldn't see even a single letter or number."

. . .

The police were helpful. Madelyn feared they might be skeptical, but by the time she and Mom had detailed their evasive maneuvers and the subsequent results, Officer Patterson, the police officer taking their statements, acted both sympathetic and concerned. "Can your husband come to the station to see you get home safely?"

Mom twisted her wedding ring. "He's out of town for the summer."

"I'm so sorry." His face started to get red. "You know, ma'am, if anyone tried to scare my wife or any of my children, I ... well, I'd have a hard time honoring my badge, is all I can say."

"Thank you, officer," Mom said, relieved.

"Do you have any idea why you might have been followed?"

Mom looked at Madelyn before answering. "Yes, I think so. My father is in prison for manslaughter." She paused to see the officer's reaction, but he didn't even flinch. "Anyway, we think he was actually set up. I believe we're getting closer to the truth, and someone doesn't want that truth to come out."

He nodded his head. "Has anything else happened?"

"Our home was broken into last week," Madelyn said, but she had to stop and think—was it really only last week? She shivered at the memory.

"Did you call the police?"

"Yes. They came out and wrote it up."

"Okay. Let me go get a copy of that report. Sit tight. I'll be right back." Officer Patterson got up from his chair, but he turned before leaving, saying, "Don't worry. You're safe here. If you don't see one of us, know that we're only a scream away."

Madelyn started to smile, thinking he was making a joke, but she caught the glint in his eyes. He was angry and clearly determined to protect them since Dad wasn't around to do it himself.

•   •   •

In the end, after calling ahead to prepare Aunt Dory and the others, they received a police escort home. After safely delivering them to the front door, the officer accompanying them said, "Ma'am," while tipping his hat, "we'll have our officers watching the house around the clock for the next couple of days. We'll let you know if we see anything. But you be careful. Don't hesitate to call us."

"Thank you so much, officer," Mom said. If it hadn't seemed inappropriate, Madelyn would have hugged him and all the other officers they had interacted with that day.

Stepping into Aunt Dory's house, the smell of it hit them. It wasn't an unpleasant smell at all—more like lilacs mixed with vanilla—but it wasn't *their* home smell. It belonged to where they were staying, where they were hiding. And while it was a sweet smell, it was darkly sweet, like a luring aroma of a Renaissance painting calling to shadowy, faceless men, who searched for them in the night. It prompted Madelyn to glance over at their house. Mom followed her gaze, and they both shivered.

It was some time before they calmed down enough to tell their story to the others and a while longer before they'd laid everything out. Mom had debated whether Jillian and Daniel should be privy to it all, but Aunt Dory said, "They're in as much danger as you. They need to know. Then they can be careful and watchful too." So, Jillian and Daniel were included in the conversation.

Even still, Mom drew a sigh of relief when the two of them went off to play in the bedroom. "I can't believe what they're having to deal with."

"Mom," Madelyn had to ask the question that had weighed on her mind, "do they plan on killing us? Are they going to kill us like they did Mr. Holliwell?"

"Oh, Madelyn," she said, throwing her arms around her.

"No, they won't." It was Aunt Dory's reassuring voice. They both turned to her, hoping her optimism was warranted. "At least not right now."

"What do you mean?" Madelyn said.

"It's because of the painting." Mom and Madelyn both registered confusion. "As long as they don't know where the painting is, they can't afford to kill you. It's why they killed George but left your grandfather alive. George was a loose end. He knew about the painting. But William Knight—well, he was another story. They needed him to lead them to the artwork. Only, clearly that hasn't happened yet."

Mom was nodding in agreement. "They can't kill Pop because they don't know where the painting is. He'll stay alive, all of us will, as long as they don't find it."

SATURDAY

It was August 9th, a Saturday, but it was anything but typical. Where Saturdays were usually days to tackle the bulk of the chores, when they woke up, Mom told them, "Just do whatever you want today. Enjoy the day." It was a false calm and joy, and they all knew it. But they weren't about to be disobedient to such a wonderful directive.

Jillian and Daniel started playing board games, but it didn't escape Madelyn's attention that it was purposely an indoor activity. For her part, she managed to sit still long enough to read her *Hobbit* chapters for the week—something she'd recently forgotten all about. But then she didn't know what to do with herself.

"Mom, I think I'll go mow our lawn. Aunt Dory, would you like me to mow yours as well?"

Mom was quick to reply, "Oh, Madelyn, I'm not sure-"

Aunt Dory put a hand on her arm. "Rachel, she'll be safe. The police are right outside. Let her go." Turning to Madelyn, she added, "I'd love to have you mow my lawn. Thank you. Maybe you can get Zane to help? He can use my mower."

Madelyn smiled at the suggestion, and before Mom could object further, she was on the phone.

•　　•　　•

While Zane mowed Aunt Dory's lawn, Madelyn mowed her own. They were often within eyesight and smiled, waved, and nodded at each other every time they were. When she wasn't sneaking a peek at Zane or spotting the police car out of the corner of her eye, she was noticing the dandelions in the front of the house—the area she and Mom had left for last. It hadn't been that long ago that they'd worked on them, but it felt like forever ago. Everything seemed to have changed since then.

As they finished mowing, Aunt Dory brought them each a tall glass of homemade lemonade. Then she proceeded to bring out two more—for the officers in the police cruiser out front.

After downing their drinks, Madelyn and Zane put their tools away. As she was closing her garage door, Madelyn was grateful to see Zane standing by waiting for her. "Thanks for your help," she said.

"Not a problem," he said, smiling in a way that lit up his whole face. "I'm glad you called."

They walked back to Aunt Dory's house, and as they did so, Zane slipped his hand into hers. It felt warm and comforting as if that was right where it belonged.

The rest of the day would have dragged on and on, stressful in every moment of it, if it hadn't been for Zane. At least that was the case for Madelyn. They talked and played games with Jillian and Daniel. In the late afternoon, they even baked chocolate chip cookies together.

It was a perfect day, except for one thing. When Madelyn said goodbye to Zane on Aunt Dory's front porch, the sight of the police cruiser could be seen right over his shoulder.

WEEK TEN – SUMMER 1975

SUNDAY

Aunt Dory decided to go to church with Madelyn's family on Sunday. "I don't usually attend church," she said, "but I'd kind of like to stick together for the moment."

"Great!" Madelyn said, happy to have her along.

Waiting for the service to begin, it dawned on Madelyn that the situation was scary for Aunt Dory as well. She was likely drawing as much comfort from their presence as they were from hers. Madelyn reached over and gave her a hug. If she hadn't been adopted into the family before, she certainly was now.

On the way home from church, Mom said, "I think we better tell your father what's been going on."

"Really?" Madelyn said. "What about not wanting to scare him when he's far away and can't do anything about it?"

"Yes, I know I said that. Maybe we don't need to share *all* the details yet." As she pulled the car into Aunt Dory's driveway, she nodded her head to the police officers parked outside and added, "Like the presence of the police out front."

They all sat silently in the car for a moment, unwilling to leave its relative safety. Madelyn finally spoke. "Okay. Then why don't you just talk to Dad? Then we won't let anything slip that we shouldn't."

"Are you sure, Madelyn? You don't want to talk to him?"

"Of course I want to talk to him, but maybe this time it's for the best to wait."

Despite deciding not to talk to Dad over the phone, all the kids gathered around when Mom did. They wanted to know Dad's reaction, and they were certain they could by watching the expressions on Mom's face.

When it was laid out step-by-step for Dad, it was surprising just how much had happened. Madelyn noticed that Mom didn't mention a painting exactly. She simply said, "a valuable antique." And when it came to the break-in at their house, she dismissed it with, "suspicious things have been happening."

She must have said, "Don't worry," about a dozen times, so Dad's reaction was pretty much what they'd expected. Madelyn moved closer and put an arm around her mom, who smiled at her in appreciation.

Mom was in the process of saying goodbye when she hesitated. "Roger, actually there's one more thing I want to tell you. There was a break-in at our house. So, as a precaution, we're staying over at Dory's." Madelyn was surprised at the confession since she'd so deftly maneuvered around it before.

She nodded her head a few times, even though Dad couldn't see it, then gave him Aunt Dory's phone number. "I know. I hesitated to tell you. I didn't want to say anything to frighten you or make you worry. But I want you to know that even though it's rough here right now, we're handling things. Really, if anything, you can feel better about us being here. We're safe." She said it with more confidence then any of them felt, but it needed to be said all the same.

They all breathed a sigh of relief when the phone call was over. Going over the details had brought so much back to their minds, as if they were reliving it all.

"Anyone up for a game?" Aunt Dory asked, trying to break the tension. Just then, the doorbell rang.

"Ma'am," the officer said when Mom came to the door. "My sergeant wanted me to give you an update. We've been watching the house all weekend, and we've witnessed no suspicious activity. He also wanted me to tell you that in addition to our car out front, whenever things are slow, a cruiser drives around the neighborhood, just in case a brown sedan has been hanging around nearby. We're happy to say it's all clear."

Mom nodded in appreciation, but the officer wasn't done. He was twisting his hat in his hands, hesitant to continue. "I ... I, uh, also need to inform you that, ... well, since nothing has gone on, we'll be suspending the watch." Mom noticeably flinched, and he glanced away so he wouldn't have to look her in the eye anymore. "We'll be here through the night, but if things are quiet, we'll shut it down in the morning." His head came up. "But, don't worry, we'll keep patrolling the area. Trust me, we'll be close if you need us."

Mom nodded again. "Thank you. You've been most kind." She was composed and calm. But when the door closed behind her, she collapsed into a pile of tears.

MONDaY

Neither Madelyn nor her mom slept much that night. They jumped at the least little creak or groan of the house. And by the time morning rolled around, they were tense, waiting for the knock on the door saying the police were leaving their post for good.

So, they both startled when it was the phone that rang first. Aunt Dory came into the room a moment later. "Rachel, it's your husband on the phone."

"Dad?" Madelyn said, having a sudden desire for the comforting sound of his voice.

"Go ahead. You can get on the other line," Mom said, shooing her off towards the kitchen. "I'll pick it up in here."

Madelyn scrambled to the kitchen, all too eager to hear her father's voice after the night she'd had. When she picked it up, she heard her mother saying, "It's good to hear your voice too. But I have to admit I'm surprised to hear from you."

"I know. I've been up half the night worrying about you," Dad said.

"I'm sorry. That's why I waited to tell you."

"Don't apologize, I just wish ..."

"I know. Me too."

"Well, the real reason I called is to offer to come home sooner. Right now, I'm scheduled to be done Friday and then on a flight first thing Saturday morning, but I could drop everything and get on a plane today." She could hear the sleepless night in his proposal. Madelyn held her breath waiting for her mother's response, pretty certain she knew what it would be.

"No. Stay. We'll be fine." It's a different answer than Mom would have given at the start of the summer, but then she was a different person now. And even though Madelyn wanted her mom to respond differently, she couldn't help but be happy with her newfound confidence and courage.

Dad was clearly surprised as well. "Are you sure? It's no trouble. Everyone here would understand."

"I know, Roger. Part of me wants to say yes, it really does. Maybe it's foolishness on my part, but I need to finish this—this summer without you, dealing with these challenges. I need to know that I can. I will always need you, and I want to face life with you together. But I'm just starting to believe in myself, to believe that I'm not stupid."

"I never thought you—"

"I know. I know. You've never treated me like I was stupid. But I've treated myself that way. I want you to come home to me when I've finished the summer, when I've finished what we set out to do, not because I gave up."

"Okay. I could argue that you're not giving up, that this is something else entirely, but I understand what you're saying." He paused, and when he spoke again, his voice was full of emotion. "I'm so proud of you, honey. You're the best wife I could ever dream of."

Madelyn felt like she was eavesdropping on this tender conversation, but she didn't want to hang up either.

"Rachel, you know I love you, right?" Dad said.

"Yes. You tell me all the time. It's one of the reasons I love you so much. My father has always loved me. I have no doubts about it. But he rarely says it. You, thankfully, are different. I ..." Mom had suddenly gone completely quiet.

"Rachel? Are you there? Are you all right?"

"Yeah, I'm here." Her voice had a distracted quality to it. "I'm okay. Don't worry about us. We'll be fine, but there's something I need to do. I'll call you tonight, okay."

"What? What's going on?"

"I'll call you tonight. I love you." And then Mom abruptly hung up.

Madelyn was still staring at the phone when Mom came into the kitchen. Mom opened her mouth to speak when a knock came at the door.

It was a different officer. "Mrs. Osborne, I just wanted to let you know it was a quiet night. We'll be leaving now. Call us if you have any other concerns."

Much as they had been dreading this moment, Mom dismissed it with a quick, "Thank you so much for your time." As soon as the door was closed, she turned to Madelyn. "Hurry and get dressed. I know where the painting is." Then without another word, she swept out of the entryway to get dressed herself, leaving not a hint of the tiredness from her sleepless night in her wake.

• • •

"Where are we going?" It was the first words Madelyn had dared speak since Mom's declaration.

Mom was turning out of their cul-de-sac. "We're going to visit Tommy."

"Tommy? I thought we were going to find the painting."

"We are. It's somewhere at Tommy's workshop."

"How do you know that?"

She was busy navigating traffic and didn't speak for a few minutes. "It's something Tommy said that didn't make sense. I was reminding him that Pop loved him, and Tommy said Pop had told him that himself, only I'd never heard that."

Madelyn remembered the conversation. "That's right. He said Pop Pop came to see him before he went away, and that he came without you." Her mouth dropped open. "Oh, wow! That's why he went to see him—to hide the painting!" Madelyn was excited and scared at the same time. "Mom, you're brilliant."

She smiled before saying, "I just hope we're not too late."

They were so excited, they failed to notice the car that pulled in behind them. It wasn't brown this time having been swapped out for a black sedan with darkened windows.

255

•   •   •

When they arrived at Tommy's workshop, it was full of the normal sights and sounds, but to Madelyn and Mom, it felt like the calm before the storm. With relief, Madelyn spotted the familiar form across the room. "Uncle Tommy!"

His head came up. "Madly! Why you come? This is Monday." Then he saw Mom right behind her. "And Sissy. Wow!"

He slowly got up from his station, carefully setting aside his work materials before starting to come their way. Despite their typical routine of waiting, now was not the time. Uncle Tommy jumped when Mom and Madelyn appeared at his elbows. "Whoa. You in a hurry today."

"Yes, we are, Tommy. We need to talk to you. Do you think we could go to your lunchroom?"

"Sure. No one's eating lunch right now."

As they moved toward the lunchroom, the ever-silent Annie saw them and waved. "Hi, Annie," Madelyn said. Annie was working next to Eliza and nudged her. "Hi, Eliza," Madelyn added. "I see you." Madelyn was in a hurry, but these people were Uncle Tommy's other family.

"I see you," Eliza answered.

As they settled into the lunchroom, Madelyn noticed that Annie and Eliza had left their work behind to hover in the doorway. She motioned for them to come in, and Annie, seeing the motion, helped Eliza to a seat nearby.

"Tommy," Mom began, "can you tell us anything about Pop Pop? Anything about before he went away?"

"Like what?"

"Well, you mentioned that he came without me once. Is that right?"

Tommy acted sulky. "I already told you about that—only you didn't believe me."

"You're right. You did tell me that, and I'm sorry I didn't believe you. Did he tell you anything special, like a secret, or something he hadn't told you before?"

He nodded, brightening a little at the admission. "He wanted to see our breakroom and my cubby."

"Why? What did he do there?"

"Don't know. He asked me to get him a drink—water in our paper cups. And he wanted paper towels from the lunchroom in case he spilled his water."

"That's kind of strange, don't you think?"

Uncle Tommy started to giggle. "That's what I said, but he said when you get older you start spilling again, just like a little baby. That made me laugh. I was still laughing when I got the water. I had to get it twice 'cause my laughing made it spill the first time." He was chuckling even harder at the memory.

It may have been amusing in a different context. Instead, Mom was biting her lip while trying hard not to pass her worry along to her brother. A look passed between her and Madelyn, and Mom whispered, "He was buying time to be alone." Madelyn nodded.

She reached over and started to pat Uncle Tommy's back. It's a motion Madelyn had seen her use to calm him many times, but usually when he was agitated not happily animated.

"Tommy, this is really important. Did you see anything that Pop Pop did in your breakroom, something you noticed when you came back?"

"Nope, Sissy. He was just waiting for me, holding his knapsack."

"He had a knapsack?" Madelyn said.

"Yeah, he brought it with him. It was cool. When I came back with the water, he let me hold it. It had a big part in the middle and then some pockets. He said I could keep it. Do you want to see?"

"Maybe later. Did it have anything in it?"

"No, don't think so."

"And you're certain you didn't see him do anything else?" Uncle Tommy just shook his head.

"I saw him," Eliza said.

"*You* saw him?" Madelyn said, knowing she couldn't have seen a thing.

"Yes, *I* saw him."

Madelyn rolled her eyes at Mom, but Mom was staring at Eliza. "Maybe she sees the way I used to read." Then to Eliza, she added, "What did you see?"

"Screws. I saw screws."

"In the breakroom?"

"Yes."

"How did you see the screws?"

"I was in the bathroom next to the breakroom, but I heard a clink outside the door—something falling. Then, when I went out, I stepped on a screw. It wasn't there before." She was smiling, clearly proud of herself.

"That's great!" Mom said, clapping her hands. Let's go to the breakroom and search for screws and missing screws. I'll bet we can figure this out."

"That sounds like a great idea," a voice behind them said—a voice just like the one they'd heard carried on the wind the night of the break-in.

There were two of them, just like before, but they were holding guns this time. Madelyn shivered, realizing they may have had guns that other night too, only she was never close enough to see. Silly that she was thinking about how much more dangerous that night had been than the situation right in front of her. With an odd detachment, she looked at the two of them to evaluate the situation.

The one who spoke was clearly in charge. He was standing erect, more sure of himself, closer to them, with a sneer on his face. Madelyn was certain he was the one who ransacked Grandpa's house. His eyes, mocking and cold, told her he would shoot anyone he thought the least bit expendable without a second thought.

But second thoughts were clearly what the other man was having. He was acting nervous, fidgeting with the gun like he didn't really want to be holding it. He was the one who had gone gently through their house the first time, Madelyn realized, and merely planted a bug the second time. But that also made him a thinker. He wouldn't act rashly. His actions would be smarter, more calculated.

She didn't know how to use what she had observed, but she was going to have to try. The men weren't wearing masks. There was no attempt to hide their identity. It's like Aunt Dory had pointed out earlier, once they found the painting, they wouldn't need them alive.

"So, shall we go find us a painting?" the man Madelyn nicknamed Sneer said.

"Come on," added the one she was calling Thinker.

They had no choice but to stand up. Madelyn did so slowly so as not to alarm the men and also to buy some time, time to figure a way out of this. She tried to make eye contact with Thinker. Maybe she could gain his sympathy. Their eyes met, but he turned away quickly, unwilling to make any connection, to even see her.

"You can leave Eliza here. She's blind, and she'll just get in the way. And Annie doesn't talk. In fact, she doesn't understand anything that goes on around her," Madelyn said.

Sneer didn't seem to care either way and said, "Fine. The rest of you get going."

Madelyn breathed a sigh of relief, hoping she'd live long enough to apologize to Annie for the lie. Just then, Thinker caught her eye. He raised his eyebrows, questioning her statements, but then he blinked and turned away, allowing Madelyn her merciful act.

Uncle Tommy's usual slow walk now felt like the last ticking seconds of their lives—step with the left, lift the right, put it down—repeated over and over, across the lunchroom, through the workroom, and down the hall toward the breakroom, even slower than normal, if that was possible. It felt like hours, each movement crushing them, hammering them into an early grave.

"What you want? Why you doin' this?" Uncle Tommy said.

"Shut up, stupid. Just keep moving, and hurry it up," Sneer said.

Madelyn could see Mom's blood boil. Holding them at gunpoint was one thing, but calling her brother stupid was something she had fought against her whole life. Mom's mouth opened to say something, but then she apparently thought better of it, closing it and continuing silently forward.

Madelyn was thinking fast. "Um, it's in an air vent, so we need to get a screwdriver, and it would be a good idea to turn off the air conditioning first. The painting—it's behind, on the other side of the fan," she said.

Sneer stopped. "Oh, so you were holding out on us. You already know where it is," he said. "Well then, you better go do that. Go with her, will ya," he said, nodding at Thinker. Madelyn was happy to have accomplished what she wanted until she realized she would be leaving Mom and Uncle Tommy alone with a crazy and unpredictable Sneer, who at this point had nothing to lose.

"I ... I don't know where the control panel is or where to find a screwdriver. You should probably take him—Tommy. I think he knows where they are."

Sneer grunted and nodded his approval of the change in plans. "Okay. You stay. He can go."

Madelyn grabbed Mom's sweaty hand in hers, watching Tommy and Thinker make their way down the hallway, hoping against hope that she wasn't seeing her uncle for the last time. Tommy turned and smiled at her. Then he winked just before ducking into the workroom with Thinker at his back.

"All right, where is this air vent you were talking about?"

Frantically Madelyn pictured the breakroom and storerooms nearby, sorting through the mental images she'd stored. But she was having trouble picturing mundane things like vents that her brain typically edited out.

Thankfully, Mom spoke up. "It's either in the breakroom or the bathroom next to it. We've only been told the general area, but we haven't seen it for ourselves yet." She said it with a calm voice despite the hand that was shaking in Madelyn's.

Madelyn squeezed her hand. "Brilliant," was what she was trying to say to her.

Once inside the breakroom, Mom made a beeline for the bathroom. "I think here is the best bet." Then she pointed to the fan above the toilet. "There. If you look closely, I think you can see the package."

Greed clouded Sneer's eyes. "Let me see," he said, pushing past them into the bathroom.

"Stand up on the toilet seat. I think you'll be able to see it."

In his haste, he set his gun down on the sink while giving himself purchase to step onto the toilet. Mom let go of Madelyn's hand and inched closer. Just as Sneer planted both feet and reached up, Mom, in one swift motion, grabbed his gun and pushed Madelyn and herself back out of the bathroom and firmly pulled the door shut behind them.

"Grab a chair. We've got to wedge this door closed," Mom said while dropping the gun onto the floor like it was a hot coal.

They both moved a chair into place then grabbed each other in a tight hug. But Mom quickly pulled back. "We've got to go find Tommy."

She bent down to pick up the gun when a voice stopped her. "I wouldn't do that if I were you." It was Thinker, and he wasn't alone, roughly escorting Uncle Tommy along with Annie, Eliza, and a couple of Tommy's friends Madelyn didn't know by name.

Thinker was behind them with his gun, but his right eye was swollen and starting to turn purple. "Carefully slide that gun over to me," he said to Mom. Defeated, she did as he said.

"Now, you," he said, pointing at Madelyn, "move that chair and let my friend out." As Sneer came out of the bathroom, Thinker corralled the others into the far side of the room where he could keep an eye on them.

Sneer and Thinker were conferring with each other, so Madelyn sidled up to Uncle Tommy and whispered, "What happened?" nodding at Thinker's emerging black eye.

"Annie and Eliza told everyone something was wrong, so my friends," he said, nodding at the other two young men, "were waiting for us."

"And that's it? They were just waiting?"

"Well, that's almost the story." Madelyn turned to see who had spoken. It was Thinker himself. "Your Uncle Tommy's a lot brighter than my partner gave him credit for. He jumped me, and then his friends joined in."

"But you were behind him. How did he jump you?"

"He swung around fast before I knew what was happening. Took the gun out with his elbow." He shrugged his shoulders, but there was a hint of a smile on his face—as if he was almost impressed with Uncle Tommy.

Madelyn turned to Uncle Tommy. "I didn't know you could move fast."

He just smiled. "Well, I never needed to before." Then he shrugged his shoulders. "But I wasn't fast enough."

"He probably would have been, if I didn't also have a knife," Thinker said, pulling out a switchblade for emphasis.

The flash of cold steel made Madelyn shiver, even more than the gun had. She had such little experience with guns that the sight of it from the beginning had seemed surreal. It was frightening but in a detached way. The sharp blade, on the other hand, was right in front of her. She knew it could cut easily, as easily as she could slice tomatoes—or as easily as it could kill George Holliwell.

She shrunk back and put her arms out to protect Annie and Eliza behind her. But to her surprise, Uncle Tommy leaned toward Thinker. "Are you okay? I didn't want to hurt you, but what you were doing wasn't nice." Thinker stared at him like he was crazy. Again, Uncle Tommy said, "Are you okay?"

"Uh ... yeah, I'm okay," he said, still studying Uncle Tommy.

"All right, everyone. Who's going to tell me where we can find ourselves a painting?" It was Sneer. He was fuming after being locked in the bathroom, appearing even more dangerous than he had before. He was waving his gun around at everyone, and his eyes were black and cold. "Hop to it. My patience is gone. Now, someone mentioned something about screws before?"

"I did," said Eliza. She stood up and walked over towards the other side of the room, apparently unperturbed by the guns or knife—although she probably couldn't see them Madelyn realized. "A screw was on the ground after Tommy's dad was here. I stepped on it."

"All right, everyone, start looking for a panel or something that's missing a screw. And no funny business. I start shooting the extras if you mess up." Madelyn caught his glare. All of them were considered "extras," she realized, and the thought made her shiver.

With earnestness, they spread out, scouring every inch of the room for the tiniest screw hole with no screw inside. Madelyn and her mom kept giving fearful looks to each other, but much as their searching glances asked, neither had an answer to this situation.

It appeared to Madelyn that Uncle Tommy and his friends didn't seem to appreciate the gravity of their situation, talking cheerfully while they looked. Better that than knowing what fate awaited them, she finally concluded.

The thought, however, was soon overtaken with something out of place around her, only she wasn't sure what it was. She stopped searching and with heightened senses tried to pinpoint what was different. She noticed Mom had done the same.

There were voices—not the muffled voices of the workers, but voices both clear and commanding. Madelyn caught Mom's eye. It couldn't be, could it? she mentally asked.

Soon, the voices reached them from down the hall. By now Sneer had heard them as well. "What's going on?" he asked, but his voice came out hoarse and shaky. He motioned for all of them to move into a corner of the room while Thinker softly closed the break room door.

Everyone tensed up, knowing the moment of truth was coming. All of them, except for silent Annie.

The scream must have erupted from the very pit of her belly. It was loud and long and shrill. And the second it started, Eliza jumped up and head-butted Sneer right in his gut. With a groan, he fell backward, the gun falling from his hand. They all stared dumbfounded at Annie and Eliza. Who knew they were capable of that?!

Then Madelyn remembered Thinker. She turned around to see the door swinging open. He was gone. The thought of him being on the loose should have scared her, but it didn't. He may not want to be caught, but he also had no taste for blood—just as she had hoped.

Pounding footsteps could be heard coming down the hallway. "What's this? Are you okay?"

It took a bit of sorting out, but Eliza and Annie, it turns out, had wasted no time warning the others while also managing to call the police. Apparently, Annie had dialed the number while Eliza did the talking.

"I'm sorry to say we thought it was a prank call. The voice was garbled over the line and not very specific. I think all she got out was the name of this workshop and then the line went dead. All the same, we check out every call."

"Thank goodness you did, officer," Mom said.

"Well, to be honest, we'd pretty much dismissed it once we arrived. Everyone must have scattered because there was no one in the workroom. We were just about to leave when we heard that scream. I've never heard anything so blood-curdling before, even as a police officer."

Madelyn hugged Annie. "Thank you," she whispered in her ear.

"You're welcome," she whispered back, much to Madelyn's surprise.

Sneer, or whatever his real name was, had lost a lot of his bravado once the handcuffs were placed on his wrists. He was sitting in the back of the police cruiser while several officers took statements and wrapped things up.

No longer afraid, Madelyn approached him. "So, the appraiser, Howard Cramer, did he send you?" Sneer glared up at her but said nothing. "Or was it your friend, Mr. Musil?" His expression didn't change. Puzzled, she mumbled, "I didn't think Peter Bruce was smart enough." His eyes flickered, and his face went white for a split second. Quickly, he regained his composure, but it wasn't quick enough.

"Officer" Madelyn called, "I think I need to tell you something."

As if she needed confirmation, Sneer muttered, "He's such an idiot. Without us-" He stopped talking as soon as he realized Madelyn was still standing there—and that she was listening to every word.

. . .

The police officers present ended up calling in detectives from the squad room to take Madelyn and her mom's statements. As more officers gathered, Madelyn and Mom began to recognize most of their faces. The police soon dispatched a car to arrest Mr. Peter Bruce on suspicion of a whole slew of charges.

As the last car pulled away, Mom grabbed Uncle Tommy with one hand and Madelyn with the other. "Come on. Let's go find the painting for real!"

Uncle Tommy laughed. "I already did."

"What?" Madelyn and Mom said in unison.

"When we were looking before, I found the right spot—but I wasn't going to tell those guys."

Giddy with excitement, the three of them raced back to the breakroom. "Where is it? Where is it?" Madelyn squealed.

"See here, at the back of my cubby." It was hard to tell if the panel had been there all along or if Grandpa had installed it at the back. Either way, there it was with screws in three corners and an empty hole in the last one.

"Now we just need a screwdriver," Madelyn said.

"No, we don't. I have a nail file in my purse. It should do," Mom said. And she was right. After all the screws were removed, she pulled out a well-wrapped parcel. Madelyn and Uncle Tommy watched as she carefully took off the outer fabric covering, revealing a small rolled-up canvas.

Mom's hands were shaking again. "I can't believe I'm holding this."

"Wow," was all Madelyn could say.

"Hello? Anyone here?"

"Who's that?" Madelyn asked, but the others shrugged their shoulders.

A woman who seemed vaguely familiar stepped into the break room. "Oh, my goodness. Are you all right?" When she saw their confusion, she added, "Mr. Musil sent me. I'm his secretary."

Madelyn relaxed as recognition dawned. "Daisy? Daphne?"

"Very good. Daphne. Anyway, we just got a call from the police. I can't believe what happened. Is everything all right?"

Mom was nodding. "Yes, I think it's okay now."

Daphne's eyes darted to the scroll. "Is that it?" The gravity of the moment hit them all. "Have you looked at it yet?"

"No, we haven't. Would you like to see it with us?"

Daphne nodded. "Mr. Musil wanted to make sure you had it in safekeeping until we could get it returned to France. But I don't imagine it would hurt if we took a peak first."

Uncle Tommy cleared off a nearby table, and Mom carefully set the rolled-up canvas down. Daphne reached out to open it.

Surprisingly, Mom gently but firmly pulled the canvas back, holding it close to her chest. "You know, maybe we shouldn't."

"But Mom," Madelyn said. Only Mom wasn't looking at her.

"You have a very nice manicure. Is that mauve fingernail polish?"

"Thank you," Daphne said. "It is—kind of my signature color. But-"

"It's understated yet striking," Mom continued.

"Again, thank you. But, the painting?" Daphne said, reaching for the canvas.

Mom held it even tighter to herself. "I'm curious. Why did you pass Mr. Bruce a note saying *keep him close?*"

Daphne chuckled uncomfortably. "I did that for you, so you could see him more often."

"No, that's not true," was Mom's cold reply.

"Well, sure it was. And he was a friend to my boss, Mr. Musil. I know he wanted to see your father. I assumed you would too. So, why don't I take that now," she said, indicating the canvas in Mom's hands.

"No. I don't think so."

Daphne was starting to redden around the collar. "It's what your father would want. He wanted it returned to France. We need to keep it safe. I mean after multiple break-ins to your house, I'd think your safety would be important."

"How did you know about the break-ins?" Mom said.

Daphne was growing impatient. "Your father spoke with Mr. Musil. He told him all about them."

"He couldn't have. We never mentioned our break-ins to Pop, did we, Madelyn?"

"That's right," Madelyn said.

"Okay, so we're not going to do this the easy way, are we?" And with those words, Daphne pulled out a gun of her own.

Madelyn should have been scared by it, but she felt like if you've seen one gun you've seen them all. "Really?" came out of her mouth before she knew she was voicing her thoughts. No longer afraid, she ventured to ask, "So, you needed him close so you could keep pressuring him to tell you where the painting was, didn't you?"

Daphne reached up with her hand to tap her nose—right on the nose. "I convinced my boss that I should be the one visiting your grandfather in prison. I told him he was too busy and that your grandfather was like a beloved uncle to me. He didn't like the idea at first, but I wore him down. And you know what, I thought he was going to tell me. He seemed to be softening since I was the only one visiting him," Daphne said, throwing Mom a nasty look. "Then he says, 'I'll take care of it.' I pointed out that was a little difficult to do from where he was sitting, but he says, 'I've written my daughter.' Just like that. I was dismissed because he had a *daughter*," she said with disgust.

Madelyn smiled at Mom, thinking being a daughter was a pretty good thing. Then, since she was willing to talk, Madelyn said, "So, were you the one who invited them out that night?"

"Aren't you the clever one." She laughed. "As a secretary, I'm invisible. I call and say, 'Mr. Musil wants to meet with you,' or 'Mr. Musil wants to invite you out for drinks,' or 'Mr. Musil recommends this defense attorney.' No one thinks *I'm* doing it. It's the attorney, the great Mr. Musil." Her laughter turned to snickers. "What a fool. My boss was actually going to return that painting to France. They aren't even searching for it. They assumed it was lost long ago in the war, never to be recovered. It was the perfect opportunity, and he wouldn't see it for what it was."

"Who did it? Who actually killed him? Who killed Mr. Holliwell?"

"Those two so-called witnesses. It was a two-for-one deal. They're in the wind now, on to their next job, I suppose. I got to set up your grandfather, get him out of the way, and take care of a loose end all at the same time."

Just then, one more person entered the room—Thinker.

Daphne smiled. "Let me introduce you to Robert Forrest. He's been a great help to me."

She reached over to kiss him on the cheek, but he pulled back. Instead, he grabbed her gun and turned it on her. "I think this stops here." The surprise on her face made him laugh. "You never fooled me, you know. I'm not the boyfriend. That would be your beloved Peter Bruce, now wouldn't it?"

She again registered surprise and tried to mutter a denial.

"You didn't think I knew, did you?" He said. "I've gone along for the ride on this one, but I'm done."

"But ... but, you came and got me. You told me they were here finding the painting. You ..."

He laughed. "Yes, I did, didn't I? I've been camped out in the hallway, just waiting for you to spill the whole story. I figured you couldn't resist bragging about your own brilliance."

"I never, I..." Her face was red.

"Officers? Have you heard enough?" Robert called to the hallway. Several officers came into the room, with handcuffs and grins.

Madelyn surprised Robert—who would forever be Thinker to her—by throwing her arms around him. "Thank you!"

He looked chagrined. "You shouldn't thank me. I was knee deep in this myself, until ... well, until today."

"Why until today?"

"I have a sister who has Down syndrome. She's an adult, but she'll always be a child, a very special child. This place ... this is a wonderful place. I couldn't go through with it. I fought back when your uncle attacked, but then I was sorry I did. I started wishing he had come off victor."

He was shaking his head. "I'm ashamed of my actions. Your uncle is just as loving as my sister. I had to make things right for him—for my sister. She would never understand what I've gotten myself mixed up in." He gave Madelyn a rueful smile. "I'm still likely going to jail, but I'm okay with that. I'll do my time. But after that—never again."

"I believe you," Madelyn said, and he smiled in appreciation.

. . .

The rest of the day was a blur. They took Uncle Tommy back with them to Aunt Dory's for the night. Even though their home was now safe, it was comforting to stay there. She did have to scramble a bit to make another bed for Uncle Tommy, but she arranged some blankets on the floor of the family room and called it good. He was just another one of the family, and she was glad to have him.

There had been a hurried call to Dad, but it consisted of Mom saying, "Just want you to know everything's fine. All the danger is past, but I'm too tired to explain. I'll call you tomorrow."

Everyone had questions, but they put them off for just one day.

"Dory, you may as well call and invite Zane and Delia to come over in the morning too," Mom mumbled, just before drifting off into a heavy sleep.

TUESDAY

Retelling their story to everyone present turned out to be almost as exhausting as living it, but without any of the worry since they knew how it would all turn out. As they were finishing their tale, there was a knock at the door. It was Officer Patterson, the police officer who had taken their statements the day Mom and Madelyn had been followed.

"I just thought you'd like to know that everyone is behind bars including Peter Bruce and the two witnesses who actually killed Mr. Holliwell. It turns out they weren't in the wind as much as Daphne McDonald believed."

"What happened to Thinker? I mean Robert Forrest?" Madelyn said.

"Well, we've been interrogating everyone much of the night. Mr. Forrest was quick to turn on the others. I can't say for sure yet, but it's likely he'll get off easy because of it." Madelyn smiled.

"It turns out Peter Bruce is guilty of incompetence and giving his girlfriend, Daphne McDonald, the names of former clients to help with her scheme," he continued. "But he didn't actually know anything about the painting or even the murder. Miss McDonald has been manipulating him all along. He is, however, facing serious charges for aiding and abetting, as well as encouraging those former clients to break parole. At the bare minimum, he'll lose his law license."

"How long has Daphne, Miss McDonald, been planning this?" Mom said.

"She claims that originally she wasn't going to steal anything. But it appears once the appraiser's report crossed her desk, greed got the better of her. That report said the artwork was likely a long-lost Renaissance painting. The artist wasn't known in his own right, but he painted in Leonardo da Vinci's studio. That's enough to make it very valuable."

"No kidding," Aunt Dory said. "Just the thought that Leonardo may have hovered over that work, adding a stray brush mark, or directing parts of its composition ... Can you just imagine? That would make the public salivate."

Officer Patterson was nodding. "Miss McDonald knew it, and she couldn't let it go. Her plan, as we've pieced it together, was to find the painting and hold on to it long enough for William Knight to disappear— one way or another. The appraiser was next on her hit list, once he verified she had the right painting."

"Oh, I was wondering about him," Jillian said. Young as she was, she appreciated the gravity of the situation.

"Yes. Then Miss McDonald's plan was to claim finding the painting in an attic. The ensuing feeding frenzy would have her set for life."

None of them could disagree. "Thank you for being kind enough to personally come by to tell us," Mom said.

"My pleasure, Ma'am," he said, tipping his hat on his way out the door.

"Well, I was going to call your dad tonight and tell him everything," Mom said, "but now there's a whole lot more to tell."

. . .

The one mystery that remained was the painting itself. They all wanted to see what the fuss was about, even Uncle Tommy, who was usually eager to get back to the workshop and his routines. But even though they'd waited this long, they decided to wait just a little bit longer.

Tuesday afternoon, promptly at 3:30, Miss Jane Wentwood rang the doorbell of Aunt Dory's home. When they called the Denver Art Museum that morning, it had taken some doing to get them to believe the story they were relating. But once it was believed, they were treated like royalty. Miss Wentwood jumped at the chance to come personally to secure the health of the "painting in question," as she called it.

Jane, as she told them to call her, gloved her hands then laid out a protective coating on the dining room table. They could tell she would have preferred doing this in a museum setting instead of an unknown environment like Aunt Dory's kitchen, but it was the deal they offered her.

Even Daniel drew in a breath as the painting was unrolled before them. Small, yet with exquisite detail, it was a portraiture of two figures—a woman and a child. Madelyn's gaze was first drawn to the woman's fingers. They were graceful and delicate, hanging in the air, yet posed as if she might pluck a rose to smell. Her wrist was touched with lace attached to a vibrant green dress. Sparkling jewels—how a painting could portray sparkling jewels was beyond Madelyn's understanding, but sparkle they did—were sewn in a line the length of the sleeve. They ended at the neck, where the scooped-out neckline was filled in with the daintiest of lace, painted in elegant detail. Her auburn hair was pulled back under a lace cap, and her expression was one of pure contentment.

The other figure, though smaller, was just as richly attired. She wore a rose-pink gown with white lace at the wrist, around her waist, and along the neckline. A thin gold necklace lay on top of her dress, and her hands were folded neatly in her lap.

The second figure was clearly the woman's daughter. She was gazing up at her mother with adoration and something Madelyn could only describe as trust. Madelyn glanced up at her own mother. Mom's eyes left the painting and connected with Madelyn's.

"Wow. They're just like you, Madly and Sissy. Only they're a lot richer," Uncle Tommy said.

Madelyn's eyes never left her mom's. There were many ways to be rich, and she was feeling pretty wealthy at the moment.

WEDNESDAY

Madelyn answered the phone around lunchtime the next day. On the other end was a cheerful Officer Patterson. "Thought you'd like to hear how things are wrapping up."

"Yes. Do you want me to get my mom?"

"It seems to me you've been in the middle of this enough. I can pass it along to you, if you'd like."

"I knew I liked you," Madelyn said. "Go ahead."

"Well, last night Mr. Bruce learned Robert Forrest was talking. Once that happened, he started to spew forth anything he could think of. It seems potential jail time as a crooked lawyer wasn't one of his life goals." He chuckled. "He hadn't been let in on any schemes, but he figured out a lot of it on his own."

"That's surprising."

He laughed again. "That's what I thought. And, of course, Daphne McDonald, as a lawyer's secretary, won't be in much better shape in the general prison population, and her crimes were far worse. So, you can guess what that means."

"She's tattling on everyone else, trying to blame them?"

"Exactly. It seems everyone involved is having a contest to see who can throw whom under the bus the fastest. However," he continued to chuckle, "according to the district attorney, none of them will be getting off. Robert Forrest is the only one being accorded that privilege."

Mom walked into the room where Madelyn was on the phone. "Who's that? I need to use the phone."

"Just a minute," Madelyn whispered to her. "Thank you so much for the update. My mom's going to love it."

"You're most welcome," Officer Patterson said before saying goodbye.

Mom was pleased, as was everyone else. But after sharing her information, Madelyn noticed her mom quickly picking up the phone to make several phone calls.

"What's she up to?" Madelyn asked Aunt Dory.

"There's a lot to be worked out. You know how we let Miss Wentwood take the painting for safekeeping yesterday?" Madelyn nodded. "Well, they're having people authenticate it today then they're offering to clean and restore it. So, your mom's been on the phone off and on with them all morning."

Just then Mom hung up the phone. "Madelyn, I'm heading down to Ross Musil's office in a few minutes. Would you like to go with me?"

"Sure," Madelyn said, but then a picture came into her head of Mr. Musil's office—including his secretary's desk, the desk of the woman who had caused them so much trouble and heartache. "You know, I think I'll stay here instead."

"Are you sure? If it weren't for you, we wouldn't have figured any of this out."

"Yes, I'm sure."

Once Mom left, Madelyn wandered aimlessly around Aunt Dory's house, eventually making her way to her own home. She walked in and out of rooms, turning on and off lights, touching doorframes, walls, pictures on the wall. It was as if she were claiming it again, making it hers, making it ready for her family again.

She paused at the door to Dad's study. It would be good, yet odd, to share it with him again. She had slipped *The Hobbit* into her pocket, and now she pulled it out. Stepping just inside the room, she opened it at the bookmark. The second to last chapter stared back at her—*The Return Journey*. Madelyn pulled it in close and made her way to one of his easy chairs, sinking into its comforting embrace.

Before beginning to read, Madelyn reached up to release her hair from its ponytail—only to discover it wasn't in a ponytail at all. In fact, other than keeping it out of her eyes while weeding, Madelyn couldn't remember the last time she'd actually put it in one.

Snuggling down into her chair, Madelyn settled in for her last read. When she finished the last page some time later, she hugged the book to her. "I can't wait to tell Mom," she said, hopping up out of the chair.

She found her in Aunt Dory's laundry room, washing a few of their things. "I see you're back. When I got home and you weren't here, I wondered where you'd gone, but Daniel came and told me," Mom said.

"He knew where I was? How? I didn't see him."

Mom laughed. "He was probably spying through the window or something. What did you expect from Daniel?"

"Oh, right. I guess it's good he's back to normal, isn't it?" Madelyn said, and Mom nodded. "You know, I think I'll go find Jilly. She might like to play a game, or maybe I can braid her hair." Madelyn started to walk out of the room when she remembered the book in her hand. "Oh, Mom, look," she said, holding up *The Hobbit.* "I finished it. It's all done."

"That's great. What shall we do to celebrate?"

"Why don't I start reading it to you? And then you can read something to me."

"I'd like that," Mom said.

THUrSDaY

After breakfast on Thursday, Mom announced, "Today is moving day. It's time we live in our own home again. Dory's been wonderful, but we've stayed here long enough."

Aunt Dory surprised them by tearing up. "I can't say it won't be nice to have my house back to myself, but I'm going to miss having you all around."

"Well, we're just next door—and we're not strangers anymore," Mom said while the others leaped up to embrace Aunt Dory.

"Oh, and one more thing. Zane and Delia will be here right after lunch to help." Madelyn had trouble hiding her smile.

.   .   .

When Zane and Delia arrived, Mom was just getting off the phone. She was trying to keep a straight face, but the light in her eyes gave her away.

"What's up, Mom?"

"Well, 1 just had two phone calls. First, the museum called to tell me about the painting. It's been authenticated. It really is from an artist in Leonardo's studio."

Everyone cheered. "That's great, Mrs. Osborne," Zane said.

"Yes, it is. And they also said the restoration should go quickly. They expect to be done by the end of September. Fortunately, this dry Colorado air was a godsend. You couple that with the careful and, until recently, undisturbed wrapping, and the painting is in remarkable shape." Then she got a twinkle in her eye. "But that's not the best news."

"It isn't?" Madelyn said. "What is then?"

"That last phone call was from Ross Musil. Pop's coming home!" She couldn't continue as tears streamed down her cheeks. The only sound for the next several minutes was the sniffles as everyone choked back tears or, in Madelyn's case, let them flow unabashedly.

When Mom found her voice again, she said, "Mr. Musil has been very helpful. This isn't his specialty, but he's been hovering over the lawyers working on Pop's case. He should officially be cleared and released in the next few weeks. And then-" she paused, looking around at the group, "on Monday, October 13th, our whole family, including Tommy and Dory, of course, will be accompanying Pop as he returns the restored painting to the church where it hung before the war."

"That will be the painting's true restoration, won't it?" Madelyn said. Mom nodded.

. . .

Moving took much of the afternoon, but it was pleasant, and they didn't hurry themselves along. "I can't believe we ended up with this much stuff at Aunt Dory's," Madelyn said to Zane, as they carried yet another load of clothes and towels.

Zane shrugged his shoulders. "At least you had someplace to go. It's not that big of a deal to carry it all back."

"I guess you're right."

"Hey, have you thought about what electives you want to take? School registration is next week."

"I completely forgot. I haven't even looked at the options. What are you going to take?"

They settled into an easy banter. Madelyn had been dreading high school, but now ... well, now it was looking pretty good.

When everything had been moved back and put away in its proper place, Mom ordered pizza for everyone. After eating, Daniel and Jillian played games while the others talked into the twilight hours.

Friday

Morning came early with a gentle shake from Mom. With the surreal experiences of the week, they'd forgotten what their real lives were all about. "Dad's coming home tomorrow," was all she said. It wasn't a statement of excitement, it was a reality check.

"The yard! The dandelions!" Madelyn said. Mom just nodded.

Maybe at this point it shouldn't have mattered anymore, but he was coming home, and they wanted the yard to look as good as possible. They'd long since stopped caring what anyone else thought, but they wanted to let Dad know they cared. If it mattered to him how the lawn looked, then it would matter to them too—just for him and him alone.

The sun was barely up, and the other two family members certainly weren't. They'd find their own breakfast without a problem, especially seeing Mom's initial summer enthusiasm about cooking breakfast had lasted a mere week or two.

They stepped out onto the front porch, surveying the impossible to ignore blooms and all they implied. With all that met their eyes, Madelyn was grateful they had agreed the backyard was hopeless, pronouncing the dandelions victors and walking away. But the front and side yards were still in contention, and Mom and Madelyn were determined to win.

Armed with a bucket between them, and each with some garden tools, they started where their efforts had last left off, even though much of the yard was still in shadow. They'd spent weeks moving from the fence on the side around to the front, declaring the side of the house finished before life intervened. They'd neglected their dandelion war, but now they were going to finish the front half in a day because tomorrow he would be home.

The day marched from the early, quiet hours to hot mid-morning to scorching noon and an afternoon they couldn't even describe using polite words. Sweat dripped down the inside of Madelyn's shirt, and she kept wiping her forehead, leaving a line of smudged dirt across it.

They talked early on, but soon the task overwhelmed them, and they had no energy left for words. Dig a dandelion, throw it in the bucket, move to the next—that was the rhythm of their gift for Dad that continued throughout the day.

The sun was close to slipping from view when Madelyn stood up, not seeing another dandelion in front of her. She looked over at Mom. She was pitching one last weed into their overflowing bucket when Madelyn caught her eye.

"Is that it?" Mom said with a whisper as if she might jinx the moment. All Madelyn could do was nod. Mom stood, stretching and working out the kinks in her arms and legs.

They turned to see what they had accomplished in one day. It was amazing. "We did it, Mom. We did it." Madelyn found herself whispering too.

"I know. I can't believe it. I never knew we could ... that I could ..." And before she could stop them, her face was flush with tears, and Madelyn knew they weren't talking about dandelions anymore.

Madelyn grabbed her in a hug. "I love you, Mom."

"I love you too." They started to dance in the fading light, so happy for all they had and who they were and who they had become.

It was only as they twirled and danced around the yard that Madelyn saw something she hadn't before. Stopping dead still, she said, "Mom?" her smile was gone.

"What is it?"

Madelyn lifted a shaky finger to point. "Look."

Little bits of sunlight were trickling through the trees, leaving streaks upon the grass, but perfectly highlighting the side yard where yellow blooms dotted the lawn, the part they thought was finished before they began their epic quest that morning.

They both stared open-mouthed, stunned at the sight before them—dandelions, too many dandelions to even count. Madelyn looked at Mom, waiting for her direction. Would they keep working all night? There were a few hours in the morning before they had to leave for the airport to meet Dad's plane. They could work then.

Mom stared back at her for just a moment then threw back her head and laughed. It was a laugh that came from her toes all the way up to the top on her head. It shook her body and sent ripples through the air, touching her skin, making her hair dance and her heart sing.

Madelyn gave in and laughed with her, laughing so hard she doubled over and fell to the ground, laughing up at the sky above her and the grass beneath her. Soon Mom was lying by her side, laughing so hard that tears were streaming from her eyes.

They laughed at the absurdity of trying to kill off a living, vibrant weed that only wanted to survive. They laughed at their summer and themselves, at when they didn't understand what mattered in life. They laughed at their notion that dandelions did. They laughed at their follies and their failings and their fears. They laughed for joy at what they'd found—how to overcome and how to survive, and the knowledge that they could only do it together. They laughed until their voices went hoarse.

The front porch light went on, and Jillian and Daniel peeked out. They'd brought them food and water and emptied their weed buckets throughout the day, but had known better than to have disturbed them. But now their faces were etched in confusion, not understanding the mirth before them.

"Are you okay?" Jillian tentatively said, certain that they must be suffering from sunstroke or some such thing.

They tried to answer but couldn't stop laughing long enough to form the words. Daniel started to twitter just a little, and before long he and Jillian had both joined in the contagion of laughter, not even certain of its cause.

They soon lay all together on the ground, wrapping their arms around each other. Madelyn didn't know how long they laughed, but it was fully dark when they finally sat up, wiping the tears from their eyes.

Mom took a deep breath and smiled. "Some battles you just never win, but then again, some of those battles aren't worth fighting—I guess I forgot to make that distinction." She looking at Madelyn and added, "Thank you," and her voice caught, "thank you for helping with the one that mattered."

Madelyn hugged her and whispered, "You're welcome."

SATURDAY

Welcoming Dad home happened in a rush. It seems like one minute they were waiting for his plane to land then watching for him to emerge from the gate, so anxious and excited. Then before they knew it, he had encircled them all in one big hug, squeezing like he'd never let go.

Madelyn didn't remember the drive home. She had lost her front seat status, relegating it to Mom again, but that was all right. She was where she should be, and Madelyn was content.

Dad pulled into the garage and walked into the house, never once taking his eyes off them to examine the yard. He was saying, "Daniel, I believe you've grown three inches. Jilly, when did you get to be so pretty? Madelyn, you did it. I'm so proud of you." And all the while he was holding Mom close.

They worked on filling the day with things he had missed. Mom read a book to him—the highlight of the day. Daniel managed to pull a prank, swapping out a cup of soy sauce for the cola Dad was expecting to drink.

"We've had so much going on that there hasn't been time for pranks," Madelyn whispered to Mom. "I think Daniel's worried he's getting rusty and might forget how." Mom nodded in agreement.

Jillian followed Dad around like a puppy dog, fetching his slippers, water—especially after the soy sauce incident, anything she could think of. In the evening, Madelyn read *Watership Down* to everyone, although they had neglected it lately. At least they weren't so far along that Dad couldn't get caught up to the story. It was a perfectly mundane, perfect day.

. . .

Mom and Madelyn never told Dad about the dandelions. It wasn't so much that they were ashamed or trying to hide anything from him, it was something more and something less. It's almost as if putting it into words would shatter the moment, and its meaning would be lost. Or maybe it wasn't possible—the words just simply did not exist. But ever after, whenever Mom was low, all Madelyn had to do to cheer her up was smile and say, "Do you remember the dandelions?"

And for her and Mom, those words said it all.

ACKNOWLEDGEMENTS

I may be the author of this book, but I did not "author" it by myself. Much research went into the writing of this book, so I need to thank the internet. Some arcane details like criminal justice in Colorado in the 1970s or the diagnosis and treatment of cerebral palsy in the 1940s would have been hard to come by without the internet.

I'm grateful to Ruth Erickson for her insights on group homes and sheltered workshops, based on her own experience with her beloved daughter Beth. On a lighter note, I'd like to thank Jennifer Amorino and her twin boys (affectionately known as Mischief and Mayhem) for their real-life antics that inspired some fictional ones here.

I'm not sure where this book would have ended up (probably not in print) without my many beta readers, editors, and proofreaders. Specifically, I'd like to thank Paula Kriz, Kent Harrison, and Amy Barnes. Their editing and insights have been invaluable (but if there are mistakes, they are mine, not theirs). My fellow authors and the staff at Black Rose Writing have also been fabulous in their support, feedback, and encouragement.

Especially I want to thank my family. They are amazing in every regard. My mother has been supportive, even though in the throes of dementia she's not exactly sure what she's encouraging. My children are my bright spots. My husband Allen has been my biggest supporter since the day he said, "Why don't you just write?" Writing was my first love, but I wouldn't have had the courage to pursue it as more than a hobby without his support.

And lastly, I want to thank Lyla Heward. It can be hard for people you grew up with to believe you can do great things—they know you too well. But that's not the case with Lyla. In her own quiet way, she's been one of my greatest cheerleaders.

ABOUT THE AUTHOR

Mary Ellen Bramwell, an award-winning writer and author of *The Apple of My Eye* and *When I Was Seven,* has been writing short stories since she was ten. She is the mother of five and currently lives with her youngest son and her husband of over 35 years in the Mountain West. She enjoys reading and playing games but is passionate about her family and alleviating the suffering of others.

CPSIA information can be obtained
at www.ICGtesting.com
Printed in the USA
LVHW091600260719
625485LV00001B/49/P

9 781684 332793

7